AB VE THE LAW

DUTCH

ABOVE THE LAW

BY

DUTCH

ISBN-10: 0-9887621-5-3
ISBN-13: 978-0-9887621-5-2

Library of Congress Control Number:

Paperback Edition, April 2014

Publisher's Note
This is a work of fiction. Any names historical events, real people, living and dead, or the locales are intended only to give the fiction a setting in historic reality. Other names, characters, places, businesses and incidents are either the product of the author's imagination or are used fictiously, and their resemblance, if any, to real life counterparts is entirely coincidental.

DC Bookdiva Publications
#245 4401-A Connecticut Ave
NW, Washington, DC 20008
www.dcbookdiva.com
facebook.com/dcbfanpage
twitter.com/dcbookdiva

Above The Law

Chapter One

Chicago – January 16

"Don't move! D.E.A.!"

"Show me your hands!"

"Slow! Slow!"

The barking commands and grenade-like explosions jolted Marlon from his slumber; he was disoriented and fuming. The glare of the large, military-style flashlights crisscrossed the room. All were aimed squarely at him and balanced above the barrels of assault weapons.

He always slept with his gun under his pillow, so he instinctively reached for it. The AR-15 muzzle to his jaw quickly contradicted the logic of his instincts.

"Give me a reason asshole," the D.E.A. agent seethed. His aura emanated intense adrenaline; Marlon could smell the stench.

The agent snatched Marlon out of bed while his cohort tossed his pillow and grabbed the gun, while yet another one turned on his bedroom light. Marlon wore only a pair of navy blue Polo boxers while being slammed face-first into the wall and cuffed.

"You're making a big fuckin' mistake!" he gritted.

"Shut your mouth!"

"What the fuck is going on?"

"I said shut up!"

"I'll tell you what's going on," a high-ranking agent of the D.E.A. said as he stepped into the room. He held up his gloved hands and in them were two packages about the size and thickness of a Webster's dictionary, wrapped in plastic and duct tape.

"Fresh uncut heroin, straight from Mexico," he smirked and mockingly sniffed one of the packages, "I can still smell the wetback. Found it in the couch cushion."

"Heroin?" Marlon echoed. "No fuckin' way! This is a set up!"

"Marlon Porter, you're under arrest for —"

"This is a mistake! I'm a Federal Agent!"

His accuser wore a menacing smile and responded with a gloating tone.

"I know; that's the best part."

By the time they reached the MCC Federal holding facility at the intersection of Clark and Van Buren streets, Marlon was enraged. He didn't know what was going on and intended on quickly getting some answers.

His perp walk upon entering the facility with his hands cuffed behind his back and a D.E.A. agent at each elbow was embarrassing to say the least. The first set of eyes he met were those of the Special Agent in Charge, Phillip Ortega. Everything about Ortega screamed F.B.I., from his inexpensive navy blue suit all the way down to his spit-shined Florsheims. He gave Marlon a penetrating gaze and approached him with his trademark military gait.

Above The Law

Ortega crossed the room and accosted the D.E.A. agent in charge.

"What the hell is goin' on, Frank? You go after one of mine and I gotta find out through a goddamn back channel? Ortega was furious.

Frank gave him a shrug and a smirk.

"What can I say, Ortega? Your guy stepped in it big time. A reliable source says your guy's dirty and we hit pay dirt. We found three kilos of heroin and seventy thousand dollars."

Ortega hit Marlon with a harsh look of anger and betrayal that made it difficult for Marlon to hold his gaze. Marlon fought the wave of guilt in his heart and stood steadfast.

"Mr. Ortega! This is bullshit! It's gotta be a plant! It's all bullshit!

Ortega turned back to Frank without responding to Marlon.

"Let me talk to him."

"Phillip, he's in custody. You have — "

"Frank!" Ortega sharply barked. Frank visibly jumped, while several people looked in their direction.

Frank sighed. There was a natural rivalry between the D.E.A. and the F.B.I. It wasn't as intense as the Yankee-Red Sox rivalry, but it definitely didn't pull on the D.E.A.'s heartstrings to see the Feds with egg on their face.

Still, Frank knew Ortega was taking it hard. A dirty agent was bad enough, but a dirty agent on your own watch was a hard pill to swallow. He eventually relented.

"Ten minutes, Phillip," Frank replied. He flashed five fingers twice to emphasize his point.

Ortega took Marlon by the arm and guided him into the first available office he found. He shut the door then turned to Marlon.

"You son of a bitch," Ortega hissed. "How long has this been going on?"

"Sir, you tellin' me you believe this bullshit?"

"What am I supposed to believe, Porter? They found it in your apartment!"

"Mr. Ortega, you know me. You know my work. I'm not dirty. I..." Marlon tried to explain, but Ortega cut him off.

"Then how did three kilos of heroin from evidence...from a case the D.E.A. was working, end up in your possession?"

Marlon was stunned to a mumble.

"Evidence? How..."

"Is that why you're so good undercover? You not only know how to be like them, you are them!" Ortega huffed. The thought of one of his trusted agents going rogue broke his heart.

It was hard enough for Black and Latino people in the F.B.I. Ortega really believed in Marlon, despite his background. Now he was beginning to think that maybe the old saying was true. 'You could take the man out of the ghetto, but not the ghetto out of the man.'

"Mr. Ortega...Please, listen to me," Marlon said. He looked him squarely in the eyes. "Those bricks...kilos...are not mine. You have my word. All you have to do is check for my fingerprints. If I put 'em there, then I had to touch 'em," Marlon proposed.

"That's meaningless Porter. Maybe you wore gloves. You're not a dumbass."

"I didn't steal no goddamn heroin out of evidence and hold it in my apartment! Who does shit that dumb?" Marlon indignantly roared.

Ortega had been a Federal agent for eighteen years; in those years, he had heard tons of bullshit. He also prided

Above The Law

himself on his sixth sense to know when someone was telling the truth.

It was screaming at him at that moment.

Before he could respond, a D.E.A. agent stuck his head in the door.

"Porter, your lawyers are here to see you."

"I don't have a fuckin' lawyer," Marlon growled.

Things were getting crazier by the minute.

Ortega knew Marlon had been brought to the MCC directly from his home. He would've never had a chance to call anyone, let alone a lawyer.

"Porter, what the hell is going on?"

"That's what I've been tellin' you from the start! I don't know," Marlon replied; he could tell the confusion was mutual.

"Then let's find out."

They walked out to find Frank waiting for them.

"Wow, for a guy that says he's clean, you sure do keep a mouthpiece close, huh?" Frank quipped sarcastically.

Ortega squeezed Marlon's elbow subtly as he slowly guided him down the hall. Marlon had no response to Frank's obvious taunt.

"Where are they?" Ortega asked.

"Follow me," Frank replied.

They came to a small room at the end of the corridor and walked in. Inside sat two well-dressed white men. Both were blond and blue eyed from pure Nordic stock. They each had athletic builds under silk Armani suits. They exuded an air of arrogance that Ortega was used to when it came to high priced criminal attorneys.

One was sitting at the small desk in the middle of the room. The other was standing. They both looked at the door when it opened.

"Mr. Porter," the gentleman who was standing greeted. "Good to see you. I'm Steve Shapiro and this is my partner, Henry Allen."

Henry nodded at Marlon.

"Who are you? I never called for a lawyer; I don't need one. Who sent you?" Marlon questioned.

Steve condescendingly smiled.

"A mutual friend thinks you do."

"What mutual friend?" Marlon wanted to know.

Steve looked at Ortega.

"Thank you officer, we…"

"Agent, Special Agent Phillip Ortega."

"Excuse me, Agent Ortega, but we have it from here. We'd like to speak to our client alone," Steve said.

Ortega's eyes met Marlon's for an instant, and then he reluctantly walked out and closed the door behind him.

"Have a seat Mr. Porter," Henry finally spoke. His voice emitted the vibe of authority between the two.

"Nah, I'm good. Like I said, who sent you?"

"A mutual friend."

"We've been around this mulberry bush before," Marlon sniped.

Henry chuckled and looked at Steve.

"Aaron Snead," Steve replied as he eyed Marlon for a reaction.

Aaron Snead was one of the subjects in an undercover investigation. He was a mid-level dealer from the East Side of Chicago, often called the "Eight-Trey." It was the Black P. Stone's territory, and they were the main subjects of the investigation.

However, how would Aaron know Marlon had been arrested? Was he being followed? Did the Black P. Stones have someone in the D.E.A or F.B.I. on their payroll? The gangs of Chicago were known to be very powerful in the Windy City, so the thought wasn't far-fetched. Marlon reasoned that if they did have a Federal mole, he would've been dead. The whole situation wasn't adding up.

"Look, I don't know what Aaron told you, but this is a big mistake."

Since Ortega left, Steve was callously walking around the perimeter of the room and looking at his watch. He looked up and gave Henry an almost imperceptible nod. Henry then stood up and knocked on the door. Ortega opened it in an instant.

"You done?" Ortega anxiously probed.

"Not at all. We would like to be assigned another room...one without an audience," he smirked.

Ortega looked from Henry to Marlon and then to Steve. He thought to himself, *How did they know?* He convincingly played it off with a shrug. "Whatever floats your boat."

When they arrived in the next room, it was identical to the first one. However, this one was void of furniture. Steve, again, walked the perimeter and looked at his watch. He stopped abruptly near the door and gave Henry the thumbs up.

Marlon watched as the mask of arrogance, usually associated with attorneys, melted from their faces. They were replaced with cold and calculating expressions of indifference. Marlon then realized that these guys were not lawyers.

"Porter, we know who you are."

Since they mentioned Aaron Snead earlier, he didn't know if his arrest had blown his cover. He also knew that he wasn't about to blow it himself, if it wasn't. He simply answered, "Yeah? Who am I?"

"Marlon Porter, born September 3rd 1983. Born and raised in Philadelphia, Pennsylvania. Both parents deceased; raised by your mother's sister. An average student, with minor brushes with the law-but no convictions. Eschewed college for the Navy and joined Naval Intelligence. You then matriculated up or down the ladder, depending on perspective, and joined the F.B.I. Your first assignment was the Atlanta Field Office."

After his spiel, Henry calmly eyed Marlon and awaited his response. Marlon didn't say a word, a fact Henry noted and enjoyed. He then continued.

"But that's just the sanitized version. The Marlon façade, shall we say? Steve... Give him the x-rated version."

Steve leaned from the wall and approached Marlon. He spoke in a sharp low tone.

"Marlon Porter, born September 3rd 1983. Born and raised in North Philadelphia's notorious Richard Allen projects. Member of R.A.M., the Richard Allen Mob or Mafia, loosely affiliated with the Junior Black Mafia, and by extension, the original Black Mafia of Philly circa the 60's and 70's. Am I right so far?"

Now it was time for Marlon's mask to melt away; the mask of the indignant, falsely accused Federal Agent. It quickly evolved into the stone expression molded by the projects.

"I don't know what the hell you're talking about."

"Fine, I'll continue. Maybe the name Ronnie "Bank" Johnson and September 1997 rings a bell. The police, the Feds, and the media thought a rival killed Bank in a drug war. But we both know what really happened, right Porter?" A mocking smirk could be discerned in Steve's eyes, but didn't reach his lips.

"It's your story. I just hope it ends with you tellin' me what the fuck is going on," Marlon growled. The men definitely had his attention.

They were talking about things that only Naval Intelligence, not the F.B.I. had found out. It only intensified his burning question... who the hell were these people?

"After that incident, you desperately needed to get out of Philly. The Navy was an easy way to do that. Besides, what better place to hide from the law then within it? They didn't even know who to look for; I love the logic in that," Steve chuckled.

Above The Law

"Yeah, you should. It's your own," Marlon retorted. "Now get to the point. I'm tired and these cuffs are getting tighter by the minute.

"Get used to 'em, because without us they'll stay on for the next ten years," Henry coldly warned.

He stepped up to Marlon. They were about the same height, but had yet to see eye to eye.

"Okay, you want the point...Here it is. You and I both know that the three kilos aren't yours. But we also know the seventy grand was," Henry said, with an ironic sneer on his face. "Stop me when I'm wrong."

Marlon's expression didn't change, but the look of defiant pride in his eyes told Henry he was on point.

"Those six kilos of cocaine in that Atlanta bust that never made it to evidence...That $1.7 million seized that was actually $1.8 million in Gainesville...my point...Again, although the three kilos aren't yours, it would be poetic justice if you went down for 'em, don't you think?" Henry quipped.

The only thing that kept the sweat from lathering his forehead was the ice water in his veins. Marlon's mind was reeling from the accuracy of their analysis. How did they know so much about him? Where had he slipped? Did they have an undercover on his undercover assignment? No. If they did, he knew they would've busted him a long time ago. They weren't there to bust him, so he decided to play their game.

"I still have no idea what the hell y'all talkin' about, but if I did...What're you asking?"

"We can make your problem go away if you agree to work for us," Steve proposed.

"Who is us?"

"N.T.K.," Henry answered.

"What's N.T.K.?"

"N.T.K.," Henry repeated with a subtle shrug.

"What will I be doing?"

"Same thing you're doing now, just on a deeper level," Steve responded. Marlon could tell that statement was loaded. He considered the proposal for a moment, but his mind kept coming back to one question.

"Man, who the fuck are you guys?" he questioned in an aggravated tone.

"We can tell you this much," Steve conceded. He looked at Henry who gave him a subtle nod, "It's deeper than 9-11."

The phrase 9-11 was one phrase Americans, rich or poor, Black or White all collectively shuddered. It was the phrase most invoked by law enforcement and politicians. It was the "never again" symbol for the new millennium America, but it also had a special meaning for Marlon.

"We know you lost your Aunt Fatima to those planes, Porter. We know how it made you feel...How it made you hate Muslims," Steve surmised.

"I don't hate Muslims. I hate cowards with a cause," Marlon replied, while eyeing Steve squarely.

"Well that's what this is about. More cowards with a cause," Steve replied.

Marlon was trying to read their angle, but with poker faces like the ones they were wearing, he knew they wouldn't show their hole card by tipping their hand.

"And the three kilos disappear?" Marlon quizzically asked.

Henry nodded then added, "Exactly."

"One other thing, Porter. If you do this, you do it *our* way on *our* say. There is no Plan B and no walking away...*Ever!*" Steve warned him.

"But trust me...you won't want to walk away," Henry smirked; he was balancing his threat with reward.

Marlon smiled to himself. He recognized the subtle game of "bad cop/good cop," but he let it go.

Above The Law

"Why me?" Marlon wanted to know.

"If you're smart enough to fool Navy Intelligence and the Feds for all these years, you can definitely fool a terrorist."

Marlon couldn't help but smile.

"Can I think about it?"

"Take all the time you need, but you don't leave this room without an answer."

"Cowards with a cause, huh?" Marlon said, while contemplating aloud.

Images of his aunt's face and of the plane hitting the building flooded his thoughts.

"I'm in," Marlon announced, but his mind echoed, *in what*?

Steve placed a pill in the web of Marlon's left index and middle fingers.

"When you get to your cell, take that."

"What is it?"

"If we wanted to kill you, you would've been dead," Steve chuckled.

Before Henry knocked, Marlon said, "Tell me this."

They turned to face him.

"The three kilos…which one of you decided to put it in the couch cushion?"

"We don't know what you're talking about," Henry said, but his smirk told a different story. They turned and exited the room.

"Who were those guys?" Ortega asked when he was finally able to enter the room.

"Lawyers," Marlon mumbled, but he couldn't look the old man in the eye. He hated the fact that he had to lie to him.

"Porter, I know those guys weren't your lawyers. Now, what the hell is going on?"

"Everything's cool," Marlon assured him as he headed to the elevator on his way to detention.

"Cool, huh? It's cool that Aaron Snead is sending you lawyers?" Ortega sarcastically remarked as the door of the elevator closed in his face.

So, Ortega had been listening after all. Marlon also recognized that Steve said Aaron's name precisely *because* he knew they were being monitored. He wanted the Feds to think that a gang lord and drug dealer sent Marlon a lawyer. That way, if Marlon said no, he would've looked that much worse.

The dirty muthafuckas, he thought to himself.

The starkly eggshell white room looked like a laboratory cubicle under the bright fluorescent light. In one corner was a toilet and sink combined in one steel module. Over the sink was a dull mirror that was really only highly polished steel and reminded Marlon of a silver serving dish. His reflection was blurry and grey.

He looked down at the orange jumpsuit and plastic flip-flops he had been given to wear, then at the thin plastic mattress that reminded him of school gym mats. This was jail; the thought of spending years in a cell identical or similar to it had him feeling claustrophobic.

If, whoever those guys were, could help him beat this, then he was all for it. He hit the button on the sink and the faucet sputtered to life with cloudy water that cleared up a little the longer it ran.

He looked at the small white pill and wondered what the hell it was it for. Why did he have to take it? Then Steve's voice reverberated in his mind saying, "You do it *our* way on *our* say…If we wanted to kill you, you would've been dead."

Marlon looked at himself in the mirror. They had him over a barrel with his ass out. They knew about enough to put him away for a long time. They even knew what really happened to Bank. They were holding all the cards and all he was holding was a pill.

"What do I have to lose?" he shrugged.

Above The Law

He tossed the pill down his throat then bent to drink from the faucet. Upon seeing the green slimy goo caked around the nozzle and the cloudiness of the water, he opted to dry swallow the pill.

Nothing happened. He sat on the bed for a minute.

Two minutes...

He stood up to pee and he began to feel it. He immediately got lightheaded. He urinated all over the toilet seat. He grabbed the sink to help with his balance; he wet the floor. He staggered around the tiny six by eight foot cell. The room was spinning like a disco ball at a junior high prom. Marlon felt himself slowly going down. He heard a faint gargle in his throat. The last thing he remembered was the C.O. looking down at him.

"Hey! Hey! You okay? We got a man down! Man down, cell 18. Shit! I think he's...."

January 17
Inmate Commits Suicide in Federal Detention

Officials at Cook County Federal Detention Center say the body of Marlon Porter, 27 was found earlier this morning from an apparent suicide.

"I've been a C.O. for over twenty years and I can usually pick out the ones that aren't stable. This guy didn't seem like the type," said Officer Howard Dunes.

Porter was charged with possession after three kilograms of heroin and seventy thousand dollars was found in his apartment.

That was as much of the article as Ortega could read before slamming the paper on his desk. He looked around his plush office and was surrounded by all the accoutrements of federal seniority. He had a large glistening desk with a matching credenza, a dark-red high-backed leather chair, and with every step, his feet sunk into the plush navy blue carpet. His walls were full of photographs and plaques, showing off his accomplishments from over the years. The large F.B.I. seal sat squarely on the wall behind his desk between the United States and F.B.I flags.

His office screamed that he was in charge, yet the situation made him feel outside of the loop. He couldn't put his finger on what exactly was going on.

"Suicide," he mumbled to himself while shaking his head and running his hand through his coarse salt and pepper hair.

He heard the news as soon as he stepped foot into the building; it was the talk of the office. He saw the article in the paper, gathered the reports, and even talked to the officer that found Marlon's body. However, he still couldn't wrap his mind around the suicide.

"Everything's cool sir," Marlon's last words to him echoed in his mind, but he could tell that something was amiss. Marlon couldn't even look him in the eyes, something he'd never had a problem doing before.

Was it guilt? Guilt because he was really dirty and he couldn't live with the shame? Was it fear of going to prison and being possibly housed with men whom he locked up? No, that wasn't Marlon; nothing about the situation made sense.

Ortega's assistant, Janice, strolled in with his coffee and morning briefs. She was a middle-aged, redheaded woman with a jovial nature and attractive face.

"Morning Chief, how are you? I heard the news about Porter. It's really a shame."

He took the coffee and the briefs.

"Yeah, it is."

"The Director called."

Ortega was expecting him to do so. Washington wanted to be brought up to speed on the situation.

16

Above The Law

"Ah Janice, I have a couple of names I need you to run, Steve Shapiro and Henry Allen. They are supposedly lawyers from Chicago, but don't restrict the query."

"No problem, Chief. What, in particular, am I looking for?"

"Addresses and photos," he replied.

Janice nodded and walked out.

Shapiro and Allen were the last two people to really talk to Marlon. He intended to get some answers.

Ortega perused the article again, that time he read it in its entirety, twice. Ortega noticed the article never mentioned that Marlon was a Federal Agent. A story like that would usually cause reporters to have an orgasm. Government law enforcement agent arrested for drugs kills himself in jail...

How could they miss that part? Or did they? Ortega picked up the phone and called D.E.A. Agent Frank Carlucci.

About the same time he was picking up the phone, Marlon was opening his eyes. His head was pounding and his mouth was as a dry as a bag of cotton balls. He tried to sit up, but it only made his head hurt worse.

"Shit!" he uttered.

"Here, drink this," Henry offered. He handed him a glass of water and helped him to sit up on the gurney. "Welcome back to the land of the living," he smiled. He gave a facetious sweep of his hand gesturing around the room they were in.

It was the morgue.

Marlon noticed the walls lined with small doors, like a room full of ovens, or like an oversized filing cabinet.

"What the hell am I doin' in a —," Marlon began to ask; then the realization hit him. "I guess this is how it all goes away, huh?"

Henry nodded.

"You committed suicide; they found you last night. Now, let's get out of here before they find you again."

Henry helped Marlon to his feet and walked him out of the morgue. When the morgue attendant came back from getting his morning coffee, he stopped short in front of the empty gurney.

"I coulda sworn..." he began to mumble to himself. Then he shrugged, sipped his coffee, and chuckled, "I guess he walked away."

Outside, Henry and Marlon got into a black Porsche 911 with jet-black 5% tinted windows.

Henry pulled off and casually shifted gears as they sped down West Harrison Street. He glanced over at Marlon.

"For all intents and purposes, Marlon Porter is dead. Your past and everyone in it is dead. You can never go back or reveal yourself to anyone, for any reason, at any time. Are we clear?"

"You didn't tell me that," Marlon shot back.

"You're a smart guy, Porter. The devil's always in the details."

Marlon laid his head back against the headrest, trying to calm his raging headache and to let Henry's words sink in.

As for the past, that was something he could easily forget. The memories that he cherished would always be with him, but the mistakes and memories that burned within, he was happy to have expunged.

Marlon sighed.

"Okay...What's done is done. I can live with that. What next?"

"Just a few formalities and then we interface and engage."

"With who?"

"N.T.K."

"Aye yo, what the fuck is this N.T.K. shit you keep talking about?" Marlon questioned in an aggravated tone.

Henry looked at him with a sinister grin.

Above The Law

"It's the first cousin of plausible deniability…the Need to Know."

Marlon nodded. "Where's Steve?"

"Tying up some loose ends."

The Loose Ends

Thank God for Facebook. I would've never known white boys were so fuckin' green!

These were the thoughts of Shaneka, a hood rat from the Southside of Chicago. She was loud, weaved up, and extremely colorful. She was a total contrast to the Clark Kent looking white boy in the driver's seat of the beige Jaguar X7. Shaneka knew that hood shit was what his jungle fever ass craved. He asked a lot of questions about the Black Disciples, the gang that ran her neighborhood. She would've thought he was the police, if he didn't smoke so much weed. So when he asked, she answered because she loved to talk and gossip. Shaneka was Google for any topic in her hood.

She inched her fingers up Roger's thigh and gripped his dick. *Who said white boys got lil' dicks,* she thought with a smirk.

"Don't do that," he nervously giggled, "you know I have to concentrate."

"Walk and chew bubble gum, baby," she cooed.

He made a left and headed toward Cicero.

"I thought we were going to get a room sweetie?" Shaneka inquired.

"Oh, we are," he replied while pushing his glasses up on his nose. "But I have to see someone in Cicero. So I figured, why not get a room out there."

"Whatever you say," she said, giving his hardening dick a squeeze. "You didn't forget about the three hundred I said I needed, did you?"

"Of course not," he answered. He handed her his wallet. "Go ahead and get it."

Shaneka took out three hundred dollar bills; then snuck two more before putting it back in his pocket.

They turned into the motel parking lot. Shaneka squinted her eyes when she saw the white Escalade with "Missy" on the plate. Beside it sat a candy apple red '64 Impala drop-top sitting on gold '74 Daytons.

"I know this bitch ain't!" she squealed with an indignant tone and delight.

She wasted no time pulling out her cell phone and punching in a number from memory.

"Baby, is anything wro…"

She held up her index finger and exited the car. This was Black Disciple business. The white boy didn't need to hear her conversation.

"Yeah," the gruff, male voice answered.

"Tony! Boy I can't believe this shit, but Missy out here wit' Aaron!

"Out where?"

"In Cicero, at the Day's Inn! Boy, he slippin'!"

"You sure?" he wanted to know, already grabbing his car keys and hitting the door.

"Of course I'm sure nigga, 'less somebody else 'round here drive an Escalade with Missy on the plate and a red Impala on Daytons! I'm out here with this lame ass white boy I been juicin'," she boasted.

"Stay there! Don't let 'em leave. I'ma be right there!"

"Don't let 'em leave? Boy, I ain't got nothin' to do wit' this shit. You betta hurry yo ass up."

Click!

Roger got out and rounded the car.

"Shaneka, if there's a problem we can just…"

Above The Law

"No, no sweetie, no problem," she sweetly replied. She leaned in and pecked him on the lips with a quick kiss. "Just be a good boy and get the room. I'ma wait right here."

She never took her eyes off the two vehicles.

Shaneka wasn't only a ghetto gossiper; she was also a police informant. Not formally, but she knew the Crime Stoppers' number by heart and had been vital to a few murder and drug cases.

That was how Steve found her. Meeting her was easy. He posed as Roger and contacted her through Facebook. From surveillance of Aaron, he knew Aaron was fucking Tony Coleman's, a rival gang member's, girl. He would be the patsy to dispose of Aaron when the time came.

Steve had GPS devices attached to all three of Aaron's vehicles. He knew where he was at all times. Aaron knew what Marlon looked like and about Al-Nymayr, so he had to go. Steve knew Shaneka would run her mouth. She saw exactly what Steve wanted her to see and did what he wanted her to do. A wise man can play a fool, but a fool can only be played.

Shaneka was fooled.

"Just be a good boy and get the room. I'ma wait right here," said the fly to the spider.

Her legs were up on Steve's shoulders when they heard the metallic roar of automatic weapons.

"Oh shit!" she gasped.

The dick was good, but death's spectacle was better. She ran to the window in time to see Missy and Aaron's body do the death dance, jerking and twitching like epileptic puppets on electrified strings.

"What's going on?" Steve asked, as if he didn't know.

"I...I don't know, Shaneka lied.

Steve was behind her. He could break her neck and cut all ties, but he decided against doing so. If ignorance was bliss, Shaneka was in Heaven, so he gave her a pass.

"Then come back to bed."

Chapter Two

"Chief, I've got the query you asked for," Janice announced as she crossed the room and approached Ortega's desk.

He was just hanging up with the F.B.I. Director Horace Casey. The Director thought he was Hoover's incarnate, so he took any smear to the agency's image as a personal affront to his Directorship. That's why the news never mentioned that Marlon was a Federal Agent. Casey had that damaging information squashed in-house.

"The son of a bitch is dead and good riddance. No need to sully the Agency, Ortega," Casey spat.

Janice handed him several pages of computer printout.

"I came up with several Shapiros in and around Cook County..."

"Of course. Shapiro and lawyer are synonymous," he dryly cracked.

She smirked without comment and continued.

"But none had the first name of Steve. So like you said, I didn't restrict the query and I came up with six Steve

Shapiros, Attorneys at Law. Two are dead, one is retired; the other three are still active."

"Thank you Janice," he replied. Ortega quickly flipped through all six photos. He shook his head in disgust. "I knew it."

"Chief, anything wrong?"

He started to explain, but his instincts thought better.

"It's nothing I can't solve. Call down to the N.C.I. and tell them I want stills from their surveillance cameras of the two guys that came to see Porter."

"Right away."

His intuition was once again on the money. None of the Shapiro's pictures matched either of the two so-called lawyers. *However, if they weren't lawyers,* he thought, *who were they?*

"I'm damn sure gonna find out," he answered himself aloud.

January 18

"What's that for?"

"Lie detector."

"I thought you guys already knew everything."

Steve shrugged and gave Marlon a casual grin.

"Routine. In our line of work, these are like piss tests for operators of heavy equipment. The things we do, the things we know, a lot of people would love to compromise us. So periodically, you'll have to take one of these," Steve explained.

Marlon gave him an indifferent nod of the head, then sat down and let Henry hook him up to the machine.

"Not much of a safety measure though. It ain't hard to beat the machine," Marlon commented, while Henry wrapped the blood pressure band around his arm.

Above The Law

"True…to an extent. The machine can be beat, but it's the questions you have to worry about," Henry explained. "There are many angles to the truth."

Marlon conceded the point.

"Ready?"

"Handle your business."

Steve checked his blood pressure, 110/80. It was normal. He gave Henry the nod.

"Do you drink water?" Henry asked.

"Yes."

The needle bumped, slid then went back to sleep.

Normal.

"Is your name Marlon Porter?"

"Yes."

The needle bumped, slid, and slept.

Still normal.

"Are you a homosexual?"

"Fuck you."

"Just answer the question."

"No"

The needle comfortably rested.

"Have you ever had fantasies of sucking a man's penis?" Henry asked without a hint of humor.

Marlon grilled him."Yo, what kind of shit y'all on…"

"Just answer the question."

"Fuck no!"

"A simple yes or no will suffice."

"No."

"Did you kill Bank?"

The question caught Marlon by surprise. He hadn't come to grips with that part of his past. He glared at Henry.

"Did you kill Bank?"

"No," Marlon growled.

The needle woke up and dipped an inch or two; it was swerving like a drunk driver.

Steve checked his pressure again, 130/110. Not normal, he was lying.

"As a Federal Agent, have you ever stolen from the Government?"

There was an elongated pause.

Icy stares were exchanged.

"No," Marlon replied.

The needle danced as if it were headed down the Soul Train Line. His blood pressure rose to 135/110. He was lying.

"Have you ever harbored ill-will or enmity towards the United States?"

Marlon smirked.

"What Black man hasn't?"

Chuckles filled the room and lightened the tension. Henry rephrased the question.

"Have you ever committed an act of aggression against the United States?"

"No."

The needle bumped and slept. He was truthful.

"Are your mother and father deceased?"

"Yes."

Bump, slide, sleep, truth.

Henry might've defeated him, but Marlon beat the machine and kept his secret.

Henry turned off the machine and extended his hand.

"Don't worry. What happened in the past died in the cell last night. You'll do a lot worse things in the future. But it'll be in the name of your country. Welcome to the team."

Marlon levelly eyed him and then shook his hand.

January 20

He absolutely had to be there. Henry and Steve told him he couldn't, but he already knew that he would. The temptation was too great. Who wouldn't want to attend their

Above The Law

own funeral? The idea of being a fly on the wall and having a chance to see his own memorial service consumed his mind. Who really would miss him, who would come, or maybe more importantly, who wouldn't come? What would they say about him?

Marlon couldn't resist.

He dressed in a basic disguise, a nappy matted Afro over his 1-guard temple tapered waves. He wore a groundskeeper's one-piece blue jumper with a padded pouch to give his six-pack abs a beer gut appearance. He stood in the distance on a knoll in the cemetery. He had a rake in one hand and a small pair of binoculars in the other. He was watching his own funeral. What he didn't know was that Steve and Henry were watching him. It was the first time Marlon had been out alone since the "suicide," so that gave them a chance to observe him in a public setting.

Steve handed the binoculars to Henry as he sat in the driver's seat of the bread truck they were using.

"I don't know about this guy...too many shadows, too many blind spots in the file that we don't know about," Steve skeptically remarked.

Henry shrugged and peered through the binoculars.

"The General says this is our guy. I just follow orders; I don't make 'em,"

"I mean, I'm just sayin'...He fit the profile to a T, but what about these clandestine calls he makes so frequently? He goes through a lot of trouble to keep them off the radar with those pre-paid cells. He always pays in cash. He keeps the calls too short to be traced *every* time. That is not a coincidence. Then he destroys the phone after a single call.

"Who do you think he's calling, Al-Queda?" Henry cracked.

They looked at each other and laughed at their inside joke.

"Anyway," Henry added while stretching in his seat, "his status is for temporary measures." He glanced at Steve with a smirk, "So when he's done..." Steve liked the idea and gave Henry a devious nod.

Marlon was a little agitated to see that only Ortega, the Reverend, and his girlfriend Asia were in attendance for his service. They had only known each other for less than a year, but they were practically inseparable when their schedules permitted. She was a broker with one of the largest African American-owned investment groups in the country, Renaissance Investments.

Marlon had been working in the Chicago field office for eight months, but it seemed like they met on the first day. They met at a local jazz club, The Backroom. It was on a Wednesday, open mic night. The two were a couple from that night forward. Now that Marlon was gone, all Asia had left were fond memories.

Her eyes may have been hidden behind oversized Gucci frames, but nothing could hide the tears that poured from them and streaked her honey-brown face. Ortega put a fatherly arm around her and gave her upper arm a reassuring squeeze. Underneath his anguish over Marlon's senseless suicide, he was disgusted with the funeral on his behalf. Since the Bureau covered up the fact that Marlon was one of them, they certainly weren't about to give him a proper burial. Ortega had to fight tooth and nail so it wouldn't turn into a pauper's funeral.

He understood that Marlon was charged with some serious crimes, but that was just it, charged and not convicted. They didn't give Marlon a chance, but then the thought hit him, Marlon didn't give himself a chance.

He decided to take the easy way out, so his suicide would forever be used as admission of his guilt.

The Reverend ended his brief eulogy with generalities and Ortega and Asia both threw a handful of dirt on the coffin as it was lowered into the ground. Ortega, a staunch Catholic, crossed himself then turned to Asia.

"Can I walk you to your car?" he asked.

She smiled through her tears.

"Yes, please do."

"I know this is hard on you, if you need anything, don't hesitate to call," Ortega expressed while giving her his card.

"Thank you, Mr. Ortega. I...I'll be okay," she sincerely replied.

He nodded as they reached her forest green Mercedes Benz C-320. She chirped the alarm to unlock the doors.

"Just..." Asia hesitated.

Ortega urged her to finish. "Yes?"

"I mean...why wasn't anyone here? I guess I expected more. Maybe not a twenty-one gun salute considering the circumstances, but something more than this. I don't know, didn't Marlon have any friends in the Bureau?" she asked.

He started to fudge the answer, but decided she deserved the truth.

"Marlon's death is being treated like the plague in the Bureau. What few associates he did have, don't want it to look like they were involved."

She nodded as if an epiphany had been revealed.

"Evidently, that didn't matter to you."

"I'm old," he chuckled lightly, "I've reached the top of the ladder."

"But...do you think he did it?"

He looked her in the eyes and answered, "No Ms. Walker, I don't."

She squeezed his hand in a gesture of appreciation and then opened her car door.

"Ms. Walker..." he began. He had been debating during the funeral, whether or not to broach the issue here...now. *Now seems as good a time as any other*, he thought to himself. "Even though I don't think Marlon is guilty of the drugs and money found in his home, I do think something else is going on."

"Something else like what, Mr. Ortega?"

"Not now. There are still a few dots that I'm connecting. But sometime soon, I was wondering if I could come by and talk to you about Marlon."

Asia sighed deeply and looked off into the distance. She saw a pudgy grounds keeper with a rake; then she turned to Ortega. "Mr. Ortega, what Marlon and I shared may've been short, but it was more than sweet, it was fire. That pinch me, I'm dreamin', type of connection that comes once in a lifetime if you're lucky. Now that I've had it, I have a Marlon-sized hole in my heart. One I'll never be able to fill, therefore I can't dwell on it. Do you understand what I'm saying, Mr. Ortega?"

"Yes, but…"

"If there's a 'but' you can't understand," she cut him off smoothly and gave him a condescending smile. "It's over, Mr. Ortega. The Bureau has already convicted Marlon. Whatever you find out won't help or hurt, so what's the point?"

She kissed him on the cheek and got into the car.

"This is my life," Marlon said to himself with an exasperated chuckle. No one to mourn me but a supervisor and a woman I've only known less than a year.

Asia was far more than just "a woman." In many ways, she was *the* woman. Marlon was not the player type, despite the fact that he was 6'1", with an athlete's physique of 200 pounds. He had a dark chocolate complexion with light brown eyes, bushy eyebrows, and he drove females crazy. He was more like a wolf. When he mated, it wasn't just for the night. He'd experienced his share of trysts, from ménage a trios to missionary, but women weren't his weakness. However, *the* woman was.

Above The Law

Asia wasn't only beautiful; she was brilliant. In many ways, she was smarter than he was. She was intuitive and funny. Their likes and dislikes meshed and consummated their connection. She was everything he wanted in a woman, and when it came to sex, like Sade said, "Every night is a New Year's Eve." Every time they were together sexually, it was a celebration of fire and passion. No woman had captivated his attention so completely. To be so close to her, yet so far away was tearing at his heart. He cursed himself for putting her through this charade, for being so selfish and not even once stopping to think how his decision would affect her.

He wanted to go to her.

He knew he couldn't.

He watched her from a distance.

When she glanced up in his direction, his stomach stopped. A part of him wanted her to be able to see past the distance, see through the disguise, and come to him. But another part was glad when she turned away. It was better that way.

The Marlon Porter she knew was dead.

As she drove away out of sight and out of his life, his thoughts turned to the last time they were together and the domino effect of the events that led to that moment...

Three Days Earlier
January 17

"Damn Playboy, y'all muhfuckas eatin' this shit in East St. Louis or what? Goddamn you come back quick," Lil' Fred commented. He displayed a combination of admiration and casualness that all hustlers possessed. Standing 5'2" in his socks, he wasn't big enough to be much else. His slow Midwestern drawled slang was never rushed, like every word was a gift from him to you. He handed the shopping bag to Marlon.

31

"Come on pimpin', recognize. Ain't nothin' slow about East St. Lou but our walk. We gets dat money," Marlon bragged, with hints of Midwest inflections to mask his East Coast accent.

Lil' Fred chuckled. "Man, fuck East St. Louis. The only thing goin' on there is the road that lead heah."

Marlon laughed. "A'ight, watch yo' mouth."

"I know that's right."

"But dead ass, tell A I'm ready to do big thangs, you understand, but I need a better number on these bricks. I could easily get better numbers wit' the Mexicans," Marlon negotiated.

"But you wont," Lil' Fred chuckled casually. "You know Big A got that shit that the fiends checkin' for. That Mexican shit is mud."

"Well tell Aaron I need to holla at him," Marlon said. He purposely mentioned the name for the wire.

Lil' Fred shrugged and rested his wrist on the steering wheel.

"Call 'em, but he ain't gonna tell you nothin' different. Them Muslim cats pushed the number up on him, so you know what it is for you!"

"Muslim cats?" Marlon echoed. Lil' Fred nor Aaron had ever mentioned their supplier. He attributed it to the fact that Lil' Fred was getting comfortable with their lucrative relationship.

"Yeah, and them jokers got it, ya heard? I'm talking like water. Since Bush sent them Army muhfuckas to Afghanistan, shit been beautiful. I hope that war never ends," Lil' Fred cracked.

Marlon nodded in response and filed that vital piece of information away in his mind. That's what investigations were about, little pieces of information that came together to tell the entire story. Lil' Fred was a small fish, what Marlon called his "point of entry."

Above The Law

He would work Fred until he took him down, then he would lean on Aaron. Hopefully, Aaron would give info on the Muslims. Then, like dominos, they would all fall. Marlon would ultimately take a piece for himself. He didn't see himself as dishonest or dirty, but why turn in millions to the government when they were the ones who fronted the money? They didn't need it.

He made $63,000 a year and took advantage of any extra money he could find. He worked for the government, but he still paid government taxes! No, he wasn't dirty, but he was nobody's fool either.

"Muslims? What Muslims?" the agent in the van a block away from Marlon commented to his partner.

The surveillance van was decked out, front to back in the newest surveillance technology. That night was the night they were supposed to take down Lil' Fred. Two more unmarked vehicles were awaiting Marlon's signal to move in.

It never came.

Boom! Boom! Boom!

"Oh Shit! What…"

That was all the surveillance team heard. Lil' Fred's brains were blown all over the dashboard, windshield, and Marlon.

The two of them never saw it coming. Lil' Fred was about to say something and Marlon glanced in his direction. He saw a shadow in his peripheral creeping up on the driver's side of Lil' Fred's rented Dodge Charger. Before he could warn Lil' Fred, the shadow stuck a chrome .357 snub-nose to the back of his head and blew his brains all over the inside of the car.

Boom! Boom! Boom!

"Oh Shit! What…" Marlon started to say, but he was stopped short when he felt the barrel of another gun at the back of his head.

"Don't be a hero," the gunman sneered.

Marlon slowly raised his hands.

"You got a winner, playa."

The gunman snickered and then faded away.

"Alpha team! Alpha team! Move in, move in!" the surveillance agent barked into his headset, and the two unmarked cars sprung into action. As soon as Marlon heard the crunch of footsteps on gravel recede, he snatched his gun from his waist and said into the wire, "Move in! My mark is hit! Move!" he said as he hopped up, ready to pursue the men, but the skidding tires in the distance told him they were gone.

Before he finished his statement, the Alpha team was already skidding up, lights flashing and guns drawn. In the blink of an eye, Marlon's mind thought of Lil' Fred's stash house. It was in a part of Chicago called the Wild 100's. He knew exactly where it was because Fred had taken him there several times. He had even been able to steal the combination to his safe, one number at a time, on three different occasions.

As the Alpha team moved towards the Charger, Marlon ducked back into the car. He reached into Lil' Fred's pocket and cuffed his key ring a few moments before the Alpha team reached the car.

"Shit! Somebody used an axe on this mosquito," one of the agents remarked, seeing the bloody stump of a head that was left of Lil' Fred. The killer had used dum-dum bullets that expanded on impact and left a bloody mess of whatever they hit.

"You think you were made?" he asked.

"If I was, I would've been dead too," Marlon replied. His adrenaline level was still so high it was whistling like a teakettle in his ears.

He gave a preliminary report at the scene, but his mind was on the other side of town, Lil' Fred's safe. He knew he couldn't go right away, but he also knew he needed to move quickly before someone else beat him to it or Ortega sent a team to search his place. If he couldn't go, there was only one person he trusted to go in his place.

Asia.

Marlon stepped away from the lights, cameras, and action of the newly established crime scene and dialed Asia's number from memory. He hated speed dial because he felt it made your memory lazy.

"Hey sexy," Asia cheerfully greeted him.

Hearing her voice always made him smile.

"Hey beautiful, listen baby, I need you to handle something for me."

"Sure, what is it?"

"It's...a friend of mine. He's in a little bind. I need you to go to his place and pick up something," he explained.

"No problem. When?"

"Now."

"Must be a helluva bind," she quipped.

Marlon didn't comment. He glanced over his shoulder at the crime scene and said, "I'm over here in Eckersall Park. Can you meet me on Yates Boulevard and the corner of East 87th?"

"Okay."

Marlon noticed a flutter of hesitation in her voice.

"You sure?"

"Yes, I'm sure. Give me a few minutes. I'll text you when I'm on my way."

Marlon hung up.

Once she texted him, he left the scene using one of the unmarked cars of the Alpha team. He was headed back to the office, but he made a stop on Yates. He pulled up behind Asia's Mercedes and went to sit in her passenger seat. She leaned over and kissed him as a greeting.

"You okay?" she inquired in a motherly tone.

"Yeah," he replied, while studying her soft features.

Marlon loved to look at Asia. When he first saw her, she reminded him of Sanaa Lathan, except her eyes were a little more cat-like.

"Is that what happened to your friend?" she asked with a slight toss of the head, referring to all the police activity. She'd seen the commotion and the lights when she drove by.

Marlon could tell by her tone that she knew something was up. He searched her eyes for even a hint of disapproval, but he didn't find any. Now he realized why it was so easy to trust Asia, because they were always on the same page. It didn't take words or even gestures. Where he led, she instinctively followed.

He handed her Lil' Fred's keys and a small piece of paper.

"That's the combination to the safe. It's behind the dresser in the bedroom. Pull the dresser out and you'll see it," he instructed her.

"How much is supposed to be there?"

"I don't know. Just get it all," he smirked.

Asia giggled, started the car, and then joked, "The things us women do for some good dick."

"Oh for real? Well check, it's a bank about a block from here…"

"No baby," she kissed him and sucked his lip. As she pulled away she said, "It ain't *that* good."

Marlon laughed.

"A'ight, you got that. I deserved it."

"Yes you did," she snickered. "I'll meet you at your place."

"He exited her car, hopped back into the unmarked Explorer, and pulled off in the opposite direction.

Marlon went into the office to brief Ortega, assuring him that he didn't feel that his cover was blown.

"Well, why didn't they kill you too?"

Above The Law

"Good question," Marlon admitted, although he had already considered the answer.

Ortega sighed.

"I'm pulling you in… just for a little while, so we can assess the situation. If it's not blown, I'll send you back in. If it is, we'll have to proceed from a different angle."

"Leave me in the game, Coach," Marlon smirked.

"Get outta here, Porter," Ortega chuckled.

The sounds of R. Kelly's "Your Body's Callin" greeted Marlon as he inserted his key and entered his apartment, causing the frown on his brow to melt away.

"12 Play" meant Asia was there. He had been trying to call her, but her phone kept going straight to voicemail. It had made him a little worried. But now, hearing her favorite album and smelling her Chanel Number 5 in the air, his senses relaxed, and he headed for the bedroom.

He could hear the shower now that he had left the sounds of R. Kelly in the living room. The bathroom door was ajar and the steam from the shower filled the room. He shook his head. He could never understand how Asia could take showers with the water scalding hot. He never took a shower with her, and she would tease him and call him a punk for it.

Marlon walked in and watched her shapely silhouette from behind the shower curtain. She heard him walk in and felt his warming presence.

"What happened? Your phone kept goin' to voice mail. I was worried," he said while leaning against the sink.

"Battery died," Asia replied, raising her voice above the shower. She pulled the curtain back. "Besides, I'm a big girl. I can take care of myself," she winked and handed him the soapy washcloth.

He took it and began to wash her back while she held her ponytail out of the way.

"If you're such a big girl, you should start washing you own back," he smiled.

"I mean, there are a few things I keep you around for," she retorted.

"I know that's right," he chuckled.

Marlon lathered and caressed her from her shoulders to her lower back, while silently admiring her scrumptious 32-22-38 body. In the back of his mind was the question, which she answered without him asking.

"Everything's good, baby. I put the bag under your bed."

"Was it worth the trip?" he probed.

Asia looked over her shoulder and replied, "Definitely."

"Good."

He slapped Asia on her wet ass, making her jump and suck in her breath.

She swung at him, but he dodged it easily and headed for the bedroom, laughing as she cursed him out from the shower.

He leaned over, probed for the bag until he felt something, and pulled it out. He grabbed it from the bottom and dumped the contents out onto the bed. Stacks and stacks of rubber-banded bills covered the middle of his waterbed in a small pyramid that bobbed up and down with the bed's motion. Just by looking at it, he estimated it to be over a hundred grand. He was actually really close. It was one hundred and seven grand.

Asia came out of the bathroom wearing nothing but a smile and drying her hair with a towel. Another one of Asia's idiosyncrasies, she loved to drip dry.

Asia walked up behind Marlon, wrapped her arms around his waist, and pressed her naked body against him.

"Can I ask you something?" she asked.

He shrugged. He had anticipated the question.

Above The Law

"I'm an agent, not an angel," Marlon simply answered. "A badge doesn't change a man's heart; no more than a ring will change a man's lust."

"At least I know what to expect if we get married," Asia quipped playfully.

"You know what I mean, Asia," he replied. He turned to her and wrapped his arms around her waist.

"Hm-hmmm. But I wasn't asking you why, that's obvious. I mean, the reasons are spread all over your bed. I was gonna ask why you trusted me to know?" she inquired.

Marlon looked into her eyes and replied, "Because, I'm trusting you with something more than just my lil' secret."

"And what's that?"

"My heart."

The look in his eyes told Asia how sincere he was. She saw that act of trust as a confirmation of Marlon's feelings for her. He was letting her into his world. She kissed him deeply.

"I promise your heart is in good hands. But I can also help with that," she told him. She was referring to the money. "I can create a couple of accounts, invest it, and clean it up for you. Ain't no angels on Wall Street either, baby," she winked.

His hands lustfully caressed her body while hers began removing his black Levi jeans. Asia fell to her knees and slowly planted wet kisses up his thigh until her tongue reached the length of his thick throbbing manhood. She hungrily took him into her mouth. Marlon grunted in ecstasy. After ten minutes of mind-blowing head, he was ready to slide inside of her throbbing wetness. He lifted Asia up and off her feet while she instinctively wrapped her legs around his waist. She greedily kissed him in anticipation of his insertion. Spreading her voluptuous ass cheeks as he pinned her against the wall, Marlon deeply penetrated her. He took her breath away with each long, powerful thrust of his hips.

"Oh my God," she gasped. She tried using her legs to leverage herself up and squirm away, but Marlon was unrelenting. Each time he forcefully brought her back down to meet each powerful stroke that had Asia on the verge of tears.

"What...what are you doing to me?" she groaned, feeling his dick in her intestines.

"Whatever you want me to, baby...whatever you need. Just don't leave me," he whispered in her ear between grunts of carnal emphasis.

"Never," she vowed, "I promise."

Those two words, I promise, echoed in Marlon's mind as he stood on the knoll overlooking his own burial. That was the last time he saw Asia. She was away on business when he was arrested. Now, she had come home to this. He felt like he had betrayed her. As he reluctantly turned away, he felt a burning desire to somehow rectify the situation with Asia.

He couldn't let it end like that.

Chapter Three

January 20

"The lab finally matched those photos for you, Chief," Janice said as she placed the photos on the desk.

"Thanks Janice," Ortega replied.

She nodded politely then exited the office and gently closed the door behind her.

Ortega removed his half-moon shaped reading glasses and pinched the bridge of his nose. A heavy sigh escaped his mouth and nose. He was a man in need of some good news. After hundreds of hours of surveillance and resources, the Black P. Stones investigation had died with Aaron Snead, Lil' Fred and the undercover, Marlon Porter. They had made good progress while investigating the connection between the Black P. Stones and certain city officials. Now he would have to start from scratch.

However, with pressure from his politically minded Director, he didn't have time to start from scratch. It was an election year and the Director wanted results; he wanted a few politicians doing the perp walk on the front page of the Tribune. Not because they were elected officials that committed crimes, but because they were Democrats. The Bureau's bread had always been buttered by the Republicans.

Ortega didn't so much mind his field office being used for such overtly political purposes, hell he was staunchly Republican himself. He just hated the thought of being the scapegoat if the investigation was unsuccessful.

He placed his glasses back on his face and opened the folder that Janice had just given him. He looked down at the face of the man he knew as Steve Shapiro and smiled. The Bureau's face recognition software had saved many cases. He looked at the second sheet and saw the face of Henry Allen. Both of their files were thick. Both had served in the military. Steve Shapiro, whose real name was Edward Mahoney was an ex-Navy Seal. Henry Allen, real name Michael Rosenberg, was an ex-Marine and narcotics detective. What caught Ortega's eye and made him remove his glasses was the fact that both were supposed to be dead.

"Holy shit," he mumbled.

He sat back and tried to gather his thoughts. He read the words 'Deceased' again under the two bios.

"Impossible," he uttered to himself.

There were three possibilities that came to Ortega's mind. One, the face recognition had erred, some kind of glitch. He quickly dismissed that option, possible, but not probable, and easily verifiable. The second thing was that those two, Shapiro and Allen, or whoever they were, both had identical twin brothers, even less probable than a computer glitch.

The third possibility, and the one that resonated the loudest with Ortega's assessment from the beginning was that this was something big, something very big, and very silent, and he was not in the loop. A place he didn't want to be too much longer.

Above The Law

When Marlon tried to grab his Pepsi can, he was reminded why he was using a straw. He almost dropped his soda; his fingers were in extreme pain. Steve had told him that they would be like that for at least ten days after chloroformic acid was used on his fingertips to remove all traces of his prints.

He looked at his fingers. They were red and puffy, but they were smooth and print-less. His fingerprints weren't the only thing removed. The veil of what real law enforcement was about in America was beginning to be removed as well.

"Our job description is simple. We're supposed to protect the country by any means," Henry told Marlon as they drove along US Route 30 in Canton, Ohio heading for New Jersey.

Steve was driving the black Dodge Durango and Henry was in the passenger seat looking back at Marlon.

"Homeland Security," Marlon nodded, as if he understood, but he had no idea.

"Yes and no," Henry replied. "We're a department called The Division, but you won't see that listed on Homeland's website, nor are we listed as official employees. For all intents and purposes, we don't exist, not as individuals and not as a part of our government," Henry explained. Steve glanced in the rearview mirror from time to time to gauge Marlon's reactions.

"Ghosts," Marlon replied.

"Exactly," Henry smiled.

"The world thinks we're dead, so we don't have to obey the laws of the living, so to speak. There are no Congressional Oversight Committees, no political strings dangling budget carrots in our faces. We're free to pursue terrorists by their own rules. Lies, deception, torture, even death. No trials whatsoever and punishment is swift."

43

"Torture? How can we get away with that type shit after all the fuckin' ruckus over waterboarding?" Marlon skeptically asked.

Steve and Henry exchanged conspiratorial smirks.

"Let me ask you something," Steve said, making eye contact through the rearview mirror. "If someone broke into your house and raped your wife and killed your kids, would there be any law in the world to stop you from killing him?"

"Shit, he dead just for breaking in," Marlon replied.

"Exactly, so do you think the government would do any less? Do you think the absolute defense of this nation depends on whether or not we get a warrant for a wiretap? Or if we had probable cause to search? No fuckin' way! We'll hook a battery cable up to their fuckin' nuts if we have to! And you know what? That's exactly what the American people want," Steve expressed.

Marlon couldn't disagree with the logic.

"But of course no one will actually say that, you know!" Henry added. "No politician can really say 'fuck it, let's murder those cock suckers', so we do what no one else has the guts to."

"We murder the cock suckers," Marlon nodded, he was feeling the idea 110 percent.

"If you're a terrorist and you're in the country or anywhere near it, we catch you, we murder you. No Miranda rights and no trial. We *are* the law," Henry boasted.

"Above the law," Marlon mumbled with a smirk.

They had opened his eyes to many things including the real meaning for the alphabet boys, the C.I.A., F.B.I., D.E.A., A.T.F., etc… What really got his attention was when they told him how they were funded.

Since The Division could never be acknowledged officially, they couldn't leave a budgetary paper trail. They couldn't even be funded by the infamous 'Black Budget,' which many covert operations were funded through. Nothing

Above The Law

about The Division could be traced back to the government. The blow back would be catastrophic.

So they were allowed to get their budget off the books. The Division was allowed to make their money in the underworld.

Laundering money for international cartels, smuggling drugs, gunrunning, and drug dealing were among the most lucrative financing vehicles. The approach made sense because international terrorism and criminal syndicates were becoming more and more intertwined. Therefore it was logical, if not exactly ethical, to have players with one foot in international crime and the other established in the high stakes game of national security. Then again, nothing about The Division was ethical.

"Look, we could walk in a bank, rob it, get caught, and be out tomorrow with the money," Steve told him.

"As long as no civilians are hurt," Henry added, "Because if that happens..." He shook his head, letting Marlon know that was the one law they weren't above.

"Marlon? You still with me?"

Marlon looked up from his soda at Henry sitting in front of him.

"Yeah, no doubt. Just thinking."

"You ready?" Henry questioned.

"What you got?" Marlon replied. He started to grab his soda, but changed his mind and sipped it through the straw.

Henry slid three black and white photos in front of him.

These are the Abdullah brothers, the nucleus of e Al-Nymayr, one of the most powerful Al-Qaeda cells in America," Henry explained.

"Al Nu-who?"

"Numayr, it means panther in Arabic. The reference to the original Black Panthers is intentional. They combined black militancy with fundamentalist Islam.

Marlon nodded while looking at the individual pictures. The first was of a brown-skinned dude heavily jeweled on the wrist, neck, and left ear. He was dressed in a white fur with a matching hat and held a cell phone to his ear.

"That's Fuquan Abdullah, the youngest of the Abdullah siblings. He is the least religious of the clan. Besides no pork or alcohol, he doesn't observe any of the other Islamic tenets. He is also the one with the most street cred as they say, and he has several gang affiliations," Henry informed him.

The next picture was of a brother with a trimmed, well-kept beard in a double-breasted Armani suit and sunglasses. He was shaking hands with another man in front of what looked to be a Mercedes convertible.

"Ali Muslim, the next older brother. He's the family lawyer as well as chief administrator of all the Abdullah's legitimate interests. Extremely intelligent and very well-connected with the New Jersey political scene."

The last picture was of a bearded brother dressed in traditional Muslim garb of a black Khamua, a long half-collared shirt that extended as low as the knee and a pair of loose fitting black pants. On his head was a gold and black kufi.

"Aziz Abdullah, also known as Brother Imam. He is the leader of Al-Nymayr. This guy knows his stuff and he's fluent in Arabic. The type of connection into the Black Muslim community that Al-Qaeda thrives on," Henry briefed as he eyed Marlon.

"This is the deal. Someone high-ranking in the Numayr organization is a Federal informant. We don't know who, but we do know that Numayr is planning a terrorist attack on American soil and the informant is playing double agent and feeding the Feds bad information."

"So why not just tell the Feds their snitch is full of shit?" Marlon proposed.

Above The Law

"Because then they'll pull 'em, or worse lean on 'em harder- which would scare him away and then we lose our only link to exactly what's going on," Henry reasoned.

Marlon shrugged.

"So snatch up Brother Imam.   He's bound to know something."

Henry shook his head.

We'd still be tipping our hand.   We snatch up one of the Abdullah brothers and Al-Qaeda will know we're on to them.   No, we need you to go in and find the snitch so we can talk to him.   We're not the Feds.   When we lean, we lean hard," Henry smirked then reached back to shake Marlon's hand.

Marlon started to shake his hand, but the contact made him flinch.   They settled on a fist bump.

"Give it a few more days," Henry said.

As soon as Ortega arrived in D.C., he knew what kind of meeting it would be.   Director Edwards had chosen to have their meeting at the posh 1789, a fashionable restaurant in Georgetown, which was frequented by Washington insiders and the power-lunching corporate crowd.   The tables were spaced well enough to make discrete conversation possible, but it was certainly no place to have the kind of talk Ortega had to come for.   He was keenly aware of the Director's intent in choosing the place.   If the conversation had meant to be frank and, if necessary, deniable, it would've taken place at the Hoover building, in the Director's private dining room.   By having the meeting in an elite, but unsecured public place, Ortega knew nothing of significance would be forthcoming.

"Good afternoon, Mr. Ortega," the Director greeted with a firm, vigorous handshake.

For 68 years old, the Director was still a bulldog of a man with heavy jowls.   His receding hairline had almost disappeared and what was left, was as white as cotton. His hawk-like eyes focused on Ortega as the two men sat down.

"Good afternoon Director Edwards. How are you? You're looking well," Ortega replied with a genuine smile.

"And I see that you are still one of the Bureau's best fabricators," the Director mockingly bowed, forcing a chuckle from Ortega. "I took the liberty of ordering for us both. Taking into account your elevated cholesterol level, I thought a soup and salad would suffice."

Ortega smiled to himself. With the Director, there was always double speaking. By ordering for Ortega, he was conveying the fact that he knew him well enough to know his taste and his concerns. The mention of cholesterol was to let Ortega know that he had eyes and ears everywhere in the Bureau, as Ortega had seen the doctor just two days prior. The soup and salad meant the conversation would be brief, no appetizers, therefore no beating around the bush.

"Thank you sir."

"I detect a hint of amusement in your tone."

"I applaud your astuteness."

"Ah, so it is."

"I would like..." Ortega started, but stopped short as the waiter brought their food.

Ortega hadn't been away from D.C. long enough to forget that you never talked around D.C. waiters. They had ears like listening devices, trained to pick up snippets. They listened for enough to pass on to appreciative receivers. As soon as the waiter walked off, Ortega slid the folder over to the Director.

"I would like for you to take a look at this."

"Director Edwards glanced at the folder as he ladled a spoonful of soup into his mouth.

"And this would be?"

"Sir, I was hoping you could tell me."

Above The Law

The Director dabbed his mouth with his napkin, then replied, "My wife informed me that our grandchildren are coming to visit, therefore it is fortunate for you that I'm feeling indulgent."

"Very fortunate," Ortega remarked with just the right amount of humility to take the sting out of the sarcasm.

A subtle grin played across Director Edwards' lips. Ortega's intent was received. He placed his reading glasses over his aging eyes, and then leisurely perused the file. He put it down after a few minutes and ladled his soup.

"I don't believe I've had the pleasure of making their acquaintance."

"These are the two men that posed as Marlon Porter's lawyers, before his...suicide," Ortega informed him.

The Director speared a tomato in his salad.

"Posed?"

"Under assumed names."

"Hmmm, interesting."

"They were supposed to be dead."

"Interesting *and* disturbing. Disturbing to think God's idea of an afterlife is Chicago in January," the Director quipped.

Ortega didn't feign amusement.

"I would like to know what's going on sir."

"Is that a statement or a question?"

"It's a respectful request for information," Ortega shot back a subtle nod. The Director speared another tomato and dabbed his mouth with the napkin again. Ortega recognized he was buying time, formulating a proper response.

"Neither of these men is, nor have they ever been in the employ of the Bureau. This much I can assure you."

Ortega assessed the Director's response. He had purposely allowed him an "in," but Ortega knew he had to proceed with caution.

"Besides my cholesterol, is there anything else up in Chicago?" Ortega quipped, referring to the Director ubiquitous ears and eyes.

"Your suspicions."

"And yours would be as well. I'm operating blindly and I don't like it. I feel like I'm being made a patsy for something I'm not privy to," Ortega expressed.

"Richard, you're not a patsy."

"I mean, I don't mind taking one for the team. But if I'm going to take a dive, at least let me know I'm in the ring. Don't let me get sucker punched. I don't deserve it," Ortega firmly stated.

Director Edwards smiled warmly with a touch of condescension.

"Richard, I have the utmost confidence in you as my man in Chicago. If the Bureau had something going on there, you'd be the first to know," the Director assured him.

"Then why the cover up concerning Porter's death? Not even a peep about him being a Federal agent? There's no way the media wouldn't have ran with that."

The Director bristled at the use of the phrase 'cover up' and sternly replied, "You're becoming redundant Richard, as we have already discussed that." His tone lightened when he added, "The Porter situation is unfortunate and the failed investigation is even worse, but this in not TV. and we can't always get our man in sixty minutes," the Director grinned. "My advice to you is to go back to Chicago, get back on your horse, and renew the investigation from a fresh angle. You win this one, many doors will open."

The Director signaled for the waiter.

"That's where your attention should be."

"Yes, sir," Ortega answered, but his mind wasn't satisfied.

The Director had all but told him to leave the Porter situation alone, but Ortega felt there were answers there. If

Above The Law

there was anything he learned in all his years with the Bureau, it was C.Y.A., cover your ass.

Chapter Four

Phase Two

January 28 – Newark, N.J.

In the streets of Newark, he was known as The Prince. Even his haters and detractors couldn't deny the fact that he always did it big. Shining wasn't something he did for the moment, it was a way of life for the youngest boss of the Abdullah family, Fuquan Abdullah. He controlled the New York/New Jersey branch of a heroin distribution network that spread like tentacles to cities as far away as Atlanta in the south and Portland, Oregon in the West.

The Abdullah family was atop a pyramidal structured organization of Muslims called Al-Nymayr or The Panther. They were the largest, but least known Muslim group operating in the United States. The media barely knew they existed, and they definitely wouldn't call them radical or militant based on the limited information they had. That was by design; Al-Nymayr's goal was to fly under the radar. Brother Imam Aziz ran a tight ship that stayed undetected like a black ant on a black rock on a moonless night.

Above The Law

On that night, Fuquan was radiating as he pulled up to the 118 Lounge on Stockton Street. Heads turned, eyes popped out of sockets, jaws fell agape, and pussies ran wet as the crowd outside visually feasted on the first two million dollar car Newark had ever seen.

It was a Bugatti Veyron 164 Grand Sport Vitesse. It was brand new, 2011, and burgundy and black. The base price was 2.25 million dollars. Fuquan paid 2.6 million once he included all the amenities such as the 2.7-inch camera in the rearview mirror, the Puccini sound system with digital processor, and other custom fittings like bulletproof glass. Not to mention the $280,000 special edition Bugatti Type 310 wristwatch he had purchased to match the car, a red gold cylinder-shaped design that sported a see-thru top to match the Bugatti's exposed twin engines.

He parked the Bugatti in the middle of the street and left the door wide open to show off the burgundy leather interior with black piping. He had a full-length black sable in the driver's seat; he took it off while he was driving and a chink-eyed red-bone in the passenger seat.

Despite the night air, Fuquan hopped out of the car wearing only a white Tee, Levi's jean shorts and butter Timbs. His 40-inch platinum chain and 8-inch Arabic Bismillah pendant were swinging with his swag.

"Goddamn Fu! You snapped, ock!" Day Day laughed as Fuquan approached. Day Day and several other dudes were standing beside his Mercedes Gullwing with the doors in the air.

He gave Fuquan a pound and a gangster half hug.

"I know that ain't the Bugatti!"

"Muhfucka, what you thought, I was talkin' just to talk? My word is money, yo," Fuquan arrogantly replied.

The group of guys slowly migrated from Day Day's car to Fuquan's. Day Day wasn't feeling the fact that Fuquan was stealing his shine, so he attempted to co-opt it and split the billing.

"Word up my dude, we doin' it big tonight!" Day Day exclaimed, but Fuquan looked at him like, "We?" He laughed in his face.

"Yo, dude, my watch cost more than your car, real talk. How much you pay for that cheap ass shit?"

"Cheap? Get the fuck outta here. I paid three hundred k," Day Day shot back. He really only paid $225,000, but he knew the Bugatti watch cost $280,000 and he was mad Fuquan pulled his card.

"Word? Then you got robbed. See me next time, I coulda got it for two and a quarter," Fuquan shot back with a smirk; he quoted the exact price he knew Day Day paid for the car.

"You know the difference between my shit and yours?" Fuquan rhetorically asked. "A zero!" he laughed.

The group snickered at Day Day's expense, infuriating him, but he held his composure. He didn't want Fuquan to know he was getting to him. Day Day was a major coke supplier in the city, so his name wasn't lightweight. Still, he knew he didn't want it with the Abdullah family.

He bent down and winked at the sexy red-bone in Fuquan's passenger seat.

"What's up Yvette, you can't speak? Day Day crooned.

She started to speak then looked at Fuquan.

"Oh, you know shortie?" Fuquan asked Day Day.

"Somethin' like that," Day Day replied with a mischievous smirk.

"You hit it?"

Day Day wanted to say yes, but he knew Yvette would blow his spot because he hadn't. The hesitation was enough for Fuquan to know the answer.

"You want to?" Fuquan asked. "Fuck it, I'll trade you."

Above The Law

Before Day Day could say yay or nay, Fuquan bent over and looked at Yvette. "Yo ma, you goin' wit' my man?"

Yvette didn't hesitate, not because she wanted to go with Day Day, but because she would do whatever Fuquan told her.

Fuquan turned to Day Day. "What's shortie's name?" he asked, referring to the Spanish chick in Day Day's car.

"Maria."

He took the Spanish chick's hand sitting in Day Day's passenger seat and said, "Ven aqui, Maria, you already know my name so don't even act like you ain't wit' it."

The Spanish chick smiled seductively as she got out of Day Day's car and walked with Fuquan holding her pinkie. It had all happened in such quick succession that Day Day couldn't protest now. It would make him look like he was feeling the Spanish chick, a definite no-no for a dude who took pride in his reputation as a cold-blooded womanizer.

Fuquan smiled and winked at Day Day. He knew Day Day was trying to play him by speaking to Yvette and implying he could have her, if he wanted. Fuquan had preempted that by giving her away and at the same time taking his chick for the night. To anyone looking, Fuquan had shitted on Day Day-and to Fuquan, image was everything.

"Trust me my dude, the broad gives top-notch head. Yvette, do that thing you do with your tongue. Day Day gon' love it," Fuquan said as he got in the car. As he pulled off he mumbled, "Stupid ass Kafir."

"They call Fuquan The Prince," Steve told Marlon as they drove along Route 22 heading towards Bound Brook. "He's an arrogant son of a bitch, but he's no dummy. He's a manipulator."

Maria studied Fuquan's profile as he drove; just looking at him made her moist. It was not so much because he was that fine. He stood 5'9" and weighed a muscular 180 lbs., with a cinnamon complexion and light brown eyes. Fuquan was definitely a cutie to the ladies and had no trouble pulling the finest women. However, his arrogant swag and the fact that he oozed charisma put him head and shoulders above other dudes. It was as if he could do anything and have anything or anyone. Some men wore the cologne named Power, but it was no substitute for the aroma of the real thing. Fuquan was a major player and those around him could feel his power.

"Yo, your man's a clown, you know that right?" Fuquan cracked, turning down Jay-Z's *"Reasonable Doubt"* CD to a tolerable level.

"He ain't my man," she shot back, sassy and flirtatiously.

"But you ain't deny he's a clown," he retorted.

She giggled.

He didn't.

"Real talk, Ma-Ma, you judged by the company you keep. So if you fuck with clowns, I'm thinkin', maybe you in the circus, too. Like the bitch that swallow swords," Fuquan remarked.

She didn't miss the implications of the analogy he used.

She sucked her teeth, and then said, "Please, I ain't in no nobody circus, but if that's what you thought then why did you holla at me in the first place?"

Fuquan shrugged. "Cause you got potential."

"Potential? Whateva nigga," she waved him off, because she knew she was a dime plus. People mistook her for Eva Longoria all the time, but she had hazel eyes and a fatter ass. Besides, she was rocking the Chanel outfit, Gucci sling-backs, and a Prada purse, not to mention the diamonds on her wrist, ears and neck. She felt like Ms. Thank New Money.

Above The Law

"It ain't your fault though. You been dealin' with low caliber type dudes who think that shit is acceptable. There's no way I'ma let you walk around mixing designers. Add to that, your diamonds are cloudy. Nobody ever taught you the four C's," he replied smoothly. He looked over at her and added, "You could be a five star chick, Ma-Ma, you just need the right coach."

Fuquan could tell he had made his point because the sassy look was gone and replaced with one of subtle insecurity. He was a master at tearing women down and revealing their insecurities. Then he would build her back up in his image.

After Fuquan's assessment, she felt as if she was wearing knock off bootleg clothes and cubic zirconium, even though her shoes alone cost five hundred dollars.

"So...you gon' be my coach?" she seductively asked while grabbing his thighs.

He pulled off from the red light and replied, "I'm sayin' yo, I live a crazy life and I ain't got time to repeat myself, ya heard?"

"You don't have to worry about that. I see you're a man that wants the best, and with me, that's exactly what you're getting. I felt what you said and you were right about something else."

"What's that?"

She smiled and unbuckled his pants.

"I do swallow."

xxxxxx

"So Fuquan is my point of entry?" Marlon questioned.

"Affirmative," Steve answered.

"What's my cover?"

Steve glanced at his watch.

"Any minute now, Fuquan should be getting a call from a guy named Malik, one of his lieutenants."

xxxxxx

Fuquan couldn't front. The Spanish chick had a head game that curled his toes. She was putting her all into it. The sounds of her slurps and his grunts filled the car. He was so much in the zone that he had to pull over to avoid having an accident. He knew the traffic was light at that late hour.

His cell phone rang with his Brick City Brigade ring tone and he reluctantly answered.

"Yeah," he grunted while gripping a handful of Maria's hair.

"Yo, Miguel got bagged," Malik barked.

Malik's words brought Fuquan completely out of the zone. He immediately sat up and accidentally crushed her head against the steering wheel.

"Owww!" she groaned.

"Shhhh!" he told her, pushing her head away. "When?"

"Like ten minutes ago."

"God Damn it!" Fuquan hissed. "A'ight, beep me when you get to Newark."

"As salaam alaikum."

"Wa alaikum salaam."

Maria sat quietly; she asked no questions, and Fuquan appreciated her silence. He speed dialed Ali Muslim, the phone rang six times, and he finally picked up.

"As salaam alaikum," Ali groggily answered.

"Wake up and meet me at the spot."

"Now?" Ali Muslim asked in an irritated tone.

"Now," Fuquan replied to stress the urgency of the matter.

Above The Law

"Rocks beat scissors," Ali sighed and relented to the request. He knew something was up. "Give me fifteen minutes."

"Wa alaikum salaam," Fuquan said as he hung up. He turned to Maria, "Where you live shortie?"

xxxxxx

"The call is gonna tell him Miguel got busted. He was their gun connect. Malik was supposed to meet him in a parking lot in Jersey City, only the Jersey City police got an anonymous tip. What, where, and when," Steve smirked. "But it was timed to make sure the bust happened before Malik got to the rendezvous."

xxxxxx

Miguel sat behind the wheel of the nondescript 1993 blue Ford Taurus smoking a Marlboro. He didn't see the police pull in until it was too late.

They came in at an angle, one in front, and one in back. Someone had snitched him out. He figured it was Malik, but he figured wrong.

"Now Miguel is a two time loser, one more strike and it's hasta luego for muchos anos. You follow me? Now with a trunk full of semi-automatic handguns, what do you think he's gonna do?" Steve rhetorically asked.

"Look man, this thing is bigger than me okay? What you got is just the tip of the iceberg. I'ma give you the whole Titanic," Miguel said. He spoke rapidly as he sat in the interrogation room of the East District Precinct in Jersey City.

Two detectives, Detective Gomez, a Puerto Rican and Detective Rossi, an Italian, sat across from him. They actually looked like they could be brothers.

"It's bigger than six Desert Eagle 9 milli's and four Riot Pumps?" Rossi replied with feigned skepticism.

59

"Mucho," Miguel replied, using his cuffed hands to signify he was holding something big.

"Start talking," Gomez replied. He turned on the small tape recorder on the table.

"He's gonna tell the cops who he was going to meet," Marlon answered Steve's question like it was obvious. Steve vigorously shook his head from side to side.

"He doesn't know who Malik is," he advised Marlon.

"Who were you selling the guns to?" Rossi asked Miguel.

"I...I don't know. He's some black gang banger; I think he's a Crip."

"He thinks Malik is a gang banger from maybe Newark or Jersey City," Steve further explained.

"Okay then, well I don't know, I guess that only leaves his connect," Marlon surmised.

"Bingo," Steve affirmed.

"So this white guy in Bayonne, you say he's the one supplying you?" Gomez inquired between fits of yawning.

Miguel nodded.

"And he's got it all, I'm tellin' you! Semi-automatics, automatics, anything you want. He even has grenades."

"Grenades?" Rossi echoed as he glanced at his partner.

Gomez sat straight up in his chair; Miguel had their full attention.

"You're sure?"

"I'm positive."

"And you got an address on this guy?"

Miguel nodded, he grinned as if he had the secret to life.

"What's his name?" Rossi asked.

Above The Law

"You're his connect?" Marlon surprisingly asked. "He's gonna give you up?"

"That's the plan," Steve replied.

"I don't get it," Marlon admitted.

"You will."

"You think this guy's tellin' the truth?" Gomez skeptically asked.

Rossi shrugged his shoulders and answered, "What's he gaining by pulling our chain? He's so scared he'd tell on his mother right now," he chuckled. "My question is with the supplier. Could he really be that stupid to take a guy like him to his cache?"

"Stranger things have happened. I'll alert Bayonne PD."

Marlon smiled. He finally understood. Steve was supplying Miguel, while Miguel was supplying the Abdullahs. Miguel thought he was selling to gang bangers. Steve knew Miguel would turn him in when pinched. It was all a part of the plan. When Miguel turned Steve in, Steve's unknown partner, Marlon, would surface.

"Okay, so I go at the Abdullahs spazzin', like how my man got popped and your man didn't. They were going to meet each other." Marlon regurgitated the plan back to Steve.

"Exactly, it puts them on the defensive. They'll be too busy denying to accuse."

"Because I ain't accusing them of snitching, but somebody damn sure is."

"And that's when you offer to solve the problem," Steve added.

"Solve the problem? How do I do that?"

"You kill Miguel," Steve replied without hesitation.

"Kill 'em?"

Steve nodded, eying his reaction.

"No way they'll think you're a cop with blood on your hands, and you eliminate a loose end. You literally kill two birds with one stone," Steve chuckled.

Steve pulled the car into the parking lot of a posh townhouse in Scotch Plains, N.J., a small town about thirty minutes from Newark. He parked next to a cocaine white 2011 Lexus LFA. Marlon admired the car and contemplated what Steve said.

"No problem," he nodded.

"You sure?" Steve probed him with a condescending tone.

Marlon simply eyed him. "That's what I said, right? I mean, what does it matter? We're all expendable anyway."

"Expendable," Steve repeated with a nod.

"Everybody?"

"Everybody."

Marlon knew that Steve didn't like him for some reason, but that was okay; the feeling was mutual. Steve handed him a ring of keys and a cell phone.

"Malik's number is in the phone. I'll call you from the county jail and then you're on your own."

Marlon opened the door and put one foot outside of the car. He turned around and asked, "Steve, where you from? You got the Boston ahh's, you know. The open mouth A's. You Irish?

"Everybody from Boston ain't Irish."

"Yeah, there's always the Black Irish and Wops," Marlon chuckled.

"Fuck you, Porter."

Steve wasn't amused by Marlon's banter.

Marlon strolled away laughing heartily.

Above The Law

"What the —? Fuquan, what is this?" Ali Muslim barked as he exited his Platinum BMW 750 LI. He was grilling Fuquan as he stepped out of the Bugatti.

Fuquan huffed like, "Here we go," then walked over to Ali Muslim.

They were meeting beside the Weequahic Park lake on the Route 22 side.

"As salaam alaikum, ock," Fuquan greeted his older brother. Despite the nine-year difference in their ages, there was no denying they were brothers. All of the Abdullah brothers looked alike.

"I can't believe you did something as stupid as this! Two mill!" Ali stopped, took a deep breath and said, "Take it back to where you got it from first thing in the morning."

Before Fuquan could respond, Malik pulled up in a nondescript blue Buick LeSabre. He parked, got out, and approached the two brothers.

"As salaam alaikum," he greeted them both.

"What happened?" Fuquan probed.

Malik explained how when he got to the meeting spot, the police were already all over Miguel. Two patrol cars first and then a third arrived. He called Fuquan right after the third car arrived.

"How much does he know?" Ali Muslim questioned.

"Not shit, he thinks I'm a Crip from Jersey City," Malik chuckled lightly.

Satisfied with his answer, Ali Muslim nodded, but he was still in deep thought.

"Yo...what the fuck happened? How'd they know? Who knew about the drop?" Fuquan asked.

"Come on Fu; don't even disrespect me like that. We're the only ones who knew," Malik shot right back.

Malik was a first cousin to the Abdullahs and the same age as Fuquan. They laid in the same crib and came up fighting each other more than outsiders. They were very close.

Malik was one of the few people who didn't bow to The Prince.

"Maybe someone on his end flipped. Maybe he had a busted tail light," Ali Muslim proposed.

Malik shrugged. "Maybe they thought he was an Arab or something, I don't know. All I know is that we out a sweet ass connect."

"Alright, it is what it is, Malik. You say he don't know nothing, but we don't know what he knows for sure. So be on your P's and Q's. Anything looks funny, bring it to me, you got me?" Ali Muslim instructed him.

Malik nodded. "No doubt, ock."

Fuquan may have been the prince of the streets of Newark, but Ali Muslim was the king of the nationwide network. He was a very humble brother; he didn't say much or seek attention. He didn't even curse, but he was a fifth degree Black Belt, an ex-boxer, and a cold-blooded killer if the situation called for it. When he was Fuquan's age, he was just as cocky and arrogant. That was why he tolerated his bullshit, but a two million dollar car was just too much.

He stepped up to Fuquan and grilled him. Even though Ali Muslim was a few inches taller, Fuquan refused to be intimidated. He looked his brother square in the eye.

"Fuquan, I'm not asking. I'm telling you, you're gonna take that car back. I don't care what you do with it, but I better not see it again," Ali Muslim hissed.

"As salaam alaikum, ock," Fuquan replied, cutting the discussion short and turning to walk away.

"Tomorrow!" Ali Muslim barked.

"Get the fuck outta here," Fuquan mumbled under his breath and got in the car.

In 2.5 seconds, the time it took the Bugatti to go from 0-60 mph, Fuquan was gone. He left a heated Ali Muslim in his wake.

Above The Law

"Baby wake up, your brother is here."

Fuquan felt like he had just dozed off to sleep; he was right. He cracked his right eye and looked at the digital clock on the nightstand.

7:17 A.M.

He had finished fucking Nikki about two hours earlier. He groaned and rolled over on his back, looking at the chandelier ceiling fan over Nikki's queen-sized bed.

He was in one of his 'good girls' apartments. Women who had their own things going on, far from the street life he lived. He always kept corporate women, political women, and entrepreneurs within arm's reach.

Nikki was a buyer for Sak's Fifth Avenue in New York, a prestigious position that took her all over the world. No matter how far she went or who she met, Fuquan prided himself on the fact that she always came back to his thug muscle.

Fuquan rolled out of bed and slipped on his shorts and his Timberlands. He already knew what brother she was talking about and the reason he came.

He entered the living room to find Aziz sitting on the couch, watching CNN on the 50-inch plasma screen. He'd purchased the TV for Nikki, but it was more for him.

"Bye baby," Nikki said as she put in her right earring and got on her tippy toes to give him a quick kiss on the lips. "I'll call you. Bye Aziz, nice to see you again."

"Be safe sister," Aziz replied with a polite smile, but in reality, he didn't approve of Nikki. Actually it wasn't Nikki, he didn't approve of Fuquan's relationship with her or any non-Muslim woman for that matter. He wanted Fuquan to settle down with a Muslim wife or two like he and Ali Muslim had done. But then again, Aziz figured if he was going to just sex those women, maybe it was best that they weren't Muslim.

Fuquan watched Nikki sashay out of the door; her short cut and chinky eye reminded him of Nia Long in her younger days. She shut the door behind her and Fuquan shook Aziz's hand.

"As salaam alaikum Shaykh," Fuquan greeted, using the title of respect he always afforded his brother. He not only loved and respected his older brother, he was the only man Fuquan truly looked up to and admired.

Aziz was only 36, but he had the wisdom and understanding of life that extended far beyond his years. He spoke Spanish, Arabic, and French fluently, and was schooled in many subjects. Fuquan never asked him a question that Aziz didn't answer in a detailed and accurate response. If Fuquan was The Prince and Ali Muslim The King, then Aziz was the Kingmaker, the Power Behind the Throne.

"Wa Alaikum As Salaam, Akih," Aziz smiled warmly. "Kayfa ḥālik?" he asked in Arabic, it meant, how are you?

Fuquan shrugged.

"I'm good, you hungry?"

"No, shukran Fuquan, I'm good."

"Fuquan could tell from his response that Aziz was fasting, something he frequently did.

They entered the kitchen.

"I know Ali told you about the Bugatti," Fuquan said. He wanted to get to the point and give Aziz his side of the story.

Aziz smoothly sidestepped the situation.

"He also told me about the other thing."

Fuquan nodded; he put a pack of turkey sausage in the microwave.

"It was a blow, but not a big one. That was only the third time dealing with him, so we hadn't got to the big stuff yet," Fuquan explained.

"All Praise is due to Allah. But that still leaves us without a connect," Aziz pointed out.

Above The Law

Fuquan popped two pieces of bread in the toaster.

"I gotta couple of irons in the fire, Shaykh," Fuquan smirked. "Gimme a week and we'll be back in business."

Aziz contemplated that for a moment, then replied, "Naw...fall back, practice sabr," he said using the Arabic word for patience. "The dudes who move guns usually move in small circles. When one gets busted, the rest know about it. So if one of them picks up a new customer, then it won't be hard to figure who. And if the police already got wind..."

Fuquan understood his point. "No doubt Shaykh, I feel you."

"We don't want to draw attention to ourselves."

"True indeed," Fuquan agreed.

"Especially now, too much is at stake," Aziz reminded him.

"I got you, stay off the radar."

"In a Bugatti?"

Checkmate, and Fuquan hadn't even moved his pawn. He smiled to himself as he splattered butter on the toast and a sprinkle of sugar. He retrieved the turkey sausage from the microwave and put all four hot-dog sized links on the toast and bit into his sandwich.

Aziz continued.

"Fuquan, listen, I understand because I'm older than you. I've been where you are. The same day that we hit a bump, you break out in a two million dollar car. Peep the signs, lil' bruh, life is its' own Qur'an sometimes," Aziz jeweled him and Fuquan had to admit, he had a point.

He surmised, "I'll fall back with the Bugatti...at least until the smoke clears."

"All praise is due to Allah."

They shook on it and Fuquan walked Aziz to the door.

"I'm almost dry too," he informed him.

"The eagle will be landing soon, Insha Allah," Aziz replied. He then added, "You know...I figure, seven...maybe eight months, we'll be in the position we need to be in, you know? But eight months is a long time to have two million dollars worth of anything just collecting dust. What's the point in being dressed up and no place to go?" Aziz quipped.

Fuquan shook his head. He didn't know whether to be mad or to laugh. Aziz had skillfully painted him into a corner.

"Yo, 'Zeez, that's that bullshit and you know it."

"I'm just sayin'…How you gon' stunt in a year old car?" Aziz innocently asked. He used Fuquan's own ego against him.

"I'll sell the Bugatti."

Checkmate, Aziz smiled.

"As salaam alaikum, lil' bruh."

Above The Law

Chapter Five

February 1st

Ortega sat in the expensive, but tastefully decorated reception area of Renaissance Investments. Asia's secretary told him that she would see him in a few minutes and asked if he would like some coffee while he waited.

He graciously declined and grabbed one of the "Black Enterprise" magazines from the coffee table. He lightly perused it, only needing something to focus on while he replayed the dizzying pieces of the complex puzzle that was unfolding.

Shortly after returning from D.C., Ortega had turned his attention to the Black P. Stones case. He concentrated on the surveillance photos, the files of the major players and the politicians, summary reports, and wiretaps and transcripts. The investigation was just beginning to grow legs when Lil' Fred Wright mentioned the "Muslim cats" who were supposedly supplying Aaron Snead. That development was a first. Who were these Muslims? They had to be heavy hitters to supply a man like Aaron; he had hundreds of foot soldiers across the Midwest. It was a promising lead, but before it could really be explored, Fred was gunned down, yet Marlon wasn't. Then Marlon committed 'suicide' and a few days later Aaron was gunned down in a motel in Cicero. Just like that, the case was dead.

Ortega didn't believe in coincidence, so he concentrated on the tape from that night. Replaying it like his favorite part of a movie, he memorized every word and anticipated every silence. He carefully examined every background noise. When the gunshot went off, he squeezed his finger like a trigger in total real time.

"Don't be a hero," he mouthed with the gunman.

He played it again.

"Don't be a hero."

Again…

Again…

The voice was flat and baritone. It was not too deep and contained no accent. There were no urban inflexions. The man could be black or white. The thought of the killer being white jarred him and immediately sent him to the audio technician.

"Compare this to the audio from Interrogation Room 1, January 16th around two in the morning. See if you can determine the race of the guy based on his voice."

After about two hours, the lab technician confirmed that the voice was 99% likely to be from a Caucasian male. He told Ortega that given a clear audio sample, a voice was like a fingerprint. In many cases, it was even better than a fingerprint. Even if a person tried to disguise their voice, the inflection patterns can be mapped, tracked, and matched. He studied the audio and confirmed Ortega's suspicions.

"The speaker on the wiretap is definitely one of the men that were in the interrogation room," the technician informed him.

"Are you positive?" Ortega asked; his mind was reeling by the confirmation.

Above The Law

"The computer is," the technician responded.

The lawyers, the dead ex-military lawyers, were also the hit men. The new information fit perfectly with the fact that they didn't kill Marlon along with Fred. So, was Marlon a part of it? What exactly was 'it' that he may have been a part of? And if the dead men weren't really dead, then maybe the suicide wasn't really...

"Sir, Ms. Walker is ready to see you," the secretary smiled as she hung up the phone.

Ortega thanked her with a smile and nod, and entered Asia's office. It was spacious and full of light, due to the panoramic view of Lakeside Drive and Lake Michigan. Three plush looking armchairs set in an intimate semicircle around a small stone fireplace dominated one corner of the room. Asia stood up from behind her polished redwood desk wearing a navy blue blazer, matching skirt, and beige silk top. She shook Ortega's hand and offered him a seat.

"Which one?" he quipped. "Here or by the fireplace?"

Asia giggled.

"For the clients who like a little more informality," Asia explained.

"Institutional handholding," Ortega translated.

"Exactly."

They sat down.

"So this is where you grow money on trees," he chuckled.

Asia laughed.

"Not quite, but we like to think we're close."

"Bearish or Bullish?" Ortega asked.

"I'm a contrarian, which kind of balances out. When the market's selling, I'm buying and when it's buying, I'm selling," she explained. "Not very exciting, but wealthy Black people tend to be a little...risk-averse."

"They sound a lot like us Nicaraguans," he snickered.

Asia smiled but her eyes took on a rigid look and Ortega picked up on it.

"What can I do for you, Mr. Ortega? Are you looking to invest, or were you just in the neighborhood?"

"No, I think you're a little out of my league. I'm more of a 401(k) kind of guy, but I wanted to show you something," Ortega answered. He pulled out two small photos of Steve and Henry and leaned over to place them on the desk in front of her.

Asia didn't even glance down at the photos. Her smile faded.

"Mr. Ortega, I thought I made myself clear at Marlon's funeral."

"You did, I..."

"Have you ever lost someone close to you, Mr. Ortega?" Asia questioned.

"No, fortunately I haven't."

"Then you don't know what it's like," Asia snapped. She turned her swivel chair around, stood up, and looked out over the city. The sunlight silhouetted her shapely frame.

"I dream about him then I wake up and realize he's not there. That he's not going to be there and it drains me," Asia broke it down to Ortega. "If you really wanted to be helpful Mr. Ortega, you would leave me in peace...leave Marlon in peace. Evidently, that's what he wanted most."

Ortega dropped his head. He felt terrible putting Asia through that, but he had no choice. A lot more than Marlon's memory may have been at stake.

Ortega came around the desk and stood next to Asia at the window.

"Please Ms. Walker, just hear me out. This isn't just about Marlon, it could also involve you."

"Me? How would it involve me?"

"Remember at the funeral, I told you I felt something else was going on?"

Above The Law

"Yes," she replied.

Ortega sighed. He really didn't want to tell her too much, but he knew he had to tell her something if there was a chance of her cooperating.

"The night Marlon was arrested; two men came to see him posing as lawyers."

"Posing?"

"Yeah. I had them checked out. They weren't lawyers."

"Then who were they?" she asked.

Ortega could tell he had her attention.

"That's what I was hoping you could help me with," he said. He retrieved the pictures from her desk and handed them to her.

"These are the two men. Have you ever seen them before with Marlon?"

Asia studied the photos for a moment, then handed them back.

"No...I can't say that I have," she answered. "But what does that have to do with me?"

That was where he told himself to be careful. As a Federal Agent, he couldn't discuss sensitive information about a case with civilians. "The case Marlon was working on was very...political. The people closest to the investigation are dead unfortunately, including him. Whoever's behind this seems to want to make sure that if anyone knows anything, they won't be able to tell it."

A knowing smirk played across Asia's lips.

"So that's what this is about, huh? You think Marlon was somehow involved in this mess and you think he told me all about it."

Ortega's eyes confirmed her suspicions.

"Whatever Marlon did or didn't tell me, Mr. Ortega, you can best believe I'll be taking it to the grave with me," she calmly and coldly told him. "But I can speak in general and tell you that Marlon wasn't involved in your…something else or those two…lawyers."

Ortega nodded.

"Mr. Ortega, let me ask you something."

"Are you doing this for Marlon or for yourself? Is this really about clearing Marlon's name or protecting me, or is this about clearing your name?" Asia asked with a grin that said let's be honest as enemies.

"It's a bit of both, Ortega relented."

She nodded and sat down behind her desk. Asia put on her Gucci reading glasses and stared at him.

"Good afternoon, Mr. Ortega. I hope this matter has concluded; I definitely don't intend on discussing it again."

Ortega nodded, put the pictures in his pocket, and looked at her one last time. For a reason he couldn't put his finger on, he thought about the Nicaraguan war in the '80s. He was there as a part of the C.I.A.-backed Contra fighters. He had seen a lot and done a lot. She reminded him of Nicaragua, beautiful, exotic, and tough. Asia had a kindred spirit that couldn't be broken. He knew it would be futile to pursue the matter with her any further.

"Ms. Walker, thanks for your time and have a good day."

He closed the door behind him. If he hesitated just one more second, he would've seen the tear that hugged the contours of Asia's cheek and came to rest on the legal pad in front of her.

The phone number Marlon had for Malik continually went to voicemail. He knew Malik had already tossed it. That was a smart move on his behalf; Marlon liked dealing with smart people.

He didn't really need the number anyway because Henry knew his daily routine. The first thing Malik did every

Above The Law

morning, Henry told him, was to go to the Masjid An-Nur for Morning Prayer. That was the same Masjid where Aziz was the Iman. As Marlon sat in his Lexus under the early morning twilight, he thought about the contradictions at play. These guys were men of God and religiously dedicated, yet they sold drugs and murdered in cold blood, not for Allah, but their own greed. It was hypocritical and morally flawed. However, no more than the Mafia and the Catholic Church, or the Klan and the Southern Baptists, Marlon reasoned. It seemed to him that the only people who weren't hypocrites were confessed liars.

The door opened and a crowd of men exited the building. Some were dressed like Arabs in the desert, while others had on suits like Ali Muslim. A few, like Malik, wore urban apparel. Ali Muslim said something to Malik before shaking his hand and getting into in his car. Malik looked up as Marlon approached his black Cadillac XLR convertible. Marlon saw the bulge under Malik's hoody and thought to himself, *The guy even took his gun to prayer.*

"Malik."

He put his hand under his shirt, but Marlon didn't flinch.

"Who you?" Malik growled.

"Damn ock, a muhfucka just say your name and you ready to blast? What part of the Sunnah is that?" Marlon quipped. He was referring to the practical guide of day-to-day life in Islam, called the Sunnah, or the way of the Prophet Muhammad.

Malik's scowl lessened as he heard the stranger speak of the Sunnah, but he didn't remove his hand.

"I said who are you?"

"Miguel's people."

Malik didn't have a good poker face, but he lied anyway. "Who?"

"Oh, now we playin' stupid? I ain't for no games," Marlon shot back with an edgy tone.

Malik pulled the gun and held it down by his leg. He closed the distance between him and Marlon.

"Or what?"

Again, Marlon didn't move a muscle. He looked Malik in the eye and replied, "Or we get into some gangsta shit, but beef ain't good for neither one of us."

Marlon knew Malik was a killer. Henry had given him a psychological briefing. Standing there seeing this look in his eyes was all he needed to know. He also knew Malik wouldn't shoot him in front of the Masjid, the very reason Marlon opted to approach him there.

The sun rose, turning the sky from a dawning purple to an early orange. Malik stiffly eyed Marlon. *How the fuck did they know where to find me?* Malik thought. He had never met Miguel in Newark, had never let on that he was from Newark. In Malik's mind, there was only one way they could know.

"Motherfucka, who are you? The police or something?" Malik bassed. He leaned toward Marlon and spoke loudly as if he thought Marlon was wearing a wire. "I don't know no Miguel."

Marlon smirked.

"Me, the police? Shit, I was wonderin' the same thing about you."

"What?" Malik snapped.

Marlon knew he had his attention now. He was basically calling Malik an informant, a snitch, which to a dude in the streets was the ultimate disrespect.

I got him on the defensive now, Marlon mused. He then said, "Come on yo, I look stupid? My man get knocked before he 'posed to meet you? Who else knew beside us and you?"

To succeed in the street game, you had to have a sixth sense about people and ulterior motives. Being too careful could be just as bad as not being careful enough. You never wanted to risk isolating yourself and passing up opportunities.

Above The Law

Malik, most of the time, erred on the side of caution. As he looked at Marlon, he wasn't getting a police vibe. However, he wasn't about to admit to being the one that was supposed to meet Miguel.

"Like I said…I don't know no fuckin' Miguel," Malik calmly replied while he tucked his pistol.

He started to get in his car.

"Yeah, well Miguel knows you."

"What's that supposed to mean?" He turned back to Marlon.

"The dude is a two time loser. If I know where you at, and he told me where you at, who else you think he may tell?"

Malik pondered his words, while Marlon went in for the kill.

"Miguel is a fuckin' bitch. I told my partner not to fuck with him, but he did anyway. Now, he got my partner knocked too."

"So what's that got to do with me?"

"The way I see it, Miguel is now both our problem. One I feel like we can solve together, so we can continue doing business."

"Yeah? What business it that?" Malik retorted.

Marlon stepped up closer and looked around.

"Dig ock, no more games. Miguel worked for my partner and me. The guns he sold you, I supplied 'em, feel me? Now the cock sucka is tellin' 'em everything. I can't have that, and if I was you, I wouldn't have it either. So, my solution is simple. I want you to bail the cock sucka out so I can murder his bitch ass. That way, I know you ain't a cop and you know I ain't a cop. We take care of a cock sucka that could cause us both a lot of problems."

Malik definitely wasn't expecting Marlon to bring it like that. He expected him to try and renew the relationship, but he didn't expect this stranger to offer to body Miguel. He carefully looked Marlon over. If he killed Miguel, there was no way he could be a cop.

"Who are you?" Malik asked, but without aggression.

"Jamil," Marlon replied. He had purposely picked a Muslim name. He handed Malik a piece of paper with his number written on it. Malik looked at the number and back at Marlon.

"I'ma holla at cha," Malik nonchalantly told him as he hopped in the Cadillac.

Chapter Six

February 3rd – 3 P.M.

Two days later, Malik had Marlon meet him at the IHOP on Bergen Street near South Orange Avenue. He pulled into the lot and parked next to a burgundy Maybach with temporary tags in the back window. Once inside, he saw Malik sitting with two other dudes. He recognized one of them as Fuquan. As he approached the table, Malik rose to greet him.

"Let me holla at you in the bathroom," Malik told him as he walked past. He didn't stop to look at him or exchange pleasantries.

Marlon turned around and followed him to the bathroom.

"You know the drill bruh, strip," Malik told him.

Marlon shook his head and shrugged. "You want a slow tease, or straight to the point," Marlon joked. Malik didn't even crack a smile.

When he was down to only his boxers and shoes, Malik went through his clothes with a fine-toothed comb. He took the wad of money out of Marlon's pocket and flipped through it. He examined his Android phone and removed the battery before putting it back in. Satisfied that he wasn't wired, he handed Marlon his clothes, but he kept the phone.

"What? You gon' keep my phone?"

Malik snickered at his question.

"You'll get it back. Take off your watch, too."

"My watch?"

"Technology a muhfucka, my dude. You could put a bug in damn near anything nowadays."

Marlon took off his platinum diamond encrusted watch and handed it to Malik.

"Anybody put a bug in a fifty thousand dollar watch ain't a cop, he just a damn fool."

Malik smirked as they exited the bathroom. Back at the table, Malik gave Fuquan the nod. Fuquan and the other dude in the kufi stood up.

"Come wit' me," Fuquan told Marlon. They headed for the front door. When they made it outside, Fuquan walked to the corner facing University Hospital.

"Where we goin'?" Marlon asked.

"You'll see."

"We catchin' the bus or somethin'?"

Fuquan didn't reply to the question. Within seconds, the number 88 bus pulled up across the street.

"Come on," Fuquan said.

They bobbed and weaved as they crossed the street and then boarded on the bus. Fuquan handed the driver a fifty-dollar bill.

"I ain't got nothing smaller," he arrogantly told the driver.

The bus driver shrugged and quickly pocketed the bill. He then turned his attention to Marlon. "I'm with him," Marlon said. The driver nodded him back.

Above The Law

It would be virtually impossible to tape the conversation on the bus. They may've been in the hood, but those dudes weren't just a bunch of thugs.

"My man told me what you said," Fuquan began. He leaned towards Marlon, who was sitting adjacent to him on the back bench of the bus.

"And?" Marlon replied.

"And...you do that...We can do business," Fuquan answered.

Marlon chuckled at his statement. Fuquan was making it seem like this was a test for him, instead of a mutual one. He liked him already.

"I'm sayin', I'm doin' this for me as much as I am for you 'cause, believe me, I ain't pressed for business," Marlon shot right back.

"You sayin' you ain't tryin' to get money?"

"I'm sayin' I ain't pressed for it. It's a difference."

It was Fuquan's turn to smirk. He saw Marlon had some swag to him, too much for the average agent of law enforcement. Fuquan figured if he was the police, then he would try to get them to bail Miguel out and tell them he killed him. Even an idiot cop had to know they wouldn't fall for something so lame. No, Fuquan needed proof.

"Okay, I'm wit' it. We'll do our part and then you and my man can handle your end," Fuquan proposed.

"Nah."

"What do you mean nah?"

"I don't need no co-defendants, I do my dirt all by my lonely, ock," Marlon explained.

"So how we supposed to know the problem's been handled?"

"'Cause I'ma handle it," Marlon shot back.

Fuquan laughed and leaned back in his seat.

"Fuck outta here."

"What did you expect? You think I'ma just ride wit' a muhfucka that I don't know to handle some shit like this?" Marlon stressed. "You don't know me, just like I don't know you. Shit, for all I know the cat you send might put one in my head too."

Fuquan leaned forward and lowered his tone.

"And for all I know, you might be the police tryin' to run some okey doke, yo."

They eyeballed each other for a minute. Neither let up until Marlon broke the silence.

"Dig ock...It's obvious you wanna fuck wit' me, just like I wanna fuck wit you, or else we wouldn't be here."

Fuquan's stare eased and his demeanor said he agreed.

"I already see you an arrogant muhfucka, but I hope you see that I am too," Marlon grinned and Fuquan chuckled. "So how do we meet in the middle?" Marlon asked.

Fuquan thought for a moment then he replied, "A'ight, how 'bout this. My man bails him out and drives him somewhere; when they get there, you'll waiting."

Marlon pondered it for a second and nodded. "Long as your man never sees my face."

"That's on you, bruh."

"Okay...okay, I'm wit' it," Marlon agreed and they shook hands.

They exited the bus at the next stop. Fuquan's man in the kufi was driving the Maybach and Malik was behind him in the Caddy. Fuquan's man got out of the car and handed Marlon his watch and phone. He then got into the Caddy with Malik. Fuquan and Marlon hopped into the Maybach and pulled off.

"Jamil, right?"

"That's right, and you?"

"Fuquan. You Muslim?" Fuquan inquired. He casually glanced over at Marlon as he turned the corner.

Above The Law

"My family is," Marlon replied. He was thinking of Fatima and the reason he was involved in all of this.

"Yeah, I can understand that, but like Allah says in Al-Kitab, qad aflaha mu'minun."

Marlon knew he was being tested, because only a few Muslims wouldn't know the verse.

"Successful indeed are the believers," Marlon translated in English what Fuquan said in Arabic.

Fuquan smiled as he pulled into the IHOP parking lot.

"Exactly, the believers always gon' be successful. Allah protects the Mumin, feel me? I mean, I might not be doin' right, but Allah ain't gon' let them do me wrong. Fuck these kafir muhfuckas out here; you know what I'm sayin'?"

Fuquan offered his hand and Marlon shook it.

"Make sure you're on point tonight. When we hit you, we gon' have him. Just tell us where," Fuquan instructed. He looked at the Lexus. "That you?"

"Yeah," Marlon replied.

"They only make like 150 of them shits. I was gon' cop one, but this cat they call The Mayor copped a green one first. I don't do second in anything. It's all good though, I banged right back with the burgundy on black Bugatti."

Marlon whistled, "Must be nice."

"That ain't shit. Stick wit' Fu, I'll show you. As Salaam Alaikum."

"Wa Alaikum As Salaam."

"Yeah my friend, I want to thank you and your peoples for helping me out when my so-called people turned their back," Miguel bitterly remarked as he closed his phone.

The Muslim brother driving simply nodded his head. He knew Miguel was a rat and he despised rats. He felt like blowing his brains out himself, but he knew the plan and stuck to it. He just wished Miguel would've stayed on the phone the whole ride so he wouldn't have to talk to him. Miguel made call after call after he was picked up from the Hudson County

Jail. Most of the conversations were in Spanish, but he could tell by the way that he spoke to the first person that he was talking to his girl. On the next call, he barked with authority, so he knew he was talking to an underling. It was on the third call where he heard Miguel say "Aeropuerto," and he knew it meant it airport. He smiled to himself, knowing Miguel was planning a getaway that he would never make.

"It's really coming down now, huh?" Miguel asked. He was commenting on the falling snow and trying to make small talk.

They had just reached Washington Heights, the section of Manhattan that Miguel called home. The snow was coming down steadily and getting thicker. It was drastically reducing visibility.

It was the perfect night for a murder.

"Aye, you don't talk much do you amigo?" Miguel nervously chuckled.

The driver could tell Miguel was getting nervous, so he spoke in order to try to calm his fears.

"Nah, just tryin' to concentrate. It's hard to see any damn thing."

"Si, si, and it don't look like it's about to stop. We're almost there; turn right here."

He made a right onto Wadsworth Avenue.

"You tell your guy Miguel never forgets a favor, eh? You tell him whatever ju need, call me in the morning and it's done, pronto," Miguel falsely assured, thinking to himself, he'd be back in the Dominican Republic by the next day.

He was only half-right; he'd definitely be gone, but he wouldn't be on a plane.

Miguel had been skeptical at first; he was scared his supplier, the white boy, had sent someone to bail him out. The driver convinced him that he worked for K.B., the name Miguel knew Malik by. That sealed it for him, just like Henry and Steve knew it would. Miguel knew there was no way they

Above The Law

knew K.B. He figured K.B. was pressed for the guns, had the bondsman find out who he was, and sprung him. He figured it was his lucky day.

"Right here amigo, this is my building," Miguel told him.

He pulled over and Miguel reached to shake his hand. The driver looked at him and glanced at his hand then back at him.

"Aye, what's ju problem man?" He opened the door.

"I hate a fuckin' rat," he growled as Miguel got out.

In an instant, Miguel knew it was a set up. He knew in that split-second that he was going to die. He turned around and stared down the barrel of Marlon's .45.

A soft "Oh" escaped from his lips before the three shots rang out.

Boom! Boom! Boom!

All three were head shots from close range, aimed at his forehead. The splatter from the first shot hit the windshield like an exploding paint gun pellet. The second and third shots splattered the dashboard and driver's seat and window. Miguel's body would be found late the next day; frozen stiff and brainless.

Marlon closed the door with a soft thud. A car quickly pulled up and scooped the driver. Marlon disappeared between the buildings heading to Steve's car a block away. The falling snow quickly covered the tracks left by the killers.

Fuquan received a text message and immediately opened it. It contained no words; no words were needed. He understood the meaning. It was the confirmation from the driver that the job was completed. He turned to Malik, who was sitting beside him on the couch watching "Notorious" and told him, "That brother Jamil, he definitely official tissue, ya heard?"

"Alhamdulillah," Malik conceded, he was more into the movie than the conversation.

xxxxxx

Marlon woke up in a cold sweat. He sat up in his bed, his eyes focusing on the patio door leading to the balcony. The snow was at least three feet deep. He took a deep breath, lay back down, and stared at the ceiling.

It wasn't the murder that bothered him; it was easy for him to see Miguel as a sacrifice for the greater good. He was there to stop whatever bombing Al-Nymayr was planning, so Miguel's miserable life was a small price to pay. Additionally, the part of him that was street simply hated snitches.

Fuck Miguel, he thought.

He wasn't concerned about getting involved with Fuquan and his crew of gangsta Muslims. He was from Philly where everybody was gangsta Muslims. Marlon was comfortable in that element. A few minutes after the murder, he received a text from Fuquan:

Salaam ock. Beep me 2 mor Insha Allah.
555-3308

Marlon knew he was in.

Steve and Henry knew it as well.

"Good work Porter, now find us that informant and stop this fuckin' bombing these cocksuckers are planning!" Henry exclaimed.

He wasn't worried about Steve and Henry either, even though he knew there was something they weren't telling him. He could sense that he wasn't totally in the loop; they were holding back. He was determined to find out what they were keeping to themselves.

None of those were the reason he was torn him from his sleep with his heart pounding and his breathing labored.

It was Asia.

Above The Law

For the past few nights, he had been dreaming of her. The first dream had them walking hand in hand along Lakeshore Drive in Chicago. The sun basked them in a warm and golden radiance. Asia carried her sandals in her other hand while they talked and joked. He loved Asia's laugh, it was throaty and from the heart.

"You're so silly," Asia giggled.

"No, I'm serious. This is a dream. We can do whatever we want," he replied. Then, like a magician's flare, he pulled a white rose from thin air and handed it to her.

He woke up with a smile.

The night before, he dreamed that they were in a small room with a balcony. The breeze flowed through and bellowed the curtains on the patio door. The heat was thick and jazz floated through the window and filled the room with a saxophone and piano duet. It was a sentimental mood and felt like New Orleans. Asia came toward him with lust in her eyes and sass in her strut. She was undressing as she drew nearer. She unwrapped her silk dress and let it fall to the floor. When she reached him, she was wearing only fire-red stilettos. The heat made her glisten with a sheen of sweat that tasted so sweet to Marlon's tongue. He could feel her lips, her nipples, her softness, her wetness, and he could feel her ambiance.

He woke up with his dick still throbbing from the explosion of the wet dream.

In that night's dream, they killed her. Marlon couldn't stop it; he couldn't reach her in time.

"Asia!" he bellowed, willing the sound of his voice to wrap around and protect her. The barrage of gunshots took the life from her and propelled him out of his sleep.

Marlon sat on the side of the bed with his head in his hands. He couldn't shake Asia from his mind or the sense of guilt out of his conscience. He felt like a fraud. What, or who had he been true to? He wasn't a Fed, he was a gangsta, he was...

What?

Above the law, he thought to himself. Ironically, it meant he was no one. He was dead, but he was alive. He was wrong, even though he was doing it for the right reasons. He was too good at being bad. His life seemed like one big contradiction.

However, he was clear on one thing, his love for Asia. She was the best thing that had ever happened to him and he abandoned her. He needed to make it right, but how could he go back? He longed to talk to her. He even went as far as calling her after the first dream.

"Hello," she answered, her voice drenched in sleep.

He imagined her in her favorite Jerry Rice 49'ers jersey, totally naked underneath.

Hello?" she repeated. That time her voice was filled with aggravation.

He wanted to speak, but knew he wouldn't. She sucked her teeth and hung up.

Marlon knew he couldn't talk to her, but he had to talk to someone and he knew just who. He got up and grabbed the prepaid Wal-Mart cell phone from the closet. It was brand new as always. He would toss it after one call like usual. There was no way he could be too careful, especially now.

He put the minutes on the phone from a prepaid card then dialed a number. It was answered and the person immediately hung up. Marlon knew the routine. He waited ten minutes later and the phone rang.

"Yeah," Marlon answered.

He could hear the sounds of Meringue in the background.

"Como estas," he greeted with a slight drunken slur.

"All these years and you still ain't get the accent right."

"I guess you really can't teach an old dog new tricks, huh? How are you?"

"I'm good."

Above The Law

"Then what's that I hear in your voice?"

There was a brief pause.

"I'm going back for her. I can't just turn my back like this."

"So you want me to discourage or encourage you?"

"I just figured you'd understand," Marlon replied.

He chuckled.

"Yeah, we both know I've been there before. Anyway, you've got your mind made up so there's no changin' it. You're like me in that department."

Marlon smiled.

"Just be careful," he warned. "Like I told you, they're using you. Think about when you're no longer needed."

Marlon knew they had been on the phone long enough. He didn't want to push it.

"Yeah, I hear you."

"But are you listening? I love you," he said.

"I love you too," Marlon replied before he hung up and proceeded to destroy the phone.

Chapter Seven

February 4th – 1 P.M

Freezing rain and the sharp Chicago winds were the kind of weather most people avoided. Not Asia, she had business to handle. She stepped from her Benz as the valet held the umbrella over her head. She wrapped the full-length sable around her as the doorman opened the door of Flini's, an exclusive Italian restaurant on Chicago's Gold Coast.

She entered the restaurant and the maitre'd checked her coat. She told him who she was meeting and he escorted her to the table. Her lunch guest stood while she extended her hand. He gently turned it over and kissed it.

"Once again, it is my pleasure, Ms. Walker," he said. His African accent was pronounced, but his English precise.

"Good afternoon Mr. Aweys, how are you?" Asia returned.

"Call me Ajaye," he crooned. He pulled out her chair and smoothly seated her.

Asia smiled graciously. She knew all about Ajaye Aweys. She met him in New York at an International Finance

Above The Law

conference.   The Vice- President of Renaissance had introduced her to Ajaye.

"I have heard so much about you," he smiled and kissed her hand.

The Vice President had given Asia the run down. Aweys was from Somalia and a member of the Recognized Transition Government. He was a businessman. His hand was in most of the country's natural resources.   They included uranium, bauxite, copper, and oil. He had business ties to several countries including Thailand, United Arab Emirates, Yemen, India, and China to name a few. He was working to establish himself in America and had sought out Renaissance to handle his accounts.

"You've definitely become one of our MVP's since you've been with us," the Vice President later told her. "But the Aweys' account is huge, you landing this would be like Kobe winning the championship."

Asia got the message; don't fuck this up.

She knew, when Ajaye called earlier about a lunch meeting, she had to turn on the charm. It wouldn't be hard for her. He stood 6'1" with a slim physique and broad shoulders. He had the aquiline nose of many Somalians and Ethiopians with light brown eyes and a smile reminiscent of Tupac. Ajaye was certainly easy on the eyes.

"I am happy that you agreed to meet me on such short notice. I know that your time is valuable," Ajaye remarked with a smile.

"As yours is as well, I'm sure."

He waved her off with a slight flick of his hand. "No matter, for you Ms. Walker, I have all the time in the world."

Asia smiled at his obvious attempt to flirt.

"Asia."

"Asia," he repeated, as if he was savoring the syllables on his palate. "That is a most beautiful name."

"Thank you."

The waiter arrived and handed them their menus. Ajaye turned and spoke to him in fluent Italian. The waiter was shocked, but didn't show it. Asia was impressed as the waiter walked away.

She giggled like a schoolgirl and Ajaye nonchalantly shrugged.

"Many people in my country speak the language. The remnants of colonization, I guess. It proves useful from time to time."

Asia nodded and sipped her water.

"I hope that things are getting better in your country. I really hate to see another African country's citizens killing each other."

"Yes, due to the rebels with their backwards Islamic courts and fatwa," he shook his head and added, "It's getting so that a man must come all the way to the U.S. to get a decent pork chop."

They shared a hearty laugh. The waiter came back and took their order. While they waited, they engaged in conversation about African politics, Renaissance, and its commitment to African development. They talked about each other and the more they talked, the more she grew to like Ajay. He was cultured, in a European sort of way, but he wasn't stiff. He definitely had swagger and was smart and funny. She found herself comparing him to Marlon and her heart grew heavy. Ajaye's spell was broken as she glanced at her watch.

"Ah, my time is up I see," he cordially smiled.

"No, no, I just...I had another appointment."

He held up his hand. "No need to explain yourself, Asia. As I said before, your time is valuable. Rest assured, we will be seeing a lot more of each other," he said while eyeing her over his flute as he sipped his wine.

"I would like that," she smiled, but just in case she sounded too personal, she quickly added, "Renaissance

Above The Law

Investments would consider it an honor, and I'm sure we will live up to your high standards."

Ajaye got the message and smiled. He subtly nodded for the waiter to bring the check.

"This I already know or this meeting would've never taken place. And I must say, you don't look like the dragon lady to me," he giggled and Asia smiled.

She'd earned the nickname for her no nonsense style of business and laser focus on achieving her goals.

"Well, looks can be deceiving," she winked.

"Only when the beholder is deceivable," he smoothly shot back with a subtle firmness.

Outside, the rain had turned to sleet and shrouded Chicago in a dull gray. Ajaye took the umbrella from the valet and held it for Asia. He used it to pull her close enough to kiss her softly on the cheek.

"I look forward to seeing you again soon, hopefully with much more relaxed time constraints," Ajaye uttered.

"I'm sure that can be arranged," Asia smiled with subtle flirtation in her tone.

She got into her car and pulled off as a black Ford Excursion with limo-tinted windows pulled up.

The passenger door opened and a beefy white bodyguard got out and opened the back door for Ajaye. He got in and pulled off as Asia drove away in the opposite direction. Neither of them were aware that they were being watched and photographed.

"You don't waste time, do you Ms. Walker," Ortega mumbled as he peered through the camera's scope.

He was sitting a half block away in his car after following her to the restaurant. He told himself he was doing it to protect Asia. A part of him thought she knew something; therefore, she may have been in danger. A part of him, the part that helped him survive in the jungles of Nicaragua, didn't trust her. It was obvious that she wasn't telling him everything, but it was what she wasn't telling him that ate at his gut like an inflamed ulcer.

She told him she loved Marlon and needed time to heal, but there a man was kissing her not even a month after Marlon's death. He put the camera down, until he spotted the license plate. They were diplomatic plates. That was not necessarily a rarity in a political town like Chicago. What really caught his eye and made him snap several pictures in rapid succession was the fact that the diplomatic plates were from New York. Why would someone, especially a diplomat, drive all the way from New York instead of flying? There was no logical reason Ortega could think of, except the man didn't want his presence in Chicago to be known. A flight meant ID's, traceable payments, and a paper trail. It was either that, or the guy just wanted to tour middle America in the dead of winter.

Ortega started the car and headed back to the office, he was eager to know who the mystery New Yorker was.

"Yeah, but they killed Malcolm."

Fuquan thought about Malik's words as he watched Marlon get out of his Lexus and into the car with him.

Malik said that earlier to Fuquan when Fuquan told him he would deal directly with Marlon on the guns, a job Malik usually handled.

"Nah ock, it's peace yo. I see us fuckin' wit' this dude hard body. I'm gonna take him under my wing and school 'em to what's what and put ock on the team for real."

"I'm just sayin' Fu, be careful."

"Of what? He Muslim."

"And? Muslims can be sour, too."

Fuquan shot him a look, but he held his tongue. "It's a deal, ock. Let it go. Besides, like Malcolm said, if I ain't safe around my own people, who am I safe around?"

Above The Law

"Yeah, but they killed Malcolm."

Marlon got in and shut the door, blowing in his hands and rubbing them together.

xxxxxx

"As Salaam Alaikum, Fu. Man, it's cold as fuck out there."

Fuquan nodded as he pulled off.

"You must not be used to snow or somethin', 'cause this ain't shit."

Snow drifts two feet high lined the streets of Newark as the sun beamed down and reflected blindingly off the snow. The snow in the streets had turned gray and black from the car exhaust and tires.

"Naw, I'm used to it. I just ain't a winter person."

"Where you from?" Fuquan questioned.

Marlon knew that question would come, so he was prepared. After brainstorming with Steve and Henry, he came up with his cover and made sure it was verifiable in case the Abdullah's tried to check.

"I'm from the Lou."

"The who?" Fuquan frowned.

Marlon smiled at his question. In the Midwest, Chicago was as far as the Abdullah family could reach. They depended on the Black P. Stones to handle the rest of the region. With their main outlet, Aaron Snead, dead, Marlon knew running a check would take a major effort. If he played his cards right, it was an effort the family wouldn't have reason to initiate.

"The Lou, Saint Louis, East Saint Louis to be exact."

"Oh," Fuquan replied. "You hungry?"

"Yeah, I could eat," Marlon answered.

They went to a Muslim restaurant named Kings and came out with halal breakfast burritos that they ate while they drove. Fuquan gave Marlon a virtual tour of Newark; he explained the different neighborhoods, which set controlled each, and what they sold.

"Yeah ock, in Newark, the gangs control the blocks. Some Crips, but real talk, Bloods run the game," Fuquan explained.

Marlon looked at him and smiled.

"I thought you did."

Fuquan shot back, "I said they run the game, but we own it," he laughed. "I mean, we could force the issue. But everybody is happy with the way it is. We keep our faces off the sets and keep our hands in the mix. It's a lot of Muslims that bang and they like our eyes and ears, feel me?"

Marlon nodded. "Indeed, but you...why you tellin' me all this?"

Fuquan smiled and threw his arm across the seat and put his hand on the side of the passenger seat headrest.

"Patience ock, patience. Now...the family game is strictly dog food," Fuquan began. He was referring to heroin by one of its many street names. "It's probably three or four other families, crews, or whatever, that's makin' some real noise, but we by far the biggest," Fuquan boasted. He glanced at Marlon to gauge his reaction. "But like I said, we supply the gangs, mainly Bloods. They in turn feed their dogs and also supply the Crips. Remember, blue and red makes green."

Marlon chuckled as Fuquan continued.

"But when it comes to the guns, we mainly supply the Crips and they arm themselves and also sell to the Bloods."

Marlon shook his head "Thug politics," he remarked.

"Exactly," Fuquan confirmed. "Bottom line is muhfuckas wanna eat. Green is the only color that matters at the end of the day, feel me?" 'Cause if they kill each other off, they'll be hurting their own pockets. So it keeps the violence down and that's important; beefin' ain't good for business."

Above The Law

"Plus, you keep both sides in your pocket just in case you gotta play one side against other," Marlon surmised.

They are definitely not your average thugs, he thought to himself.

Fuquan smiled at him.

"They already divided, so it makes 'em that much easier to conquer."

They shared a laugh.

"But on the real, that's why I poured you a drink on this. I want you to take over the gun side of things. We gettin' 'em from you anyway. So we cut out the middle man, which is us, and let you do you," Fuquan offered.

They drove to the sounds of "Wu-Tang Forever" for a moment and then Marlon asked, "What's the catch? What, you want my face on front street or somethin'?"

Fuquan pulled over on 12th Street behind a green BMW X-6 and in front of a two family house. He looked at Marlon like he had two heads.

"Front you off? Yo, listen here 'cause I never fuckin' repeat myself. The rest of the world can eat a dick and die, but a Muslim? Word up, a Muslim can get my last. When I go to hell, and I know I'm goin' 'cause I ain't right, the one thing Allah won't say is I fucked over His people," he hissed. He was looking Marlon straight in the eye.

"My man Malik, I grew up wit' ock, pissed the same bed wit' 'em and everything. He told me be careful with you. You know what I told him?"

Marlon didn't respond.

"Do you?"

"Nah, what you tell him?"

"I told him, like Malcolm said, if I ain't safe around my own people, who am I safe with? And he said, but they killed Malcolm..."

Fuquan got out of the car and began to walk up the steep set of porch stairs. He turned back to Marlon, "Yo, you just gon' sit there?"

Marlon got out thinking about what Fuquan said. A twinge of guilt shot through his heart. Fuquan may have been an arrogant motherfucker and maybe even a terrorist at some level, but he stood firm by his people. Marlon almost felt like he was cheating by using Islam to get under Fuquan.

But, he thought to himself, *all's fair in love and war.*

He reached the top step just as Fuquan turned the key.

"Ay Fu."

Fuquan looked at him.

"You ain't goin' to hell, ock...Probably," Marlon smiled.

Fuquan laughed. "Insha Allah," he replied. It meant God willing in Arabic.

They entered a hallway that faced a flight of stairs to the right. The sounds of the Qur'an being recited by a strong sonorous man's voice played on an unseen stereo and filled the corridor.

They went up the flight of stairs and turned on the landing. It led to another shorter flight and up to a door. The sounds of Nicki Minaj's remix of Biggie's "Warning" rattled the door with each drop of the bass. Fuquan sucked his teeth as he stuck his key in the door.

They walked in to a face full of Sour Diesel smoke, one of the many exotic brands of medical marijuana. Four females sat around the L-shaped sectional getting high.

"Fatimah! Fa'eemah! Put on some fuckin' clothes," Fuquan hissed.

Fatima rolled her eyes and passed Fa'eemah the blunt.

"Boy, you ain't nobody daddy. We older than you."

Fuquan clenched his jaw, making his jaw line flex. "Wallahi, if you don't get yo' ass up, I'm gonna smack the shit out of both of ya'll!"

Above The Law

Fuquan may've been the youngest of the seven Abdullah siblings, but he was definitely not the baby. Fatimah and Fa'eemah, the identical twins who were eleven months older than Fuquan, still heeded his word. Seeing his pressure boiling, they knew he would make good on his threat.

Fa'eemah slowly got up.

"Come on Temah, before I gotta beat his ass if he put his hands on me."

Fatimah reluctantly followed her sister.

"And take that wit' you," Fuquan hollered after them as they sashayed down the short hallway to the bedroom.

Marlon had to fight himself to keep his eyes diverted, especially since Fuquan was watching him to make sure he was. From the corner of his eye, he could see how thick they both were. The cutoff jean shorts were hugging their shapely fat asses.

"As Salaam Alaikum," one of the other girls on the couch flirtatiously said.

"Wa Alaikum Salam," he mumbled in reply.

The two females looked Marlon over as they passed the blunt back and forth. A few moments later, the twins came out in sweat pants and a t-shirt covering their tank tops. Fa'eemah handed Fuquan a book bag.

"Ali said call him, too," Fa'eemah informed him, before she took her seat on the couch.

Fatimah walked straight up to Marlon.

"Who you?" she smiled, eyeing him mischievously.

"A friend of your brother's," he replied. He glanced at Fuquan, who turned away and went in the back with his phone call.

"That's your real name or just what they call you?" she joked.

Marlon laughed at her humor. "I'm Jamil."

"Yes you are," she smiled.

Jamil meant handsome in Arabic, so he knew she was flirting with him. He couldn't lie; Fatimah was beautiful. She stood no more than 5'3", her pecan tan complexion and almond shaped brown eyes with her button nose and long silky hair made her look like a lighter version of Gabrielle Union. Even in sweat pants, Marlon could still see her Coke bottle shaped hips and ass. Even her feet with the purple toe nail polish looked scrumptious.

"You comin' to my birthday party?"

"I didn't know you were having one."

"Well, you do now," she replied. She looked up at him with eyes that were both innocent and provocative at the same time. "Give me your phone."

Fatimah was aggressive. She had the same name as his aunt, the woman who raised him, the woman who died on September 11th.

He handed her his phone. She put in her number and hit send. She let her phone ring once, then hung up, and handed it back with a smile.

Fuquan came out with a frown. He glanced at Marlon and Fatimah, but he didn't comment.

"Let's go, ock," Fuquan told him.

"As Salaam Alaikum Jamil," Fatimah sang.

xxxxxx

"So he didn't give you the Scarface, don't-fuck-with-my-sister rant?" Steve quipped.

Marlon had met with him and Henry in a darkened corner of Port Newark later that night. In the distance, across the ink-black shadow of the Hudson River, Marlon could see the lights of New York. He turned away and looked at Steve and Henry.

Above The Law

"Nah, I mean, it was obvious that he felt a way about it, but he seemed to have other things on his mind," Marlon told them.

"Other things?" Henry probed.

"His sister told him Ali Muslim wanted him to call. He called him."

"Did you overhear the gist?" Henry asked.

Marlon shook his head no.

"He took it in the back. When he came out, he was upset about something and we left. He dropped me off at my car, gave me the book bag and what he needed, then he left."

Henry nodded. Marlon had already given him the book bag. It contained twenty thousand dollars in rubber-banded bundles of thousands in small bills, all tens and fives.

"We need to get a tap on his phone," Marlon suggested.

"I'll see what we can do," Henry replied.

"Why, what's the problem?" Marlon questioned.

"It's…hard to pin these guys down. They don't keep a phone longer than a week and they use beepers heavily. We suspect they use codes because usually a face-to-face meeting ensues after a beep is received," Henry explained. He was covering up the real reason they didn't tap their phones or beepers.

Marlon seemed to accept that and Steve tossed him a set of keys.

"That goes to a storage garage in Linden, number 16. Inside it, you'll find all you need to keep those guys taken care of for awhile."

Marlon nodded in agreement. Steve applauded him in a congratulatory manner.

"You're doing a helluva job, Porter. Got your own branch of the family business, hell the sister wants you to be a part of the family. Well…a part of you anyway," he winked.

"It ain't me. The dude just has a weakness for Muslims," Marlon replied.

"Do you?" Steve asked while looking him in the eye.

"Do I what?"

Steve shrugged.

"I'm just sayin'…you look distraught, self-conscious. I mean, maybe you feel bad about betraying this guy's trust."

"That's my job, right? That's what I'm here for, ain't it? I know my job and I know why I'm here. You, nor anyone else has to remind me, you hear?"

Henry sat back and allowed the banter. He knew that despite Steve's brash manner, or maybe because of it, he was one of the best at getting in someone's head. He studied psychological assessments and profiles. He knew Marlon was so good at what he did because the lines were so blurred within him, between what he was and what he was supposed to be. They had to stay in his head; they were going to push him right up to the teetering edge and…

"Okay," Steve shrugged and backed off, "I hear you."

Henry allowed the tension to dissipate and then he turned to Marlon. "So what's your next move?"

"Climb the ladder. Get as close to Aziz as I can, as quickly as I can," Marlon replied. "It's obvious Fuquan is tryin' to bring me in, so I'll make it easy for him."

Henry nodded.

"Make it clear to them that guns aren't all that you can supply," Henry said.

"Meaning?"

"Meaning," Steve answered instead of Henry, "Let 'em know you've got access to heavy shit too. C-4, Sentex, grenades…"

Marlon looked at Henry. "Entrapment?" Marlon asked.

Henry smiled. "Remember, when it comes to national security, the only law is prevention."

Chapter Eight

February 9th – 7:30 P.M.

"Ohhh Fuuuu, yeesss you feel sooo good," Maria moaned as Fuquan vigorously long-stroked her.

He had her legs pinned over his shoulders. He was stretched out in a push up position, fucking her in the 'standing-up-in-the pussy' position. Her pussy was sloppy wet and every stroke squished and smacked as she squirmed beneath him.

"Ahh I…I feel it in my stomach," she screamed. Her pussy coated Fuquan's dick with milky fluid for the second time.

"Cum for Daddy, Mami," Fuquan growled.

"I am! Oh shit!

A door slammed and he heard the footsteps.

"Fuquan, baby you home?"

He knew it was Nikki. He flipped Maria over on her stomach and began beating the pussy harder. He could hear the tap of Nikki's heels coming nearer across the hardwood floor.

"Yes! Yes! Right there baby! Oh goddamn you fuckin' this pussy so good!"

Nikki opened the door, her eyes were wide, and her jaw dropped. Somebody was fucking on her bed, in her home, with her man.

"Fuquan," she barked. Her tone was full of shock and rage.

Fuquan didn't miss a stroke. He pushed Maria's face into the pillow and looked at Nikki. He rotated his hips and grinded Maria's pussy causing her to tremble in delight.

"Chill Ma, it ain't that serious. Come here," he offered while holding out his hand.

I...I can't believe you would do something like this to me," Nikki screamed. She loved Fuquan, but she wasn't stupid. She knew he had other women, but not there, and in her bed. She wanted to yell, fight, do something, but her feet were glued to the floor and her eyes were glued to the act.

Fuquan tried to grab her wrist, but she jerked away and suddenly became animated. She lunged at Maria.

"Bitch, I'ma kill you!" Nikki hissed. She grabbed Maria by the hair, but Fuquah snatched Nikki by the throat. His grip was vice-like, but his voice was calm and soothing.

"Ma, stop frontin'. You ain't mad; you just think you're supposed to be."

He leaned to kiss her, but she snatched away.

"I hate you!" Nikki yelled as she turned on her heels and stormed out.

The sound of Fuquan's laughter followed her out of the room.

She slammed the door and seethed with anger. She was feeling humiliated, violated, and...curious.

Fuquan was an instigator; he knew people and their limits. He loved to push them to it, especially women. He loved taking an independent, opinionated woman, and making her docile and submissive. He did that with mind games. He

Above The Law

would find the weakness that even the most beautiful woman had in their vanity and tear it down, only to build it back up in his image. He used emotional manipulation, as well as his thick, curved, nine plus inches of love muscle to drive them to sexual frenzies that only he could satisfy.

Nikki never stood a chance with her Mount Vernon suburban background, her Ivy League schooling, and her Fifth Avenue sensibilities. Fuquan knew she was bi-curious, so he knew she'd do it, even if she didn't know it herself.

"Oh God baby, I can't stop cumin!" Maria squealed. Her screams sent a tingle down Nikki's spine.

"Fuck this dick bitch! Fuck Daddy's dick!"

"Oh Fuquan, I love it. I love it."

The voyeur in Nikki wanted to watch. She softly opened the door. She saw Maria riding Fuquan in the reverse cowgirl position. Her face was a mask of sexual ecstasy. The sight, sound, and the smell of the fucking Fuquan was giving Maria made Nikki's panties wet. Fuquan smiled, he knew it would work. Maria licked her lips at Nikki. Fuquan extended his hand to her. Nikki could only smirk at his audacity, as she unbuttoned her blouse.

Two hours later, Fuquan's beeper went off on the nightstand. The three of them lie asleep; Fuquan was in the middle with his arm around both women. Their heads were on his chest and smiles adorned their sleeping faces. The beeper went off again. Fuquan, a light sleeper, saw it flashing.

"Maria," he said, shrugging his shoulder under her head.

She finally stirred.

"Hand me that."

She sat up groggily and pushed the hair from her face. "Do what? Huh?"

"That, the beeper right there. Damn," Fuquah growled. He was so impatient.

She handed it to him and then lay back down. He checked the number and vaguely recognized it. He sat up and dislodged himself from the three-way embrace. Nikki sucked her teeth in her sleep and rolled over. Maria sprawled out on her back.

Fuquan grabbed Maria's phone and dialed the number.

"Yo," he said when the number was answered.

"So this is how you muhfuckas wanna play?" Marlon bassed on Fuquan.

"What...who...Jamil?" Fuquan was confused by his tone.

"You know who the fuck this is and you know what the fuck this is about! Y'all got the right one now!"

Fuquan shook his head in an attempt to shake the last bit of sleep out of it. "Yo ock, what the fuck are you talkin' about?"

"Your boy, man, your boy!"

He was making no sense to Fuquan.

"Look, where you at? I'm on my way."

Marlon didn't respond.

"Ock!" Fuquan called out, because he tried never to use names on the phone.

"Meet me at White Castle on Elizabeth Avenue."

They ended the conversation.

xxxxxx

Marlon was shaken and heated at the same time. He just had a gun to his head with only five pounds of pressure between his decision and death.

He met the Crip dude Malice that Malik introduced him to a couple of days earlier. Everything went smoothly...at first. Marlon pulled up in Weequahic Park in a brown van, his work van. Malice pulled up in a blue chromed out Dodge Charger, with Snoop Dog's "Gin and Juice" blasting.

106

Above The Law

Malice was an older dude, close to forty Marlon surmised. That seemed amusing to him, why would a grown man be a party to the young gang madness?

However, it wasn't amusing for long.

Malice got in with Marlon and handed him ten thousand dollars in a Burger King bag. Marlon pulled a duffle bag from the back and handed it to Malice. Inside were twelve Heckler and Koch 9 millimeters. Few words transpired between the two men, but when Malice opened the passenger door to get out, a dude with a red bandana around his face pulled him out aiming a snub-nosed .357 at his head.

"You know what it is muhfuckca! Run that shit!" the masked man barked.

Marlon could feel the gun stuck in his waist. It was locked, loaded, and useless. They had caught him slipping.

He raised his hands.

"You got it, yo," Marlon calmly remarked, but inside he was steaming.

Another man appeared, took the duffle bag from Malice, and told him to leave. Malice quickly complied and jumped into his car and peeled out.

That's when Marlon realized it was a setup.

The gunman put the barrel of the gun between Marlon's eyes. "Take off the chain and the watch," he hissed.

Marlon reluctantly did so and never took his eyes off the gunman. Marlon tightly clenched his jaw, but didn't shift his gaze. The gunman rammed the barrel of the gun into Marlon's forehead, causing him to bang his head against the window.

"I said don't look at me! Open the door and get out!"

"You got everything, yo...," Marlon replied. He lowered his gaze.

The gunman patted Marlon down and felt his gun. He took it and then snatched the Burger King bag off his lap and opened the driver's door. He shoved Marlon to the ground.

The other gunman jumped in and the two of them skirted off in the van.

Marlon sat on the ground furious. Never in his life had anyone taken anything from him. A part of him wished he had bucked on the gunmen, preferring to be dead than experiencing the humiliating feeling of helplessness. He quickly dismissed it as a foolish thought because he wouldn't get to taste the sweetness of revenge.

xxxxx

Fuquan waited for a break in the oncoming traffic before he whipped the Maybach into the White Castle parking lot. He saw Marlon step out of the shadows in the rear of parking lot near the Hawthorne Avenue entrance. Fuquan parked and hopped out. They stood about ten feet from one another.

"As Salaam Alaikum ock," Fuquan greeted Marlon without approaching. He still didn't understand what was going on.

Marlon stood and glared at him.

"Jamil, what's up?"

"What's up?" Marlon shot back, his tone was confrontational and challenging.

Fuquan sighed. "Come on yo, we can box and throw rocks all day. What the fuck is goin' on?" he asked.

Marlon took a few steps closer. "Your man fuckin' robbed me," he growled. "Bitch ass muhfucka ain't have the heart to do it himself, so he had his lil' goons do it, actin' like Bloods."

"Robbed you? Who Malice?" Fuquan spat. Now he was pissed; it wasn't like Malice to disrespect his people.

Without another word, Fuquan pulled out his phone and hit the number five. It went to Malik's beeper. He punched in his number and hung up.

Above The Law

"Wallahi ock, we ain't have nothin' to do wit' that, but we do now," Fuquan vowed. He used the oath Muslims swear by, meaning 'by Allah.'

Marlon squarely eyed him. He truly didn't think Fuquan would set him up like that, but in those types of situations when you don't know who to trust, he trusted no one.

Fuquan's phone rang.

"As Salaam..." Malik started to say, but Fuquan interrupted.

"Where you at?"

"What's up? You good?"

"Nah, meet me at Pathmark on Lyons Avenue," he instructed. He hung up without awaiting a reply. He looked to Marlon, "Come on Jamil, ride wit' me."

Marlon hesitated momentarily, but slowly got into the Maybach.

Several minutes later, they pulled into the parking lot of the Pathmark Supermarket on Lyons Avenue. Fuquan cruised the parking lot until he spotted Malik's Cadillac. He parked a few rows away and he and Marlon walked over to Malik's car.

"Yo, when you hollered at Malice, what you tell him about Jamil?" Fuquan questioned. He was getting right to the point.

"What you mean what I tell him?" Malik shot back. He played stupid.

Fuquan knew his cousin too well and his impatience flared. "You know what the fuck I'm talkin' about! Malice robbed Jamil! Now, if he did it knowing Jamil was wit' us, then he got a problem. But if he did it and he didn't know, then *you* got a problem!" Fuquan barked.

"Fuck you mean, I got a problem? If he got a problem, that's *his* problem!" Malik retorted while pointing at Marlon.

"And please believe, I don't need no fuckin' body to help me straighten it," Marlon replied to Malik.

Fuquan looked at Jamil. "Yo ock, just chill a'ight? I got this."

"Man, what's the fuckin' point?" Marlon grumbled.

"Jamil," Fuquan firmly said. He turned to Malik, "Why didn't you tell them muhfuckas Jamil was family?"

"Cause he ain't!" Malik shot back. "Fuck I'ma vouch for him for. I don't know the dude and neither do you!"

Fuquan stepped up to Malik and stood nose to nose.

"You gon' fuckin' call Malice and straighten this shit out, Malik," he hissed.

"Nah Fu. I told you, I ain't vouching for this muhfucka," Malik stood his ground.

"Yo, don't even sweat that shit. I'ma vouch for me," Marlon growled. He turned to walk away.

"Yo, 'Mil!" Fuquan called after him, but Marlon kept on walking.

"Yo, Jamil! Where the fuck you goin?"

Marlon turned the corner and disappeared from view.

Chapter Nine

February 10th – 9:46 P.M.

Asia stepped off the elevator on the fortieth, the uppermost floor, in the Renaissance building. It was the top of the company, literally and figuratively. The floor was reserved for the President, his assistants, and his secretary.

Asia stepped into the plush waiting area. The secretary stood to receive her with a tight, but polite, smile. Asia sensed she was sizing her up and it amused her that the pale, skinny Norwegian-style woman would think they were in the same league.

She's probably fuckin' Mr. Templeton and thinks I'm her new competition, Asia mused.

"Right this way, Lawrence is expecting you," the secretary told her. She spoke over her shoulder as they walked into the main corridor.

Lawrence? Asia snickered to herself. *She's fuckin' him and she wants me to know it too.*

Asia subtly shook her head. *The games women play,* she thought. They came to a set of double mahogany doors with polished brass lever-like handles. The secretary knocked

111

once then entered before she heard a response. She pushed both doors and they stepped into the room.

"Ms. Walker to see you, sir," she graciously announced.

Templeton was sitting behind his large black lacquered desk. "Very good, Tina, thank you."

The secretary nodded and left. Asia looked around and was impressed. Templeton's office reminded her of the saying, 'It's lonely at the top.' Although, the view of the city was magnificent. Both outside walls were floor to ceiling windows where Asia could see the city's beautiful skyline highlighted by the majestic Sears Tower. Templeton's desk sat angled to the corner where the two windows met; the perspective one had of him was superimposed on the panoramic view of Chicago behind him. In one corner was a large cherry wood bookcase next to a small bar. Beside it was a door that led to his private bathroom. Asia saw an executive bedroom where Templeton slept over, or discretely entertained company.

He let Asia gaze around his huge office for a moment; he was pleased with her admiration. To some men, admiring the trappings of their success was like admiring the size of their dicks.

"You have a beautiful view here," Asia complimented him.

Templeton chuckled as he stepped around the desk to shake her hand. "It's not really mine, but God's letting me borrow it for awhile."

Asia politely giggled, not knowing if he was trying to be sanctimonious or sacrilegious.

"Please," he said, gesturing to the high-backed armchair in front of his desk.

She sat down and crossed her legs to get comfortable. Templeton perched himself on the edge of the desk. He

Above The Law

unbuttoned his coat to get comfortable and revealed the Tom Ford banker's vest underneath.

In the looks department, Templeton left much to be desired. He was well groomed, but paunchy and wrinkled. He was 67 years old and had started Renaissance during the 60's 'Black is Beautiful' movement. He used that mentality to his advantage, opening one of the first Black brokerage firms in the country. He was the only one who believed he would be successful and he proved the naysayers wrong. After he became the famous New York Yankees' slugger Reggie Jackson's personal money manager, his business took off. He had had accounts with some of the biggest names in Black America, from Bill Cosby to Michael Jordan, Robert Johnson, and even Oprah Winfrey. Renaissance had offices in several cities, including New York (which was the headquarters), Atlanta, Houston, and Los Angeles. Templeton may not have had the looks, but he had the things that were worth more, money and power. He wore those well.

"Ms. Walker," he began in his deep baritone voice that reminded Asia of James Earl Jones, "How long have you been with us?"

"It'll be a year this June," she answered.

He nodded and pursed his lips. "I'm impressed, in less than a year you've landed more major accounts than some people who have been with us for several years. I take my hat off to you young lady and thank you personally."

"Thank you, sir."

"Ms. Walker," Templeton said. He was looking her directly in the eyes. "Can I be very, very frank with you?"

Asia met his gaze with professional sincerity. "Yes sir, by all means."

Templeton nodded and rose from the edge of the desk. He slowly walked around to his seat and sat down. He rubbed his right temple with his right index fingertip and leaned his elbows on the desk.

"Mr. Aweys has awarded us his account."

Asia's face lit up like the sky on the fourth of July. "That's wonderful, Mr. Templeton."

His poker face told her that there was more to come.

"He also asked, no he stipulated, that you and you alone, handle the account."

Asia solemnly nodded in agreement. "I'm honored; I know that I will live up to his expectations and the company's, sir," she assured him.

"Do you know how much Mr. Aweys' account will be?"

"No, I don't sir."

"Six hundred million dollars."

Her heart almost skipped a beat; that meant six hundred thousand in her pretty little hands from his account alone. She was a little nervous, but she was prepared.

"Yes, six hundred...million. With this one account, we double our assets under management...double," he repeated to let the emphasis sink in. "I'm not going to lie to you Ms. Walker, Renaissance needs this account. With this account, we'll be one of the top investment groups in the nation, no longer just the top black-owned group. Mr. Aweys is being well-courted in Washington. The government needs him on our side with the situation in Somalia and the war on terrorism. So it's not only six million dollars, it's opening a door to D.C. and a branch office on New York Avenue in the city," he smiled. "Somebody's going to have to head that office and I think that someone should be you."

"Sir, I'm...I'm flattered," Asia could barely contain her excitement.

"Don't be," he dismissively replied. He then softened his tone and smiled, "At least not yet. Mr. Aweys has not only requested that you handle his account, but only his account.

Above The Law

As of now, I'm pulling you off everything else. You'll brief me on everything and turn it over to me."

"Yes sir."

"From now on, you are Mr. Aweys' personal portfolio manager. Make no mistakes, Ms. Walker, this account is the biggest opportunity in your career, maybe even in your life. If I were you...," he concluded with a curious twinkle in his eyes, "I'd be very willing and accommodating to ensure its' success."

He leaned back in his throne-like leather chair with his fingers tented beneath his chin. "Are we clear?"

Asia allowed a slight smile to come across her lips.

"Crystal clear, Mr. Templeton."

He's nothing but a corporate pimp, she thought.

When Asia returned to her office, she found a middle-aged white man in a chauffer's cap waiting for her.

"Ms. Walker?"

"Yes?"

"Mr. Aweys has sent me to humbly request a pittance of your time," he said with a heavy British accent.

"Well, thanks to Mr. Aweys, my calendar is totally open," she smiled.

"Excellent...May I?" he replied as he reached for Asia's sable and helped her put it on. "Shall we?"

"We shall," she replied.

They drove to O'Hare International Airport in a black Cadillac Escalade limousine and headed for the private jet hangars. Asia lowered the glass between her and the chauffer and asked, "May I ask, where are we going?"

"New York. Mr. Aweys has sent a plane so that you may join him."

The jet was a Piaggio P.180 Avanti. At first sight, Asia though it looked like a hammerhead shark because of the wing that cut across the nose of the plane. It was designed to make it more aerodynamic. Once inside, she was seduced by the luxurious ambiance of the cabin. Two sets of deep-cushioned leather chairs sat across from each other. A fully stocked bar was located behind the seats. Two 32" LED monitors on either side of the aisle provided entertainment.

Asia removed her sable and laid it across one of the seats before settling into the seat on the opposite side. A tall blond stewardess emerged from the cockpit greeted her, "Good morning Ms. Walker, my name is Sylvia. The flight should take about two hours. In the meantime, whatever you need, please don't hesitate to summon me."

"Thank you."

Sylvia warmly smiled. "No need to thank me. Mr. Aweys instructed me to take good care of you, and I intend to do just that. Now...may I get you anything? A drink, maybe?"

"Maybe just a splash of Remy Martin V.S.O.P. if you have it," Asia requested.

"I'm sure we do," Sylvia responded.

Sylvia brought Asia her drink and added, "We have an extensive library on file. Any requests?"

"Do you have "Dynasty," by Dutch? I heard it's a great series and I haven't been able to check it out," Asia responded.

"I'll check for you," Sylvia replied.

She returned in five minutes with the book Asia requested, "Is there anything else I can do for you?"

"No thanks, this will do. Thank you," Asia said.

She kicked off her shoes in order to feel the thick carpet between her toes. She began reading while sipping her drink. If that was what it was like working for Ajaye, she could definitely get used to it.

xxxxx

Above The Law

Janice went into Ortega's office and placed a folder on his desk.

"Chief, here's the file you asked for on Ajaye Aweys."

"Thanks Janice."

"No problem."

She was on her way out, but stopped and turned back to him. "Chief...can I ask you a question?"

"Sure," he replied. He kept his eyes glued to the file.

"Does all this have anything to do with the case that Agent Porter was assigned to? Why are you doing everything off the radar?" Janice asked.

Ortega removed his reading glasses and looked at her. She was his original secretary of eighteen years. They had worked together daily since he was sent to run the Chicago field office. He knew if he could trust anybody in the office, he could trust Janice. At least, that's what he thought.

"Why do you ask?"

She came closer with her hands clasped in front of her and sat down in front of his desk.

"Well...because...since Porter killed himself you haven't been yourself. It's almost like you're conducting a secret investigation."

Ortega placed the folder on the table. He folded his hands on top of it and sighed heavily.

"As my secretary, you do a lot of typing."

She didn't know if it was a statement or a question, but either way she felt it appropriate to nod.

"And in all this typing, you probably type certain words over and over, right? Like and, the, Special Agent in Charge," he smiled. "Have you ever had a problem spelling a word like that? One you've typed a million times if you've done it once."

"All the time," she agreed.

"Well, that's how this is for me. I've worked on hundreds, if not thousands of investigations, but this one...something just isn't spelled right. I've seen it a hundred times, but I keep asking myself 'Is this how it's spelled?' You understand what I'm saying?"

"Yes, but why not assign someone? You're the boss, yet you're running around here like your own lackey. Like you're me," she smiled in a self-depreciating manner.

Ortega laughed, and at the same time contemplated how to answer.

How could he tell her that the Chicago Chief of Police had been aware of the connection between the Black P. Stones organization and City officials for over a year, but decided to wait until an election year to push the issue? How could he tell her he believed he was being set up as a scapegoat for a potential Democratic regime change? The powers that be would want to clean house and his head would be the first to roll. How could he tell her that he didn't know who the Director's mole was in this season of palace intrigue? He couldn't assign anyone.

How could he tell her? He couldn't, so he didn't.

"Because maybe it's just me and the word is spelled right," he smiled. Just the same, I think I'll keep it secret as you say, for just a little while longer."

"Okay Chief," she replied and started to get up.

"One more thing Janice; get Richard Baker on the phone. Let him know that an investigation I may or may not be conducting, has turned up a connection to Ajaye Aweys. Tell him I'd like to discuss it in detail at his earliest convenience," Ortega instructed her as he smirked to himself.

Richard Baker was the Assistant Secretary of State. By giving Baker the heads up, Ortega knew he would contact the Secretary of State. If there was a problem, the Secretary of State would contact him- thereby completing the boomerang of bureaucracy. It was how the game was played.

Above The Law

"Sure, Chief," Janice smiled. She knew how it was played too. "I'll get right on it."

xxxxxx

Ali Muslim continued jumping in silence for a moment, while he contemplated what Fuquan just told him. They were in the Shabazz Gym on Howard Street. Ali Muslim went three times a week for his heavy cardio work out.

He expertly worked the rope, crisscrossed his hands and whipped the rope in front of him, then jumped back in without missing a beat. In the background the taunts and barks of trainers, the thump of the heavy bag and the steady dribble of the speed bag filled the air.

Ali Muslim stopped jumping and checked his watch; he was slightly winded.

"Now...tell me again, why should we risk business over a beef for a dude that isn't even family."

Fuquan took a deep breath and launched his spiel once again. He explained how he gave Jamil the gun side of the business, how it was a chance to lock in what he felt would be a major gun connect. He explained how he vouched for him and told Malik to vouch for him so no one would try him. Fuquan explained how his word was at stake and a Muslim's word is sacred to him. Lastly, he explained that Jamil was a Muslim.

"I'm sayin' Mu, he ain't on his deen, but Allah knows his heart. He Mumin, a Believer. I know he could bring a lot to the cause if we take him under our wing," Fuquan proposed.

He followed Ali Muslim over to the speed bag. Ali slowly worked it. He gradually built up speed before losing his rhythm and letting the bag get away from him.

Fuquan playfully pushed him aside. "Move big bruh, let the champ show you how it's done."

Ali Muslim laughed.

Fuquan tore into the bag like a pro with steady hands. He hit it rapidly with two hands. He altered force and made the bag hit the top and bounce back. After a few minutes of showing off, Fuquan stopped the bag by grabbing it with both hands and looked at Ali Muslim. "Any questions?"

The two of them shared a laugh and then Ali playfully threw a combination at Fuquan, which he easily slipped and countered. When it came to the art of boxing, Fuquan had the edge on Ali Muslim, but once Ali added his martial arts acumen, Fuquan was no match.

"You really vouch for this dude, huh?" Ali Muslim probed.

Fuquan nodded. "Yeah Mu, I do. I mean, Allah know best, but he a sound dude. Ock made his bones from the door, so I know he go hard. I'm sayin', wit' a little groomin', and once he see Al-Nymayr ain't about no suicide bomb bullshit...Yeah; I say we bring him in."

Ali Muslim nodded while thinking. "Let me meet this dude. Look him in the eyes, a'ight?"

"Done deal."

Ali Muslim's beeper went off. He checked it and smiled; it read all sevens.

"Alhamdulillah," Ali Muslim gave praise.

After Malik texted Ali Muslim all sevens, he laid the phone on the passenger seat. He was driving a rented Ford Focus and trailing a white beer truck sized tractor-trailer off the Westside Highway in Manhattan to a warehouse. The warehouse awning and the truck read the same: Zanzibar Exports, Inc.

The truck backed into the warehouse bay. Malik parked halfway down the block and casually surveyed the street. A few cars were parked along the street. He spotted a stretch Benz limousine in front of the main entrance to

Above The Law

Zanzibar Exports and smiled to himself. He already knew who was in that limousine. The eagle had definitely landed.

From where he sat, he could see the warehouse workers loading the cargo onto the truck. The cargo was in big wooden shipping crates, about five feet tall and five feet wide. Forklifts carefully lifted the crates and placed them into the truck.

Inside the crates were beautifully sculptured African artifacts and statues. Most were made of different types of wood, but some were made with ivory, brass, even electroplated gold. There were many different styles and designs, each one exquisite in their own right, but that wasn't what made them so expensive.

Inside of each statute, depending on the size, was varying quantities of uncut Afghani heroin. It was packaged by the kilo. That was the reason Malik was trailing the truck. The driver didn't know he was picking up over a thousand kilos of heroin a month. To him they were just boxes of funny looking statues.

If he only knew...

Malik looked up and saw the eagle coming out of the warehouse; he was accompanied by a gorgeous looking woman in a full-length sable. The eagle and Malik's eyes met. He gave a subtle nod and got into the limo behind the woman before they pulled off.

As the limo pulled off, Ajaye turned to Asia.

"So...did you see anything you liked?"

"Everything," she giggled. "One of those statues must cost a fortune."

Ajaye modestly demurred.

"A small fortune, but it is worth it, don't you agree? For a man to take a small piece of God's creation, mold it, shape it into his own...to give it life with his hands is more than creative, it is...sublime and worth every penny," he passionately explained to Asia.

Asia loved the lilt of his accent. She could listen to his smooth voice for hours.

"I definitely agree. They say an idle mind is the devil's playground, but the artistic mind is God's canvas."

He smiled. "Eloquently put, because even the most expensive works of art pale in comparison to the beauty God created with his own hands," he caressed her cheek and added, "For that is priceless."

Asia lowered her gaze and blushed like a shy teenager.

The driver lowered the glass partition between them. The bodyguard in the passenger seat reminded Asia of Vin Diesel. He said, "Mr. Aweys, they're ready for you."

"Excellent," Ajaye replied.

The glass partition raised. He looked at Asia.

"Now…we can get down to business."

They arrived at a windowless brick building tucked away in the Soho section of Manhattan. The driver opened the door for Ajaye. He in turn gave his hand to Asia and helped her from the car. A heavy steel door opened, allowing Ajaye, Asia, and the bodyguard to enter.

A small, pale, bird of a white woman in rectangular shaped reading glasses and a clipboard greeted them. She limply shook Ajaye's hand.

"Good afternoon, Mr. Aweys. If you follow me, we can get started."

Ajaye nodded and offered his arm and a smile to Asia. She took both and they followed the woman.

They entered a large room, the size of a Manhattan studio apartment. The only furniture was two director's chairs and between them was a small glass table and an elevated runway. It was three feet off the ground and illuminated with lights embedded along its' length.

"Please have a seat. Christophe will be with you momentarily. May I get you anything," the woman offered.

"Chardonnay," Ajaye replied.

Above The Law

She nodded and left.   Asia looked at Ajaye with a twinkle in her eye.

"Ajaye…what is going on? I thought you said this was business?"

He slyly smiled. "Christophe is serious business."

Before she could answer, a super skinny white man with fire engine red hair, a black turtleneck, black stirrup pants, and bare feet entered the room with a flourish from the opposite end.   Four of his assistants followed him.   They flocked around him like worker bees to the queen as he approached Ajaye and Asia.

"Ajaye!" Christophe sang in a high-pitched homosexual lilt.   "I love you, I hate you, I worship you, I despise you," Christophe spat. His facial expression changed to match each emotion he described. His English was tinted with the accent common to Eastern Europeans.   "These are the conflicting emotions ravishing me from within because you disrespect my artistic process with such short notice!" He stomped his feet like a spoiled child to punctuate his tantrum.

Asia curiously looked at him, but Ajaye indulgently smiled.   He was well aware of the eccentricities of the flamboyant designer.

"Notice is for mortals, but you my dear Christophe are perfection personified; perfection needs no preparation," Ajaye smoothly replied. He was placating him.

"Yes," Christophe said.   He paced the floor with his pelvis thrust forward in a languid sort of way.   "This is true. I am a God aren't I? Will you miss me when I kill myself?"

"Terribly."

"You know I must kill myself, don't you? I am an artist, it is inevitable. A true artist must create his own death as he created his life, or he has failed. So my death will be beautiful," he mused.

"The world will mourn, dashing itself on your memory," Ajaye remarked. Asia had to suppress her laughter as she watched Ajaye expertly play the man.

"Yes," Christophe dreamily replied. He was picturing the mourning.

"But before you go, please…just a glimpse of perfection," Ajaye requested.

Christophe placed his hands around his own neck like he was going to strangle himself and slowly approached Asia. He looked her over.

"And this is she?" Christophe inquired.

"Yes," Ajaye answered.

Christophe framed Asia's face with his hands.

"Absolutely beautiful…Breathtaking," he gasped.

"Thank you," Asia replied. She was amused by the designer.

Still cradling her face, Christophe asked, "Would you like to behold my spring visions as the last people on earth to see me alive?"

Before Asia could object, Ajaye cut in.

"Yes she would, Christophe, it would be an honor."

"It would," Christophe softly said. He then abruptly stepped away and began barking orders and snapping his fingers. His assistants took off in four different directions to carry out his orders.

The bird woman brought them two flutes and a bottle of Chateau Villa Bel-Air Blanc on a silver tray. She sat it down on the table between them then disappeared.

"Ajaye, he is unstable. I don't want to be the last person to see him alive," Asia protested with a worried frown.

Ajaye chuckled as he poured the wine.

"Don't worry. He won't kill himself. He thinks his death will be the greatest thing he can give to the world, so he is…how do you say, milking it for all it is worth."

Above The Law

Asia shook her head at how crazy some people could be. Ajaye handed her a flute.

"Ajaye, you don't have to do this."

"This is more than an extravagant indulge, Asia. As I said, Christophe is serious business. He is *the* most sought after designer amongst the upper-echelon of the world's elite. He once denied Melinda Gates a dress because he didn't feel like she had the right bust line for it. After that, he took off. You don't choose him, he chooses you. It makes it an honor for you to give him your money." He smirked at the irony.

"Hell of a hustler, huh?" she giggled. "He uses a feminist approach to marketing."

"Indeed," Ajaye replied. "He understands the rich very well. They have everything, so they are very insecure that they themselves measure up. Christophe has effectively created a hoop that they fight each other to jump through."

"Okay," she said. "What's the point?"

"Having a Christophe original will open many doors. He will brag to his clients about you, they will in turn inquire about you. You will meet them, they will love you, and when they find out you handle my money, they will give you theirs," Ajaye explained. He raised his glass; they clinked together and took a sip.

"How can you be so sure?" Asia probed.

Ajaye looked at her and smiled. "Because I am of that class that Christophe never denies."

She could tell he wanted her to ask, so she did.

"And what class is that?"

He took another sip and casually replied, "The international criminal class."

The lights were dimmed and the runway lights fluttered on and illuminated its' length like a miniature airport. Christophe's voice filled the room from the speakers hung in all four corners of the room.

"In the beginning...there was spring...new birth...life after death...the season of resurrection..."

The sounds of Mozart's "Requiem" replaced Christophe's voice and gave the presentation a light and springy feel as the first model stepped out. Christophe may've been an eccentric and over the top drama queen, but his talent spoke for itself. From formal gowns to cocktail dresses, business attire to casual wear and accessories, Asia found herself in awe with the colorful designs paraded in front of her.

Ajaye handed her a buzzer the size of a cell phone.

"When you see something you like, simply press the button," he explained.

"I like everything!" she gushed.

He laughed. "Then click it when you see something you love."

Asia smiled as she got the message. She could ball...but not out of control. After viewing a dizzying array of exquisite materials, classic and cutting-edge styles, symmetrical to asymmetrical, Asia settled on four designs. Two business suits, a cocktail dress, and a formal gown at Ajaye's request.

"And burn the design," Ajaye had told Christophe. Christophe burst into tears and dropped to his knees. Asia didn't understand. "Burning the design" was an option Christophe extended to all of his creations for an astronomical fee ranging between one million and several million dollars. Christophe would not make the design for anyone else. It would be not only a Christophe original, but also a Christophe exclusive. It put the wearer on a level that few would ever obtain.

Burning the design was always a negotiation. Ajaye knew the tears were a part of the sales pitch.

"No! No," he sobbed. "Any other one, but that one! It is sacrilegious! I will burn in hell if I burnt such a masterpiece!"

126

Above The Law

Ajaye squatted beside the prostrate Christophe and winked at Asia.

"But don't you see? If you hold on to this masterpiece, if you become covetous, then how can you create another? You must set it free and in the process, free yourself. Freedom is the key to creativity."

Christophe stiffened and looked up at him.

"Yes...yes, I must make room for greater perfection...but...I couldn't do it for less than...1.5."

"Excuse me? What was that? Did you say 1.3?" Ajaye said while putting his ear near Christophe's mouth.

"I hate you," Christophe hissed. "I hope you get mauled by wild boars!"

He snapped his fingers. "Children! My tape measure!"

That meant the deal was sealed.

After Asia was fitted and the delivery arranged, Ajaye took her to The Lion, a moss-covered ninth street brownstone that housed a posh little club. Over a dinner of lamb shank and branzino, she asked him the question that had been on her mind since his comment.

"So what do you mean, you're an international criminal?" she asked between sips of her Zinfandel.

He dabbed his mouth with his napkin.

"I am the Defense Minister of a country that has been at war for as long as I can remember...and I have a memory like an elephant!" He smiled then continued, "Soon, there will be peace. The more moderate rebels will make peace with the government, and then the coffers will be pillaged. The more radical rebels will say the moderates sold them out, meaning they left them out of the pillaging, and they will turn on these former allies and it begins again." He shrugged, sipped his wine, and concluded.

"Where does that leave me? Maybe, I will be executed by the rebels for ordering the killing of so many of them.

Maybe the government will execute me when they find out I have also sold guns to the rebels. I could end up ensconced on the South Pacific island of Koro, where I'm heavily invested as a developer. Naturally, I choose door number three," he smiled.

Asia sipped her wine while letting it all soak in.

"So...we're not talking about investments, are we? We're talking about laundering," she succinctly surmised.

Ajaye nodded in respect to her assessment.

"Pretty girl, whether it's dodging taxes or Interpol, anything north of two hundred million must undergo some cleansing."

She nodded while thinking. "How many accounts?"

"Five."

"Where?"

"Three in Cyprus, two on the Island of Jersey."

"I'm glad you didn't say the Caymans, too well known and well monitored," Asia remarked.

"So...I take it we have an arrangement?"

Asia raised her glass. He raised his as well.

"To the lowering of inhibitions and the increase of my management fee."

Their eyes met. His smile conveyed his respect and his agreement.

The click of the toast made it official.

She knew he would come to her. She had felt the sexual tension all day. Now, on the plane, he was making it a reality. For every button on her blouse that Ajaye unbuttoned, he replaced it with a kiss. He continued until he ran his lips from her neck to her belly button. He pulled her bra straps from her shoulders and watched her plump, succulent breasts tumble out.

Asia's nipples stood erect like dark chocolate chips. Ajaye sucked and nibbled on her nipples until she gripped his

Above The Law

ears and released a soft whimper. Her body felt good. She was totally relaxed. She had been drinking throughout the day and although it hadn't been heavy, she was buzzed and receptive to his advance.

Asia couldn't lie; she was definitely attracted to Ajaye. He had style, finesse, international swagger and was a fine looking brother. Still, a part of her felt guilty.

She thought of Marlon...

It hadn't been a month yet and she was already naked, other than her shoes, on a private plane. Ajaye's tongue was doing luscious things to her swelling clit.

"Ohhhh, you're making my pussy so wet," she cooed.

"You taste so good," he groaned while running his tongue along the length of her pussy and darting in and out.

Asia squirmed, tightening her grip on his head.

"Let me taste."

"He rose up, allowing Asia to suck on his tongue. The taste of her own juices made her lust become more intense. She devoured his tongue while her hands fumbled with his belt. He slid two fingers inside of her, twisting them on the thrust. He made her suck in her breath and cream on his fingers.

"Put it in Ajaye, please just put it..." she deliciously groaned. She wasn't able to complete her sentence as her wish and her wet pussy were filled simultaneously. She was laying back in the chair with her legs cocked wide open, both her arms on the chair. She watched Ajaye's thick eight-inch sausage snake in and out of her wetness, the base of his dick was already white from her juices.

"Oooh, yessss baby, right there!"

"Tell me this dick is good to you."

"It's...it's soooo good baby, don't stop!"

"Tell me again."

"Oh baby, please don't stop!" she gasped.

She came while riding him, screaming as she gripped the carpet of the sky. She came when he bent her over and pounded her supple ass from the back. She came when she was sitting on his face and Ajaye hungrily munched on her womanhood. She needed it; Ajaye was her release. He was attentive, passionate, hung, and had a strong back. The sex was mind blowing.

However, she didn't intend to ever do it again.

"Where are we? Shouldn't we be landing soon?" she asked while straddling him on the floor.

Ajaye chuckled and traced a ticklish finger across her nipples and down to her belly button.

"Asia, we landed thirty minutes ago."

She threw her head back and laughed.

"I guess the plane came down before I did."

He laughed with her before rolling over to blow her mind once more.

xxxxxx

"Good night Ajaye."

"Good night Asia."

They stood in her living room. She sniffed the air and frowned.

"Are you okay?" he asked.

"Better than okay," she replied. She threw her arms around his neck and tongued him down.

Their lips parted, both wet with passion. She cleared her throat.

"Should I go?"

"Yes, I'm exhausted."

"I make wonderful pancakes." He smiled.

"Good night Ajaye." She giggled and pushed him toward the door.

"Until tomorrow," he playfully said.

Above The Law

"Sounds good," Asia replied.

"Good night."

"You already said that."

He laughed and pecked her lips.

"I'll call you," he said as he turned and headed to the limo.

Asia shut the door and slid the chain lock in place. She thought of Marlon and sighed. A wave of guilt washed over her; then a hand locked like a vice-grip around her mouth.

Chapter Ten

"Yo Jamil! Where the fuck you goin?"

That was the last thing Marlon heard as he rounded the corner leaving the parking lot. He crossed the street and boarded a stopped bus.

"I ain't got nothin' smaller," he told the driver as he handed him a twenty-dollar bill.

The driver pocketed the bill and Marlon sat down. He could still feel the weight of the barrel between his eyes. Up until that point, he felt untouchable...a different breed...above the law. All that went out the window when the young boy with the cold eyes proved he wasn't untouchable. He was ready to prove he wasn't bulletproof too. Marlon felt like he needed to recoup...take a step back...go back...Asia.

It was the type of decision made at the spur of the moment, the kind of decision that flew in the face of logic, but just felt right. He was going to Chicago. He called Delta, the first airline he could think of. They asked for his name; he had to check his ID to give her his name. He had so many, he felt free and trapped at the same time. Asia would be the key to unlock him.

Above The Law

The bus dropped him downtown. He took a cab to the Newark Airport. He had no baggage to check. He knew it could raise a few eyebrows, but didn't worry. The ID was government issued; he laughed to himself about the phrase.

"Now boarding Flight 413 for Chicago O'Hare Airport."

It was colder in Chicago than in New Jersey, and he took a cab to Asia's building. He still had her key on his key ring. He had consciously kept it. It was like his safety net, like no matter how far that he fell, it would keep him from hitting rock bottom. He turned the key in the lock and entered. He could smell her once inside; he inhaled her scent. It was like a hungry man returning from work to a home-cooked meal. The scent comforted him and gave him butterflies at the same time.

How would he greet her? He was dead. Here I am, back from the dead? Would she yell, scream, cry, curse or...or what? It would be a shock, but that was the only way to do it. He couldn't call; Henry and Steve may've had his phone tapped. He couldn't approach her in a public place, her reaction might draw too much attention.

So it had to be there and now. She would probably turn on the lights and see his face, he chuckled, and probably faint. However she reacted, it would be a hell of a surprise for her.

What Marlon didn't know was, she had a surprise for him as well...He heard the key in the lock. He felt like the confident kid in the school play that suddenly got stage fright.

"Fuck it, I'm here now," he mumbled.

He started to approach the door, until he heard him.

"There is a banquet in Washington that I must attend next week. Will you wear the dress for me then?

"Yes."

Marlon's stomach twisted into knots like he wanted to throw up. Who was he? Marlon wanted to peek, to see his face, but they were entering the apartment. She turned on the light as Marlon slipped into the shadow of the corner; he was hidden by houseplants and furniture.

"Good night Ajaye."

"Good night Asia."

There was no formality in the salutation. It was warm, familiar...intimate. Marlon's sickness turned to rage and made him wobbly.

"Are you okay?" he asked.

"Better than okay."

And then he heard it and felt it. Closing his eyes, he even saw it. Asia was kissing a pair of unknown lips. He could hear the soft moans she used to make for him.

Marlon's fists clenched by his side. Jealousy isn't rational, nor is it particularly illuminating. It is irrational and blinding. That's exactly what Marlon felt, irrational and blinded, irrational because he was dead to her. What was there to wait for? He was blinded by jealously and started to come out and confront them both until he heard, "Should I go?"

"Yes. I'm exhausted."

He was leaving! Maybe it had only been a date. Sure, she kissed him, but Asia was putting him out, meaning he wasn't staying to make pancakes. He heard the door close and it stirred him to action. Once she started down the hall, she would see him for sure. Then she might scream and bring the man back. He couldn't let that happen. So as she locked the door and slid the chain lock in place, he moved like the ghost he was supposed to be, right up behind her, and gripped her mouth like a vice.

Asia started to scream, to bite, to kick and fight, but the scream died in her throat when she smelled that familiar scent, the same scent that made her sniff the air and Ajaye to ask, "Are you okay?" She brushed it off at first, charging it to her imagination. Now it was stronger, coming from the hand stifling her scram and she knew it was real. A fragrance

Above The Law

named Blue Nile, sold by Muslim vendors across the country. It was Marlon's favorite. Her knees got weak as her mind probed the contours of the hand over her mouth. She had touched that hand, been touched, and caressed by that hand.

Marlon felt her body sag and he understood why. He supported her weight, helped her to the couch, and whispered in her ear, "Shhh baby, it's me. I...I know it's crazy, but please...give me a chance to explain."

He sat down on the couch for the first time in almost a month.

"Marlon?" she gasped. Silent tears streamed down her cheeks. "It...it can't be!"

"It is baby," he replied and sunk to one knee in front of her like he was proposing.

"I...I don't understand."

"It's complicated, Asia. Just know that I love you and I'm here now," Marlon answered.

She shook her head. "Why did you do this to me? Why? Do you know what I went through? I thought you were dead, Marlon. You let me think you were dead," she sobbed.

Asia got up and brushed past Marlon. He took her hand as she passed and got up and pulled her to him.

"No Marlon, you left me."

He pulled her to his chest, holding her tightly.

"No baby, I swear I didn't. I'm here now and I swear I'll never leave you again," he vowed. He did not know how he would keep the promise, but he meant every word.

Asia allowed him to comfort her.

"I love you, Marlon."

He kissed her nose. He gently kissed her lips, no longer caring they had just been kissed before. She kissed him back, their tongues intertwined. She was slipping into his zone. She pulled back and broke from the kiss.

"What's wrong?" Marlon probed, he was scared of the possible answer.

"I...I can't."

"Why?"

She looked at him and he saw it in her eyes. His stomach knotted and twisted again.

"You did it, didn't you?"

She looked away; she couldn't meet his eyes.

"Asia, did you do it? Did you fuck em?" he growled.

"Yes," she hissed as she snatched away.

The fact that he had the audacity to get mad made her furious.

"You were dead, remember? You left me, okay?"

"I was coming back!"

"How was I supposed to know that?"

She was right and he knew it. Still...

"Look," she sighed, her guilt overruling her anger, "Even though I did...it wasn't...it's nothing to worry about."

"Just a quick pick me up?" he bitterly quipped.

"Fuck you," she hissed.

"A friendly fuck? Casual sex? How the fuck is it nothing to worry about Asia?"

"It was business," she firmly and defiantly replied.

"Business?" Marlon echoed. "That's what they callin' it these days?"

She wanted to slap him. She wanted to kiss him. The two impulses cancelled each other out. She walked away without a word. Marlon plopped down on the couch with a grunt of frustration. He held his head in his hands. The reunion wasn't going the way he planned.

xxxxxx

Above The Law

Marlon didn't realize that he had fallen asleep until he woke up. His neck was slightly stiff from leaning back on the couch. The sun had already risen, but was still low on the horizon. He looked to his left. Asia was curled up on the end of the couch in her 49ers Jersey sipping her morning coffee. She was watching him sleep. That used to freak him out, but now it seemed strangely comforting to him.

"Good morning," she grinned, asking for a truce in her tone.

"Morning," Marlon grumbled. His tone said he was not ready to grant one.

He went into the bathroom for his long morning pee; it was how he usually greeted the day. He washed his face and noticed his toothbrush was still in place.

At least everything hadn't changed.

While he brushed his teeth, Asia leaned against the door watching. From the corner of his eye, he admired her beauty. She was gorgeous, even fresh out of the bed. There wasn't a day that passed by where several dudes didn't try and get with her. He couldn't blame them.

"Can we talk like grown folks now, or we just gonna yell?" she asked.

He spit the toothpaste out, rinsed his mouth, and grabbed a towel to wipe it.

"I'm listening," he replied as he leaned against the sink.

Asia took a deep breath and began telling him everything about Ajaye Aweys. He was the Somalian Defense Minister with a 600 million dollar portfolio with Renaissance. She told him about Zanzibar exports as well.

"And there's a lot more going on with that. Too many young black dudes with a lot of swagger working there," she remarked.

She told him about Christophe and him burning the design. She spoke about money laundering, Cyprus, and The Island of Jersey.

By the time she finished the story, they were in the bedroom. She was sitting on the edge of the bed and he paced the floor in front of her.

"That's a lot of money, Ma. A helluva lot of money. Cats on that level play for keeps. You sure you wanna do this?"

Without hesitation, she answered, "Definitely...Now, what's up with you, Marlon? What's going on?"

He looked her in the eye and wanted to tell her everything. He wanted to unburden himself by telling the woman that he loved and trusted, but he knew he couldn't. Not yet anyway.

He crouched in front of her, and took both of her hands in his.

"Baby...have I ever kept a secret from you?"

"Now, how would I know if it was secret?" she quipped with a silly grin that made him laugh.

"Okay, have I ever acted like I was holding anything back from you?"

"No...but you're about to, right?"

Marlon sighed.

"I have to for now. Just please, trust me, okay?" Marlon requested. He was thinking how he could somehow bring Asia into his world, somehow convince Henry how much he needed her.

Asia wrapped her arm around his neck.

"That goes without saying, my love."

She passionately kissed him.

"There's something else," she said.

"What?"

Above The Law

"Mr. Ortega came by the office and questioned me about the two guys that supposedly said they were lawyers."

"What did he ask?"

"If I had seen them before, did you tell me anything about whatever they were up to. He thinks I know something about your ... extracurricular activities," she smirked.

His legs cramped, causing him to stand up. Asia stood with him.

"Okay, if he comes around again, let me know."

"How?"

He gave her a beeper number.

"A beeper, Marlon? Where you hiding out? The 80's?"

He laughed. "Yeah, that was cute. Naw, I just don't keep the same number for more than a few days," he explained.

"Can I ask where you'll be?"

There was a pause.

"Jersey," he told her.

She nodded.

"I love you."

"I love you too," he replied.

They shared a long and deep kiss, trying to get all they could of each other.

"I'll beep you," she giggled.

He smiled and winked before blowing her a kiss on his way out the door.

Chapter Eleven

February 13th – 12:37 P.M.

"When you gon' step your car game up, ock?" Fuquan asked.

"What? My shit is fire," Marlon boasted as they both got out in the parking lot of the Masjid.

Fuquan chuckled at his comment.

"Naw, 'Mil, a Lexus?" Fuquan snorted. "It ain't shit but a Toyota with an L! This shit only fly when you got like four of 'em, summer cars to match your outfit and shit. When you only have one, it's like wearing a pair of hot ass Timbs wit' a fuckin' tuxedo!" he laughed. Marlon couldn't help it; he joined him in laughter.

"Man, get the fuck outta here," he waved him off.

"Real rap though, after this I'm takin' you to see my car man, get you somethin' to go wit' your gators."

They entered the tranquility of the Masjid. They silently removed their shoes and put them in the cubbyholes where shoes were kept during the service. Fuquan rolled up his red monkey jeans, he was careful that they were above his ankle. He and Marlon then went and joined the noon prayer of

Above The Law

Zuhr, which was already in progress. There were several rows of men lined up shoulder to shoulder. The few women that were there stayed behind an opaque partition. All you could see were their shadowy silhouettes moving through the four positions of Salat.

Marlon waited patiently, remembering his aunt when she used to offer Salat in the living room. The prayer concluded and the brothers began mingling around. They were shaking hands, salaaming each other, and talking.

Marlon remembered that he left his phone on the charger in the car. He put on his shoes and went to get it. After he retrieved it and shut the door, a woman in a full black over-garment called a Jalibiyah and a vibrant yellow head covering called a Khimar emerged from the woman's door. She headed toward a white Range Rover.

"As Salaam Alaikum, brother," she said in a flirtatious voice.

It caught Marlon off guard. Muslim women weren't usually so aggressive, especially in the parking lot of the Masjid.

"Wa Alaikun As Salaam, sister," he politely replied and kept it moving. He could feel the woman's eyes on him as he went back inside. Fuquan was waiting for him to return.

"Yo, where you go?"

"I forgot my phone," he replied.

"Come on, they waitin' for us."

The 'they' that were waiting were Ali Muslim and Aziz. Marlon knew he was making progress when Fuquan told him they were going to meet the next day.

Marlon quickly set up a meeting with Steve and Henry.

"Should I be wired?" Marlon asked.

"No need to risk it at this point. Besides, if they knew who the informant was, he'd be dead already and we'd be fucked," Henry explained.

"We won't need the snitch if I can find out what they're planning," Marlon reasoned.

"True, but no wire."

Marlon thought it was strange to go in unwired.

xxxxx

Fuquan opened the door to an office in the back of the Masjid. It was small and cluttered. Books were strewn about everywhere. Aziz sat behind the desk and Ali Muslim sat on a small broken-down couch against the wall. They all greeted each other and shook hands. Fuquan perched on a milk crate full of books. Marlon stood with his back square to the door and his right hand clasped over his left wrist.

"Jamil, right?" Ali Muslim began once the Islamic formalities and introductions were over.

"Yeah."

"My little brother tells me you had a problem with an individual whom he pointed you in the direction of recently," Ali Muslim stated. Marlon smiled to himself. Ali Muslim even used lawyer-speak outside of the courtroom. He decided to play along.

"That is correct," Marlon evenly responded.

Ali Muslim firmly eyeballed him, seeming to see if Marlon was trying to be funny or not. He continued, "You feel like he's responsible in any way?"

"Responsible? Do I feel like he set me up?"

"Set you up, let it happen, turned his head, however you want to put it," Ali Muslim elaborated.

"Nah," Marlon replied.

"Then why did you bring the problem to him?"

Marlon felt like he was on the witness stand. He shifted his weight from one foot to the other. He glanced at Fuquan and then back to Ali Muslim.

Above The Law

"I'm sayin'; when it first went down, I ain't know who set it up. I was goin' in on the strength that they were Fu's people," Marlon explained.

Ali Muslim delicately smirked.

"But I'm sure you know, in the streets, your man's man ain't always your man." Ali Muslim jeweled him.

Marlon immediately shot back.

"True, but when your man is the man in the streets, you take respect as a given."

Ali Muslim contemptuously snorted.

"Those young boys don't know what respect mean."

"Yeah, well I'm about to teach 'em," Marlon angrily retorted. "Look, I ain't come here lookin' for y'all to hold me down on this, I ain't looking for no big brothers," Marlon said while looking Ali Muslim in the eye. "I came here on the strength of Fuquan, 'cause I ain't wanna bring beef to your doorstep. I'm gon' straighten this sh..." He started to curse, but remembered he was in a Masjid and caught himself. "This thing will be handled."

Ali Muslim slightly laughed at his bravado.

"You, huh? You gon' take on a whole set, huh?"

"Listen ock, I got guns they only seen in video games. After I come through, whoever's left...I promise you they'll throw their hand in," Marlon confidently growled.

Ali Muslim sat back on the couch and assessed him.

"You got somethin' to prove, Jamil?"

"Nah."

There was a long pause before the next words were spoken.

"Fu told me that you go hard," Ali Muslin smiled and Marlon knew he was talking about the Miguel murder. "You running around here puttin' your hammer game down, when you should be aiming for your real enemy."

"And who's that?"

"If you don't know, then you're already lost."

143

Another silence swept across the room.

"Jamil...take a walk with me," Aziz requested. He stood up from his chair.

He hadn't said a word for the entire conversation. He listened and observed. He moved around the desk and then he and Marlon left the room. The walked along West Kinney Street, the afternoon sun kept the winter chill at a tolerable level.

"Don't let Ali get to you. He's a beautiful brother, but sometimes he takes himself too seriously."

"It's no problem, Shaykh."

"He used to be just like you and Fuquan, wild, arrogant, and thuggish. But now, sometimes he even admonishes me! I say ock, I'm the Imam, and he says 'then you really have to tighten up'." Aziz and Marlon laughed. Aziz added, "So I guess Ali keeps us all in line. Alhamdulillah."

Marlon nodded.

"You asked who your real enemy is. Do you really want to know?"

"Yeah, sure."

Aziz smiled. He knew that Marlon was only trying to appease him, but he had more patience than Marlon had impatience.

"I could say that your real enemy is Shaytan. That is the truth, but too abstract, too ... spiritual. I could say it's the Kufar, the non-believers, but that would be too narrow. Sadly, sometimes our own Muslim brothers are worse enemies than the Kufar. No, your real enemy is ignorance and oppression. The Qur'an says oppression is worse than slaughter, worse than slaughter. In addition, Allah describes the slaughter of one person like killing of all mankind. Think about that, ock. The oppression of one human being is worse than the killing of all mankind!"

Marlon contemplated his words as Aziz continued.

Above The Law

"You know why? Because when you kill a man, you render him non-existent. No pain, no suffering in a physical sense. Some even prefer death to suffering. However, when you oppress, you retard the sour, you debase the spirit and you create disorders dis-ease or disease, and that can destroy generations. Just look at slavery."

The logic of what Aziz said struck Marlon as profound. He now had his full attention, Aziz's patience won out.

"This man who robbed you, he took something from you, from here," Aziz emphasized. He backhanded Marlon's chest, "And you want revenge, that's okay. Our innate sense of justice demands that. But think about what they have taken from us here, in America, and the land from which our blood runs from. *That* ... demands justice as well."

Marlon could see why Aziz was the Imam and commanded the allegiance of hundreds of Muslims nationwide. His words spoke to your spiritual side, which is the heart of all motivation, be it good or bad. It challenged your manhood and made you respond.

Aziz pulled out his cell phone and hit speed dial. He spoke in Arabic. After a brief conversation, he hung up and placed his phone back into his pocket.

"The man you're looking for is named Blade. Right now, he's on his way downtown to pick up his watch from Palm Jewelry on Halsey and Market Streets," Aziz explained and smiled. "Justice ock."

At first Marlon was confused how Aziz could have such detailed knowledge of the dude. Then he remembered Fuquan telling him that there were Muslims amongst the Bloods and Crips. Now he understood what was going on. The Abdullah's wouldn't get involved directly, but they would use their resources to help him, thereby gaining a friend without making an enemy. Marlon smiled at the information.

"Shukran, Shaykh," he said, using the Arabic for 'thank you.'

"Afwan."

Blade hopped from the passenger seat of the rented Chrysler 300. The redbone driving tried to pass him the blunt, but he slammed the door and bopped inside of Palm's Jewelry.

Thirty seconds later, Marlon double-parked right beside the 300. He purposely blocked it in. The woman driving the car rolled down her window.

"Um, excuse me," she yelled, with much ghetto attitude.

Marlon ignored her. She threw open her door, slamming it into his Lexus and stood outside the driver's door.

"Okay, mothafucka, I bet your ass hear me when my man get out here!" she vowed. She had no way of knowing that her man was coming out in a body bag.

Marlon calmly walked inside. Blade's back was to the door. The Asian dude behind the counter was showing him something. One other woman was browsing in the store. The Asian guy saw the gun first. His eyes widened in fear. Blade turned around to see what was going on as his girl walked in.

"This motherfucka…" she started.

"Remember me?" Marlon asked Blade.

The fear in his eyes said he did.

"I, I, got…" Blade stuttered.

"Caught slippin'," Marlon finishing his sentence.

Tah! Tah! He fired two head shots from his .40 caliber with dum dum bullets. It looked like an exploding melon. Blood splattered the counter and flew into the Asian man's mouth and eyes; he thought he was back in Vietnam. The girl screamed and remembered she dented his car. She begged for mercy as she pissed her skin-tight Capris.

Marlon winked and brushed past her. He left the store and checked the dent on his car. "Stinkin' bitch," he hissed as he glanced back at the store and got inside his car to pull off.

Above The Law

When Malice found out, he swore that he would straighten it for his "Lil' Homey." He later got a call from Malik; he told him it wasn't them, but Jamil was family. Malice still barked, still swore he would straighten it, but by now they were just words. He didn't want to lose the gun connect. He was even allowed to keep the guns and six of the ten grand he got from the robbery. Besides, he really didn't want to go to war for Blade.

"Lil' muhfucka shoulda killed him when he had the chance," he shrugged, charging it to the game.

The only color that mattered was green.

Chapter Twelve

"What the fuck were you thinking?" Henry barked on the night of the murder. They met by the lake in Roselle Warinaco Park. They had the park to themselves.

"Look, you want these dudes to trust me? You want 'em to bring me in? Then this is the way to do it, killers respect killers," Marlon responded.

"No! This wasn't about your cover or your status with the Abdullahs; this was about the bone you got stuck in your teeth because the guy robbed you!"

Marlon shrugged and nonchalantly replied, "You said we can do what we want."

Henry got in his face and poked him in the chest.

"We don't expose ourselves for nothin'! Over bullshit, this is bullshit, Porter!"

Henry angrily eyed Marlon for a moment; he paced away and then paced halfway back.

"What do you think this is, a game? You think we're outlaws?" Henry barked, he snatched the gun from his waist and used it to punctuate his statement. He never pointed it at Marlon. "If that's what you think, I'll put a fuckin' bullet in

Above The Law

your head and dump you in the lake! We are defenders of America! We may play rougher than others, but that's because the bad guys force our hands! We do not and I repeat do not, use our power or position for some personal vendetta! Am I making myself clear?"

"Yeah," Marlon replied with a stone face.

Henry came closer.

"I said, am I making myself clear!"

"And I said yeah."

They eye boxed for a round or two and fought to a draw.

"Any kills that aren't in self-defense are to be cleared first by me, understood?" Henry instructed.

"Understood."

"I hope so...for your sake."

Henry walked away and opened the driver's door of the Escalade.

"Henry," Marlon called out.

He turned around.

"I understand what you said and I agree one hundred percent. I was out of line and it won't happen again, but don't ever pull a gun on me and not use it."

"Don't give me a reason to Porter."

xxxxxx

The next day, the tape from the store disappeared from the evidence room. The detective in charge checked the evidence log. Everything appeared to be intact, the tape simply ceased to exist.

"C.Y.A.," the detective told his partner.

"I've been C.Y.A.'d," he assured him.

The murder became a cold case.

February 14th – 8:15 A.M.

"Ortega, good morning."

"Good morning, Mr. Director."

"I hope I'm not disturbing your itinerary."

"No sir, not at all."

"Then what I hear in your voice isn't preoccupation, it's the satisfaction in knowing I would call."

Ortega smiled.

"Yes sir, I was expecting your call."

"A testament to your expertise in billiards, I commend you!"

Ortega chuckled at the reference to pool skills.

"So there's no need in wasting time to tell you why I'm calling."

"No sir, it's not."

"Good, I detest wasting time."

"Then it's ironic that you called, sir," Ortega slyly replied, he was unable to resist the jab.

"We're feeling rather presumptuous this morning, aren't we Ortega?"

"I apologize sir, I meant no disrespect."

"No need to apologize, I enjoy it. A witless conversation is like a non-alcoholic beer. What's the point?"

"I agree sir."

"I thought you would. It was very astute of you to anticipate the crux of my talk would be about not wasting time. Ironic indeed," the Director laughed.

"So, Ajaye Aweys."

"Yes sir."

"Turns out he's a very interesting fellow. He's Somalia's Defense Minister. I haven't had the pleasure, but State speaks very highly of him."

"I'm sure," Ortega replied with a twist of sarcasm in his tone.

Above The Law

He knew that by mentioning the State Department, the Director was letting him know Aweys was a part of America's foreign policy plan in some discrete way.

"He's quite the international playboy, but a bit of a rogue. He imports authentic African artifacts that aren't really authentic."

"Forgeries sir?"

"Yes, but virtually indistinguishable from the real thing because pottery, ceramics, glass, or metals can be carbon dated," the Director explained.

"It must be lucrative, since it is also illegal."

Ortega could hear the shrug over the phone.

"Sadly, it's out of our jurisdiction. International law protects diplomats from such… inquiries."

"Sad indeed sir."

"Besides, he seems to be 'our man' in the Somali situation. He's very useful in keeping those Islamic hooligans from wrapping their hands around the Horn of Africa."

"Much more important than forgeries," Ortega quipped.

"If Muslims controlled the Horn, it would be like having an Al-Qaeda stronghold on the corner of 5th and Vine. You'd have a helluva time finding parking."

"I understand."

"Very good."

"And the woman, Asia Walker? Does she have any… immunities I should be aware of?"

"Who?"

Ortega smiled. He knew the Director knew exactly who he was talking about, but was giving him the green light.

"Is there anything else, Ortega?"

"No, sir. I thank you for saving me from wasting time."

"Good day Ortega."

"Good day Mr. Director."

xxxxxx

Marlon and Fuquan pulled up to the car dealership in Hoboken, New Jersey in Marlon's Lexus LPA. Ferraris, Lamborghinis, even Bentleys and Aston Martins sat facing the highway, providing eye candy for commuters.

Marlon pulled up close to the showroom, a burgundy Gull Wing McLaren sat next to a black convertible Jag with brown interior.

A short Italian dude who reminded him of Joe Pesci stepped out of the showroom. He wore a navy blue Brioni suit with matching gators.

"My man Fuquan!"

"What's up Gino," Fuquan replied.

The two men shook hands and embraced.

"Gino this my boy Jamil, Jamil this is Gino, my car man."

Gino and Marlon shook hands.

"Nice to meet cha, Jamil."

"Same here."

Gino looked at Fuquan.

"This fuckin' guy," he shook his head with a deep laugh.

"You come see me one more time in the next three months and I'm gonna retire. I swear to God, move to Miami!"

Fuquan snickered and shook his head. Gino looked at Marlon.

"First he buys a two and half million dollar car. I gotta order it and go through all the red tape...Jesus, Joseph and Mary, got me pullin' my hair out over here! Then, two weeks later, he brings it back and buys a fuckin' Maybach."

"Yo, I need you to hook my man up. Take that piece of shit off his hands," Fuquan remarked.

Above The Law

"Piece of shit? The car's beautiful," Gino replied as he assessed the Lexus.

"Ay yo 'Mil, Gino's a funny dude, ock. Ay Gino, tell him the Deniro story."

"Eh, the guy doesn't wanna hear the Deniro story," Gino waved him off, but Marlon could tell he really wanted to tell it.

"Just tell the fuckin' story, spaghetti eatin'…"

"Aye Gumbah, watch your mouth," Gino playfully shot back, throwing a jab at Fuquan.

"Tell the story."

"Okay, I'll tell the story," he chuckled and then looked at Marlon. "Okay, so I'm at Bobby's Restaurant in Manhattan, it's a beautiful fuckin' place. It ain't Italian, but fuck it, it's Deniro's place right?"

"Tell the story," Fuquan chuckled.

"You wanna tell it?" Gino quipped; he turned back to Marlon. "Anyways, I've got this broad, a fuckin' blond Amazon cunt, right? Boobs out to here," Gino demonstrated with his hands. "I ask her one time; how the fuck do you see your feet? Anyway, the cunt's a doll and I really want to hump the broad, so I'm braggin' about how I know Deniro. 'You don't know Bobby', she says. I says, of course I know Bobby. Me and the fuckin' guy are like brothers. Only, I've never met him a day in my life."

Marlon laughed at Gino's story.

"But who cares, right? So, I'm a pretty good talker and I've almost got this cunt believin' I know Bobby. All of a sudden guess who walks in?"

"Bobby," Marlon snickered.

"Worst fuckin' luck right? But hey, it's his fuckin' place. So the cunt goes, 'Hey, it's Bobby! Introduce me!' Mama Mia! What I'm gonna do? So now, my foot's in my mouth. I figure, hey what I got to lose? I go over to his table and his bodyguard stops me. So I say, Mr. Deniro, you don't know me, but I know your cousin Paulie from the Lower East Side. Which is true because... Ah, that's not important. So I explain the whole shabang to the guy and he's laughin' his ass off! He's getting a kick outta this shit. So he says, 'You want me to come over and say hi?' Fuckin perfect," Gino laughs. "So I goes back to the table and a few minutes later, he comes over with a big smile, right? He says, 'Hey Gino! How the hell are ya', old pal?' I look up at him and I go, Bobby...not now. Can't you see I'm wit' somebody?"

Fuquan and Marlon fell out laughing.

"So I blow off Deniro for this broad, fucked the cunt six ways from Sunday. The pussy turned out to be the shit after all that. And that's the Deniro story," Gino shrugged.

Marlon knew Fuquan was sharing more than a car connect or a good laugh. Little by little, he was bringing Marlon deeper into his world. Marlon ended up buying a black Maserati Quattro Porte with wine colored interior for $125,000. He paid in cash, on the spot of course, the paperwork didn't reflect the actual transaction. On paper, Gino made it look like Marlon (in the name of Sean Maddox) put down ninety five hundred dollars. His monthly car payment said twenty-eight hundred a month. The money he paid also covered the interest rate, gas-guzzler tax, and luxury tax. It looked on paper as if, after six years, the car would be paid for. In actuality, Marlon was walking out with the bill of sale in hand.

Marlon was pushing the Maserati near one hundred miles per hour across the Pulaski Skyway. He was dipping in and out of lanes and passing cars like it was the Indy 500. Fuquan sat slouched in the passenger seat laughing and enjoying Marlon's new toy.

"See, Didn't I tell you, you needed some new shoes? Got you on your grown man shit now, huh? I told you Fu was gon' hold you down."

Above The Law

"This only the beginning ock. I'm 'bout to cop two more of these, and show you how to ball!" Marlon retorted with cockiness. Fuquan's arrogance was rubbing off.

Not to be outdone, Fuquan shot back, "Show me? How? Fuquan's beyond a don. The only reason I ain't God is because Allah ain't got no partners."

Marlon shook his head with a smirk.

"Yo, you wild ock."

"A man ain't been born that can outshine me, unless the muhfucka on fire," Fuquan added while grabbing his nuts.

"I can show you better than I can tell you."

Fuquan let out a good-natured fit of laughter.

"You can try."

After the laughter died down, Marlon cut his eye at Fuquan. It was time to go for the kill.

"Yo Fu…When you gon' put me on?"

Fuquan glanced at him.

"Put you on what?"

Marlon gave him a look that said, "You know what I'm sayin'."

"What you talkin' 'bout, ock?" Fuquan asked; he was genuinely perplexed.

"I'm sayin'…I know this shit bigger than just getting money and flossin'," Marlon said.

"How you figure that?" Fuquan probed, but Marlon could tell by his tone that he knew what he was talking about.

They came out of the Holland Tunnel and entered Manhattan. When they stopped at the light, he looked at Fuquan.

"Come on ock, I read damn good, especially between the lines. That walk I took with Aziz wasn't for my health," he sarcastically quipped.

Fuquan shrugged, but didn't respond. He just looked out the window in thought.

Marlon continued, "All I'm sayin' is, y'all ain't gotta come to me, I'm comin' to you. What you think, I'm gon' talk? Run my mouth? Understand something, ock, I can't sing and I never learned to whistle. I keep my mouth shut; I even breathe through my nose. I might even keep a bitch if I licked the pussy, but I keep my tongue in check. Fuckin' thoroughbred ock, born and raised," Marlon spat with slickness and a smirk.

Fuquan cracked up and shook his head. He wanted to open the door for Jamil, but he knew it wasn't his call. However, he also knew all that was just a formality. Jamil was ready to be brought in.

"Yo ock, I don't know what you talkin' about right. But maybe if I did, we could help each other out," Fuquan hinted.

They smiled at each other like two co-conspirators playing poker, both itching to call.

"How so?"

Fuquan effortlessly ran his tongue over his teeth.

"Can you get your hands on some C-4?"

Marlon smiled to himself. The door had just been opened.

"Hell yeah, gimme 'bout a week."

He dropped Fuquan off at Nikki's. Fuquan exchanged pleasantries with the doorman and jumped on the elevator. He opened the door of the apartment and spotted Nikki's phone on the charger. He texted Aziz.

He's in...

Chapter Thirteen

Fuquan heard soft moans coming from the bedroom as he walked into the house. A devious smile crept across his face. He hurried to the bedroom and opened the door. Nikki was on her bed lying on her back with her legs wide open. Maria's face was buried in Nikki's pussy. Maria looked up when she heard the door; she wore Nikki's juices like a milk mustache.

"We've been waiting for you Daddy," Nikki purred.

"Looks like y'all couldn't wait," he replied.

The girls giggled and moved to undress him. Fuquan had officially accomplished his mission.

xxxxx

Crush the Crescent! Save the Horn!

Somali has no government, only butchers!

Islam, the religion of pieces, not peace!

Somalian government must go.

The placards and picket signs were visible along both sides of 15th Street, near The W Hotel in D.C. Protesters were out in droves. Some were pro-Somalian government and anti-

Islam, the others were mostly Muslims, and they hurled slogans and chants at each other in the cold D.C. night air. The only thing they had in common was the fact that they were all black.

The media was out in full force as well, they were not there to cover the protest, but for the Republican fundraiser being held for Senator Mark Kirk's re-election. A caravan of limos arrived carrying politicians, millionaire supporters and foreign dignitaries like Ajaye Aweys, who was accompanied by Asia.

They exited their limo and were almost immediately accosted by several reporters.

"Mr. Aweys, how do you respond to the accusation that the Somalian government has authorized, and you as Defense Minister have carried out, the use of chemical warfare against not only the rebels, but also the Somalian populace?"

"I respond with the fact that the United Nations has investigated these accusations and found them to be totally and utterly baseless," Ajaye calmly answered with Asia on his arm.

"It is true that the Somalians are torturing the populace that supports the rebels?"

"My country is at war, the priority of war is to defend the sovereignty and the people of Somalia. Therefore, torturing our own people would be counterproductive. Thank You!"

He and Asia disappeared inside, they left the reporters baying his name and useless questions like a pack of hungry jackals.

"Now see, that couldn't be me, shoving microphones in my face, and blocking my way. The media is so rude," Asia remarked.

"But a necessary evil, Asia. All one has to do is put up a picket sign or two..." Ajaye replied.

His smirk said it all.

Above The Law

"You set that up? The demonstrators for your country?" She giggled at his cleverness.

"All of them actually," he chuckled. "In America, the crux of public policy is influenced by public opinion. It's easy to manipulate the dog wagging the tail. Now, with attention sufficiently raised, we've created another campaign issue, one that is easy to support by both parties. Even wars need good P.R."

They entered the banquet room. Red and white streamers adorned the walls and doorways. The tables had white tablecloths and the servers wore white jackets with white gloves.

Looking around the room, Asia was surprised to find several black people there. She giggled to herself, thinking how the Republican Party had finally been integrated.

Ajaye helped her out of her full-length chinchilla and checked it with the coat check.

"You look absolutely gorgeous, my lady," Ajaye complimented her and kissed her hand.

"Thank you...I know," she giggled.

The Christophe exclusive was black silk, very elegant but very sexy at the same time. It had a split that allowed her left thigh to play peek-a-boo with each strut. It hugged her shapely ass and hips, crisscrossing in the back leaving her back partially exposed. She was by far the most beautiful woman in the room. Asia was turning heads and getting appreciative nods from those who knew what she was wearing.

They schmoozed and rubbed elbows with businessmen and politicians, some of the most wealthy and powerful people in the country. Ajaye's assessment turned out to be correct. Several senators and congressmen approached Ajaye with pledges of support and to have their pictures taken with him. Somalia was a "fringe country" in the so-called war on terror; it didn't garner nearly as much attention as Afghanistan or the Middle East. It was ripe for the politician that wanted to look tough on terror and like he spearheaded the call for action. Ajaye knew that when the Appropriation Committees met to discuss Foreign Aid, these politicians would go a long way in helping Somalia and Ajaye's pockets to the top of that list.

He was also right about something else. With his, and not to mention Christophe's endorsement, Asia was doing a little schmoozing on her own. Before the night was over, she chatted with several potential new clients. She understood that the initial accounts wouldn't be major, but they could give Renaissance Investments what Templeton craved, friends inside the Beltway. She could picture her D.C. office already. The night wore on and eventually Asia was ready to go. Networking was one thing, but Republican fundraising definitely wasn't her idea of a night out. Ajaye sensed it and began to wrap it up.

On the way to the coat check, Asia saw something that made her frown.

"Is everything okay, Asia?" Ajaye questioned with concern.

"That guy...never mind."

"Which guy?"

"Really, it's okay. I'm just tired,"

But it wasn't really okay. The guy she was referring to was a middle-aged white man. He had brown hair and was of medium height. He passed her as he came from the coat check without looking in her direction. But all night, Asia would notice him looking at her. It was not admiringly, it was as if he was watching her. She didn't tell Ajaye because she didn't want to seem paranoid. Besides, she wasn't doing anything in order to be watched, or so she thought.

They retrieved their coats and left. They headed directly to Dulles International Airport where the private plane that brought them to D.C. waited. This time it was a G-4. The flight attendant waited until after takeoff to bring Ajaye and Asia their drinks. She then left them in privacy.

Above The Law

"To a boring, but productive evening," he toasted.

"Very boring evening," she quipped.

"Boring is good with those kinds of people, which means its business as usual."

They sipped their drinks and Ajaye put his glass down.

"You think everything went well with the first transaction?" Ajaye asked.

"Yes," she tentatively replied.

Ajaye laughed at her trepidation.

"Sweetheart, you can talk freely. I am a diplomat, it is illegal to investigate me, let alone tap my conversations. Besides, I have more to lose in this getting out than you do."

Asia relaxed a little, enough to explain how she handled the first 100 million dollars. He wanted to make sure his money was in good hands. She finished her drink and took him step by step through the process of how to make dirty money clean and virtually untraceable.

"I not only clean it, Ajaye, I give it a face lift and a new identity," she smirked.

"I'm impressed," he smiled and moved closed to her. "And also…" he kissed her neck, "Very aroused."

His caresses felt good and although she hadn't forgotten the last flight, she knew she had to stay focused. She moved away, picked up her empty glass, and held it out to him. Ajaye smiled as he got the message. He took the glass to the bar. Chevis Regal, he handed it back to her.

"Is there anything troubling you, Asia?"

"No…yes… it's just…" she fumbled her words and looked him in the eyes. "I'm attracted to you, Ajaye. I've never met a man like you before. So…worldly, sophisticated.…It overwhelmed me, you overwhelmed me."

He lifted her chin with his finger.

"Don't let it. The money, the power, even the plane, it doesn't matter. I am only a man, a simple man, easily satisfied with the best and you my lady are the best."

He leaned in and she allowed him to kiss her softly, she then pulled back.

"The best implies there are others to compare me to. Don't deny it, Ajaye, I'm not a fool. You probably have girls on every continent. I don't just want to be another," Asia admitted. She blended just enough truth with the bullshit to make her sound sincere.

The truth was, she had Marlon, and that was enough. Besides, it was time to separate business from pleasure.

"You won't be," Ajaye assured her. They both knew he was telling her what she wanted to hear. "I have no intention of making you just another."

Asia grinned.

"So you won't mind giving me time. If you're not going anywhere, then we have all the time in the world, right?"

No matter how sophisticated a man could be, he could still fall for the Janet Jackson shit.... *Let's Wait Awhile.*

February 15ᵗʰ – 9:40 P.M.

Fuquan rented one of the biggest clubs in Newark for Fatima and Fa'eemah's birthday bash. The crowd ranged from fully covered Muslim women serving food, to females in regular clothes wearing the head covering Khimar and even the regular half-naked hood rats. The men in kufis and long beards mingled with men in baseball caps, platinum jewelry, and Timberlands. The entire Muslim spectrum was represented.

Fuquan arrived in a full-length snow-white chinchilla fur with a matching executive fedora brim. He had Nikki and Maria on each arm.

Marlon arrived a few minutes later in a three-quarter length chocolate brown hooded mink, with matching Ostrich three-quarter boots. The first to spot him was Fatimah.

"As Salaam Alaikum, Jamil," she flirtatiously smiled.

Above The Law

"Wa Alaikum As Salaam, Fatimah, Happy Birthday," Jamil replied.

She giggled and put her right index finger to her mouth.

"Shhh, don't let Fuquan hear you say that. You know Muslims don't celebrate birthdays, he says it's just a gathering. So I was like, oh this Jumu'ah?"

Jamil laughed heartily; that was the literal meaning of the Muslim 'Holy Day' of Friday.

"So why you ain't call me?" she quizzed him.

"Why you ain't call me. It ain't like you ain't got my number too!"

"Exactly, I got your number 'cause I stepped to you. It was your turn to holla back," she retorted while playfully punching him in the arm.

"I would get you a drink, but Ali made 'em take all the alcohol out. He lucky I don't drink anyway."

"I'm good."

"Okay, well come dance with me," she demanded. She sounded like a woman used to getting her way.

Fatimah grabbed his hand and led him to the dance floor. Ali Muslim came over and interrupted them on their way. She hugged her brother and in a deep voice, she mocked Ali.

"Salaam Alaikum Fatimah, Happy Birthday," she replied in an exaggeration of her own voice, "Oh thank you Ali!"

"Stop playing girl, you know we don't do birthdays," Ali Muslim responded with a smile.

"No, you don't do birthdays anymore. Remember when you turned 21?" she mischievously smirked.

"That was a long time ago," Ali Muslim shot back.

"Look, Jamil, *this* brother here at 21? Worse than Fuquan, he who Fu got it from! Ali had twenty-one chicks in thongs, each holding a lit candle for the whole night! I'm tellin' you, Muslim arrogance, ain't no arrogance like it in the world," Fatimah laughed.

Ali Muslim smiled for the first time since Marlon met him.

"Go 'head with that trouble, Fatimah. Let me holla at Jamil for a sec," Ali Muslim chuckled.

He and Marlon stepped over and leaned against the empty bar.

"Damn ock, lil' sis pulled your card huh?" Marlon laughed.

Ali Muslim shrugged.

"I mean, it ain't no secret. I was a thug, but thugs grow up to become gangstas and gangstas grow up to become me, you know? Life is growth."

"True indeed."

"But look, Fuquan says he holla'd at you about that. What's the word?"

"I still got the feelers out. My partner usually handles shit like that, but that Miguel shit still got him shook," Marlon lied. They already had access to C-4 and could get it on call, but Marlon didn't want to produce it too quickly and arouse suspicion.

Ali Muslim nodded in response.

"Yeah, I can dig it. Just stay on that and do what you can, a'ight?"

"No doubt, I got you."

They shook hands and parted company. Fatimah approached and took his hand again.

"Now, you mine for the rest of the night," she told him. She was only half joking.

They moved to the dance floor, J. Cole's "Who Dat" was playing. Marlon two-stepped and Fatimah kept a respectable distance.

"So, who older? You or Fa'eemah."

Above The Law

"Fa'eemah, by like six minutes, but I'm the pretty one," she smiled.

"My aunt was named Fatimah, she raised me," Marlon told her while thinking about his aunt's smile.

"Was?" Fatima questioned.

Before he could answer, he spotted Malik talking to Ali Muslim. By the gestures and body language, he could tell Malik was upset. The two of them stepped outside.

"Yeah, she ummm...she passed," he told her. His mind and eyes were on Malik. "Excuse me for a minute, Fatimah."

He went around her and headed across the room. Fatima didn't see Malik and Ali Muslim; she didn't know why he left. However, she wasn't the only one watching Marlon either...

Marlon saw Ali Muslim and Malik exit the side door. He saw the emergency exit just around the corner and eased it open. He knew Malik didn't like him, but he didn't know why. Was it simply that he didn't like outsiders, as he tried to portray, or was it something else? He was the initial point of contact and dealt with Miguel. Did Malik's distrust stem from something that happened before Marlon entered the picture? He had to find out, to make sure he wasn't trying to turn Ali Muslim against him at that critical point.

Marlon kept the exit door open with a bottle and crept to the corner, he was about ten feet from Ali Muslim and Malik.

"That's all I'm sayin', ock," Malik concluded.

"Nah, I hear you. I been tryin' to talk to Fuquan, but he got a head like a rock. He only listens to Aziz, but all Aziz say is 'he'll grow out of it'," Ali Muslim replied with a tone drenched in frustration.

"He too arrogant, ock," Malik shook his head. "Our shit is too deep to slip now."

"No doubt. What you think about this dude, Jamil?"

Marlon's ears perked up.

"Only thing I know is, the cat ain't police. Not the way he get down. The muhfucka go extremely hard," Malik begrudgingly admitted. "The Palm Jewelry thing? Muhfucka sick as fuck, but I'm like, who the fuck is this dude, feel me? Where he gettin' all the guns from, I mean, damn, you know? What the fuck?"

"Bottom line is, he's not the police," Ali Muslim summed up.

"Yeah, but just 'cause we know who he not don't mean we know who he is."

Satisfied with what he heard, Marlon went back inside. He found out that it wasn't so much him, but Fuquan that Malik was badmouthing. Malik thought he should be in charge of the street division and not Fuquan. He saw himself as more levelheaded, more discrete, and more dedicated to Islam than Fuquan. He was pushing for power and using Fuquan's swagger against him.

As Marlon entered the back corridor, he almost ran into a woman.

"Oh ex —," he started to say, until he looked up into the sensual smile and alluring eyes of the flirtatious sister from the Masjid in the yellow Khimar.

"Remember me," she asked.

"Should I?" Marlon quipped.

"Shouldn't you?" She smirked, "I'm Hasana."

Hasana saw Marlon when he followed Ali Muslim and Malik. She waited until she thought no one saw her and she went behind him.

However, somebody did see her...

Fatimah was watching.

Marlon stared suggestively at Hasana. Even though she wore full covering, he imagined the contours of her curves underneath and licked his lips.

"I'm Jamil."

"I know who you are. My man doesn't like you."

Above The Law

"Who's your man?"

"Malik," she answered.

He smiled, like she knew he would. Revenge, however subtle, is still sweet.

"What's that got to do wit' me?" he crooned.

"Exactly," Hasana said.

The air became charged between them and Marlon's dick started to bulge in his silk slacks.

"I'm sayin' then, where we go from here?"

"You lead, I follow," she assured him.

"I'm in the black Maserati."

"Give me ten minutes."

She turned and walked away, putting extra sway in her hips and checking over her shoulder to make sure he was watching.

He was.

Marlon stopped by Fuquan's booth and told him he was leaving.

"But you just got here," Fuquan protested.

On his way out the door, Fatimah called his name.

"Leaving so soon?" she asked with a hint of disappointment.

"Yeah Ma, somethin' came up I gotta handle." He was thinking about handling Hasana's ass.

She acted like she didn't know, but inside she was hurt and angry.

"Oh okay, well handle your business."

"As Salaam Alaikum."

"Wa Alaykum," she replied before walking away.

He frowned at her response. Wa Alaykum was the greeting Muslims used for derision. He shrugged it off, thinking he just didn't hear the last part and left the club.

xxxxxx

He sat in his car for about five minutes before a red Nissan 350Z pulled in front of him. The windows were deeply tinted, too dark to see inside. The driver's window went down and the darkness was replaced by Hasana's smile. She mouthed the words "follow me" and peeled out.

The Z was fast, but the Maserati was faster. She was a good driver, but he was better. They moved in tandem with finesse and speed, like a pair of skates crisscrossing in traffic and exchanging the lead all the way to the Marriot on Route 19.

They parked and Marlon got the room. They walked into room 112 and entered the room entangled. "Let me take a shower," she giggled. She returned wearing nothing but her Jimmy Choo's and a thong. She wasn't ghetto thick, but her petite form was proportioned and curvaceous. She crawled up on the bed like a panther in heat. He was in his boxers and already hard as a rock. Hasana was dripping wet and he was ready to devour her. She pulled down his boxers and took him into her mouth. She could feel his dick in her throat.

"Cum in my mouth," she gasped.

Who was he to deny her request? He willingly obliged. Hasana swallowed his seeds and kept working on the dick until it was at full attention again.

He climbed on top and fucked her like Allen Payne gave it to Jada Pinkett in "Jason's Lyric." After roughly fifteen minutes, they switched it up. He beat it from the back like Halle Berry got in "Monster's Ball." Eventually, he flipped her over again and punished the pussy like DMX did Taral Hicks in "Belly." After their movie was over, Hasana rested her head on his chest. She was exhausted and satisfied, her pussy still cumming.

"Damn baby, you trying to make a bitch fall in love with you? Then Malik gon' really have beef," she giggled.

"Nah Ma," he smiled, "I'm a lover, not a fighter."

Above The Law

"That's not what I heard. I heard you the gun man," she told him. She grabbed his dick and gave it a sensual squeeze, "The big gun man."

Pillow talk was a gangsta's nemesis. Malik was sleeping with the enemy, his own mouth. He was the only one who could've told her.

"Nah yo, I don't know what you talkin' 'bout."

"I'm talkin' 'bout money," she shot back with no hesitation. "You ain't the only one 'bout business. I got people in Hartford, big guns for big money in Connecticut."

He searched her eyes for any hint of deception and found them firm.

"Yeah?" he smirked.

"Yeah," she affirmed.

"Maybe we should talk."

"Oh, we will," she replied. She licked her lips seductively, "But not now; I'm ready for round three."

Chapter Fourteen

February 16ᵗʰ – 10:15 A.M.

"Sir, this was just picked up from the Walker wiretap," the agent said. He handed Ortega a printout.

"Phone numbers?"

"No sir, a page. This is the number she paged and the second number is the number she wanted called. It's not the number we have under surveillance," he explained.

"Is she still in New York?"

"Yes sir, staying at the W in Times Square."

"Get in touch with the New York office ASAP. Tell them we need someone on the ground yesterday," Ortega firmly instructed.

"Yes sir," he said it so crisply that Ortega thought he was going to salute.

Ortega went into his office and gazed at the number as if it was some ancient riddle.

"What are we up to, Ms. Walker, and who will we find at the other end of the line?" he rhetorically asked himself, he had a good idea as to the answer.

Above The Law

Unbeknownst to Asia, as the logistics and needed manpower were being arranged, she stepped out of the shower and grabbed the remote. She turned to CNN's "Money Talk." A crystal-like ring sounded from the nightstand. It was the prepaid cell she bought to call Marlon. She smiled and happily answered.

"That was an hour ago," she said as soon as she answered.

"Good morning to you too," he sleepily replied.

"Ew, you got the dragon, please talk away from the phone," she joked.

Marlon responded by blowing on the phone as if it was a Breathalyzer test.

"You so common," she giggled.

"Where you at?"

"Manhattan."

"Okay, give me an hour and meet me at The Grey Dog Café on University."

"Cool," Asia replied.

"See you then," he said.

Marlon hung up the phone and looked at Hasana.

"Wifey?"

"Somethin' like that."

"So, I guess you gotta go."

"Yeah, but not before you tell me what you talkin' about," Marlon replied. He figured that Malik had something on the side that involved her. Maybe the something on the side was where he could find his target, the informant.

"I got a brother; he a Crip. He's in Hartford gettin' money and need guns. Lots of 'em," she smiled, "Big guns."

To Marlon, it sounded like a dead-end situation. The informant couldn't be that far removed, or could he?

"When do I meet this brother?"

"What's the point? He don't know you and you don't know him. You give me the guns, I give you the money," she explained.

"Damn Ma, you were damn sure hidin' a lot under that garment, huh?"

She laughed at his comment.

"I wasn't always Muslim."

He got up and headed for the bathroom.

"So what up," she probed.

"Lemme think about it," he answered.

xxxxx

It used to be the exception to see somebody walking down the street talking to themselves, even in New York. Now, it's the rule. With Bluetooth so common, you don't know if the guy behind you is talking to his Bishop, or his broker, or reporting everything you're doing. In the case of the balding white man in the camel hair trench, it was the latter.

"She's leaving the hotel now," he reported. His Bluetooth picked up every word.

He managed to stay a comfortable half a block behind Asia. A few dozen New Yorkers helped him to hide out in the open. It was two-man surveillance, one on foot and one in a standard blue sedan, in case she hopped in a cab. It was all merely visual surveillance; the investigation wasn't New York's, so there was no expanded use of manpower.

"She's heading up University."

Asia entered The Grey Dog Café and took a table in the back by the window. She took off her leather trench and ordered two espressos and two apple strudels. The man in the camel hair trench came in.

Is he watching me? she thought.

Above The Law

She knew when a man was watching her; she had a sixth sense for it. A range of questions flooded her mind. Should she leave? Should she stay? Should she beep Marlon?

In an instant, she saw Marlon on the opposite side of the street, coming her way. He was crossing the street in his signature aggressive style. If the man was watching, he was about to see Marlon. If she went to Marlon and stopped him, he would know there was a reason to watch her in the first place.

Asia knew that yawning is contagious. She knew if she yawned and the man did the same, he was definitely watching. She decided to test her theory and yawned. She opened her mouth and the biggest yawn she could muster escaped her mouth.

Marlon entered just as the man in the camel hair coat yawned. The hairs on the back of her neck rose. Marlon smiled as he approached; he was exposed.

"Hey baby, I —," he began to say, but she abruptly cut him off.

"Baby! Do I look like a baby to you? I'm a grown ass woman and on top of that, I have a man. To the left, to the left," she said, in a voice dripping with attitude and enough volume to be overheard.

Marlon was confused for a moment, but he quickly picked up on her eye movement. She looked at him and rapidly off to the left where the man was sitting. To anyone hearing the remark, "To the left, to the left," sounded a like a reference to Beyoncé's break up song, but Asia was telling him the problem was to the left.

Marlon replied without missing a beat.

"Damn Ma, why so hostile? That's why I don't fuck with black women. Y'all got issues. Gimme a white girl any day."

Two black women sitting together to their right rolled their eyes. One white woman, sitting behind them alone, eyed Marlon flirtatiously.

"Whatever," Asia dismissively retorted as she got up to leave.

Marlon kept his cool demeanor, but inside his nerves were on high alert. Henry's words echoed in his head. 'You can't ever go back,' Henry told him. Here he was, like Jimmy Hoffa's body, about to be discovered.

He thought he would be arrested at any minute. "Dead Man Arrested in Manhattan," the headlines would read. He wasn't, and no armed officers surrounded the restaurant and forced him face down at gunpoint. The only thing that happened was that a guy in a camel hair trench got up and left a few seconds after Asia. Now Marlon knew exactly who she was talking about. While he followed Asia, he followed him. The hunted became the hunter.

Asia's prepaid phone rang and she quickly answered.

"Yeah, you're definitely being watched," Marlon told her.

She smiled and downplayed the conversation.

"I want to see you too, baby."

"There's the guy in the trench and one in a car."

"Oh, I'm not busy. I can get away. I'm looking for a cab now."

"No doubt. Take a cab to 42nd, jump out quick, and take the subway. Meet me in Harlem," he instructed.

"And I'm thinkin' the same thing. Love you," she sang.

"Be careful," he replied as he hung up.

It took virtually no effort to slip the agent in the car. Once she exited the cab and disappeared down into the subway stairs, the agent radioed in, "Subject on foot, going into the subway corner of 42nd and 8th Avenue," he then drove off.

Above The Law

Since it really wasn't the New York office's problem, it wasn't really their concern.

In Harlem, Marlon and Asia met in a small laundromat near Lenox Avenue. They sat side by side, hidden by the machines.

"Now will you tell me what's going on?" she asked him.

He had no intention of telling her the full story, so he tried to divert her focus.

"How you know this is about me? Maybe this is about your boyfriend's business," he sarcastically retorted.

"That's bullshit Marlon and you know it."

"Which part? The boyfriend or the business?"

Asia closed her eyes and took a deep breath.

"Look...Marlon...Baby...Ortega came to me asking about you, he wants to know about you, he thinks I know something about you. Now please tell me, how can I help if you keep me in the dark?" she pleaded with glistening eyes.

"You can't ever go back again..." Henry's voice echoed again in Marlon's head.

He stood up.

"Comin' back was a mistake. You've got your own problems. Just...go back to Chicago...I know Ortega. If there's something there, he'll keep coming. We just gotta fall back and make him think it's nothing there."

He started to walk away.

"When will I see you again?" Asia asked.

"I don't know Ma, soon...awhile...I don't know. Shit is just too crazy right now."

She walked over to him and pulled her beeper out of her pocket.

"Take my beeper."

"For what?"

"Because I know you're gonna dump yours. I know it's hot, but I need something to hold on to, so I know you're not gone for good," she told him.

He nodded and took the beeper. She wrapped her arms around his neck.

"Oh and F.Y.I., I don't have a boyfriend. I have a man that I love very much," she cooed.

Marlon smiled.

"Yeah? Well, I'm sure he loves you, too," he kissed her deeply, showing her just how much.

xxxxxx

"Chief, New York lost her in the subway," the agent told Ortega upon entering his office.

"Did we get anything?"

"Maybe, maybe not, they said she didn't meet anyone, but she did order for two."

"She was going to meet someone that never showed," Ortega surmised.

"Well, not exactly."

Ortega looked at him with a puzzled face. The agent continued.

"There was an incident. A young African-American male, estimated to be 6'2" or 6'3" entered the café and proceeded toward Walker. She verbally berated him then abruptly left the restaurant. I think it's safe to assume, since she left without meeting anyone, the man in question was the meet," he explained.

"Humph, smart girl."

"I wonder how she knew," he said aloud.

February 17th – 8:45 A.M.

"Ms. Walker," Asia's secretary said in an annoying tone.

Above The Law

She approached as soon as Asia stepped off the elevator.

"Good morning, Cynthia, is there a problem?"

"The detective, Ms. Walker."

The word threw her for a millisecond, but then she understood. In Cynthia's mind, any law enforcement officer in plain clothes was a detective. Asia didn't try to correct her.

"What about him?"

"He's... he's in your office," Cynthia told her. She quickly added, "I tried to tell him he couldn't go in there, but he insisted."

Asia warmly smiled and replied, "Don't worry about it, Cynthia. I'll take care of it."

Cynthia was visibly relaxed. She liked working for Asia, but she knew Asia could be cold at times. They didn't call her Dragon Lady for nothing. Cynthia just didn't want her to breathe fire on her.

Asia entered her office to find Ortega sitting in the chair in front of her desk.

"Good morning, Ms. Walker," Ortega greeted.

"It was...Mr. Ortega," Asia smoothly retorted with a slight hint of irritation in her tone.

She hung up her sable and put her briefcase on her desk before she sat down.

"And it still can be, Ms. Walker. But that is entirely up to you," Ortega smiled.

The simple smile angered Asia. It meant he was toying with her, but she held her composure.

"And I suppose that depends on my cooperation."

"Very much so."

"But I've told you all that I know."

Ortega shook his head.

"No you haven't, but then again, I haven't told you everything that I know."

"And what is it that you know, Agent Ortega?"

Ortega recognized that her calling him Agent and not Mister meant that whatever sliver of familiarity that they had shared was now replaced with cold professionalism. He didn't mind it one bit. He leaned forward, rested his elbows on his knees, and never took his eyes off Asia.

"Well, I know who to give a hundred million to if it needs a facelift and a new identity."

Her grin slowly disappeared, but she held it together on the inside. She recognized the words instantly from her conversation with Ajaye.

"Am I supposed to know what that means, Agent Ortega, or are you going to tell me?" she probed.

"No problem," he proceeded to tell her, almost verbatim exactly what she told Ajaye about laundering the money.

"You can talk freely," Ajaye assured her.

Was he setting her up? No, she dismissed that notion. As Ajaye said, he had more to lose than she did. Then how did he know? Was the plane bugged? Was her office, her life bugged?

As if he was reading her mind, Ortega said "I'm sure you're wondering how we know. First, let me assure you that no international laws have been broken. I'm sure you were planning on hiding behind Mr. Awey's immunity from prosecution. He's not my concern, Ms. Walker, you are."

The coldness in his eyes let Asia know he thought he had her backed into a corner and was going in for the kill.

She allowed him to continue with the illusion.

"What do you want from me, Mr. Ortega?"

The mister was back; she was offering the familiarity in exchange for leniency. He accepted her offering.

"Marlon, Ms. Walker. I want Marlon."

"Marlon is dead," she blandly replied blandly. There was no flicker of the lie revealed in her demeanor.

Above The Law

Damn, she's good, Ortega thought to himself, but most women were born actresses.

"No, he's not. Marlon is the man you were going to meet yesterday in New York," he smirked. "The one warned off with your charade. Then, you took the subway somewhere to meet him at another location."

Asia didn't respond.

"Ms. Walker, I'm fully prepared to play hardball with you if that's what you want, but we don't have to do so. There's more at stake here and I don't really think you understand just how much, for Marlon and for you," he explained while evenly eying her. Maybe we can help each other."

Returning his gaze and matching his firmness, Asia replied, "Believe me, the last thing I need is your help."

Ortega smiled, stood, and put his card on her desk. He left his index finger on it and said, "Ms. Walker, I'm a patient man, but not a *very* patient man. I leave it to you to understand the difference."

He slid the card in front of her and walked out.

Chapter Fifteen

February 20th – 2:35 P.M.

They sat in an apartment, seated around the table. Henry handed the packages to Marlon. They all wore gloves.

"It looks like a kilo of cocaine," Marlon remarked.

"Only this will blow more than your mind," Steve chuckled.

Marlon squeezed the package. It was as soft as clay.

"What kind of damage could this amount of C-4 do?" Marlon inquired.

Steve shrugged.

"Depends on how it's used."

"A city block?" Marlon asked.

"Easily," Steve responded.

Marlon nodded.

"These are the blasting caps. Keep them separate at ALL times. They're non-static, but you still don't wanna take any chances," Henry explained.

"I guess we won't have to find the informant after all," Marlon remarked while putting the packages in two separate shopping bags.

Above The Law

"How so?" Henry asked.

"This," Marlon replied, referring to the C-4. "They gotta be plannin' a big bang with this much plastic. We track it, we stop the bombing," Marlon concluded. His tone implied that what he said should be obvious.

"Too risky," Henry replied without hesitation.

"I agree. A bust could blow your cover," Steve added.

"We stop the bombing, I won't need cover anymore," Marlon surmised.

There was something in their silence that made him ask, "What am I missing?"

A look passed between Steve and Henry, it was quick. It was subtle, but it wasn't missed.

"Stopping the bombing is only half the battle," Henry answered. "The informant is integral to whatever the Al-Qaeda liaison is with the Abdullahs. That's what you have to concentrate on. It's our job to make sure the bombing doesn't take place on American soil."

Marlon nodded, but still something didn't feel right.

"Don't worry, we got our end under control," Steve assured him, with a smile only a mother could trust. Marlon definitely didn't trust it.

xxxxxx

Marlon sat in the parking lot of a movie theater in East Newark. The headlights were off but he left the car on for the heat. He waited and he thought. He smiled to himself at the fact that cops and criminals were so much alike. Neither of them trusted anyone. Cops call it suspicion and criminals call it being on point. Either way you cut it, the outcome was still the same; get you, before you get me. These feelings were present now. He didn't know who was doing the getting, but he intended to find out.

Fuquan pulled up in a rented Ford Focus with an Asian looking black chick driving. Her face looked familiar. Fuquan got out carrying a book bag and casually surveying the scene. He got in the passenger side of Marlon's Maserati and gave him dap.

"As Salaam Alaikum 'Mil, how you?"

"Wa Alaikum As Salaam, Fu. I'm good," he answered. He nodded towards the Focus. "Who that?"

"Oh, she good, ock. She think I'm coppin' some exotic," Fu chuckled.

"Naw, I mean who is she? Her face looks familiar."

"It should. She's a model for Roc-A-Wear. She on my dick hardbody, ock. Did I tell you about Nikki and Maria?" Fuquan asked.

"Nah."

"Yeah, both them bitches left me…for each other!" He laughed. "And I'm the one that turned the bitch out!"

Marlon smirked as Fuquan continued.

"Fuck it; let somebody else win for a change. What wrong wit' you? This shit ain't got you shook up, do it?"

"Shit, never that. I'm just sayin…," he looked Fuquan in the eyes, "You trust me?"

"I don't distrust you, ock. Trust is a big word," Fuquan replied.

Marlon nodded, "True indeed," he responded.

"But what's up though?"

Marlon reached in the back and handed Fuquan the two plastic shopping bags.

"I said I'd do my part; it's done. That shit wasn't easy, you know what I'm sayin', you start askin' for shit like that and muhfuckas don't forget, feel me? Then something somewhere goes boom and I'm caught up in some shit I didn't even know was going down," Marlon expressed.

Fuquan put the book bag in the back seat.

Above The Law

"Come on ock, you shouldn't even come at me like that, yo. Your name will never come up regardless of whatever. Wallahi, I breathe through my nose, too."

"Yeah, but you missin' the point. I'm feelin' like a pawn in this shit," he said to Fuquan. He could've been talking to Henry and Steve with the same words. "And I don't like that feeling, ock. I could bring an arsenal to the table, plus I'm a soldier. That lil' fifty grand you just tossed in the back ain't shit to me; I piss that. I'm for the cause Fu, remember, I'm Muslim too."

Marlon felt low using Fuquan's belief against him, a belief his aunt lived and died for. However, the truth was relative; the ends justified the means.

Fuquan listened to Marlon's pitch and ingested every word.

"Be careful what you ask for, ock," Fuquan warned.

"It's whatever with me," Marlon firmly retorted.

Fuquan nodded and extended his hand. Marlon shook it as Fuquan smiled.

"I always knew it was more to you than this gangsta shit, ock. Qad Aflaha Muminun," Fuquan recited.

"The Believers are already successful," Marlon smirked.

"As Salaam Alaikum."

"Wa Alaikum As Salaam."

Fuquan got out and headed to the Focus. He and the girl pulled off. Marlon quickly exited the Maserati and walked two cars down to a rented Dodge Magnum he had waiting. His plan was to follow Fuquan and get a lead on where the C-4 went. Hopefully, it would lead him to some answers. He just didn't know how deep the answer would be. The icy rain combined with the cover of night made it easy to follow the cautious model.

They drove to Elizabeth, the Jefferson Park section. The streets were quiet, making Marlon more obvious. He drove past as another car pulled up passenger window to passenger window with Fuquan. Looking through the rearview mirror, Marlon saw Fuquan pass the bags. They both drove off. Marlon made two quick lefts and rounded the block. He caught the headlights of the other car turning onto North Broad Street.

They entered another neighborhood and the car pulled over. Marlon parked and sat down the block. The passenger entered a house carrying the bags. Ten minutes later, he came out without the bags.

"Bingo," Marlon smirked to himself.

He found the safe house.

However, that wasn't all that he found.

Satisfied with his discovery, he was about to pull off, when a white U-Haul sized truck came rumbling down the block. It parked in front of the house. Emblazoned on the side was Zanzibar Exports.

He thought of Asia. He thought of Ajaye Aweys. He remembered Asia's words, "There's a lot more going on than that..."

Was he about to find out that she was right?

The driver got out and went to the back of the truck. He raised the trailer door. Inside were rows of boxes and several identical statues about three feet tall. He took out two, put them on the ground, and locked the trailer. He took the statues to the door and disappeared inside.

He emerged twenty minutes later carrying the same two statues. Marlon perked up. It wasn't hard for him to figure that the C-4 and the blasting caps were now inside the statues. It was a hunch, but one he intended to verify.

The truck pulled off and he did the same. They cut through downtown Elizabeth and crossed Route 19. They headed into Port Newark.

Above The Law

Port Newark is a large industrial park that spans many acres. It sits against the Hudson River and is a major shipping port of call for automobiles, large appliances, clothes, and furniture from overseas. Marlon saw that the Zanzibar driver was planning to make a deposit.

Was the C-4 heading overseas?

Marlon backtracked and rewound the trek from East Newark in his mind. He rearranged the pieces in every way, but they kept pointing to the same conclusion. They were smuggling the C-4 out of the country, or maybe it was headed for another port in America. That could be the safest method to smuggle, he had to know for sure.

He got out and made his way toward the docks. Several longshoremen were milling about. He hopped a fence and tore his jeans in the process. He cursed the fence in anger and crept along stacked trailers waiting to be hoisted by the huge mechanical crane before placed on out-going ships. In the distance, a dog barked and another dog answered. Marlon pulled out his gun and took it off safety.

He was several rows away from where the Zanzibar truck was parked. Even if he could get right up to it, what would be the next move? The trailer was locked. He didn't know for sure, he moved on gut instinct, the instinct of an agent and a criminal.

Two rows away he could hear voices and laughter. The wind brought the smell of cigarette smoke to his nostrils. He crept closer and could hear the sound of a trailer being opened. He hoisted his neck to get a better listen and to see what was going on. The Zanzibar trailer was open. The small black statues lined up like little African warriors stared at him defiantly, daring him to come closer. He decided to take the challenge. He saw several men huddling in an office trying to get some warmth. He wondered if he could make it or if he should even try. He'd never find out.

"Don't move," were the words he heard at the same time he felt the hard steel of a barrel to the back of his head. The last thing he saw was the African statues before he felt a blow and everything went black.

xxxxxx

The bodyguard that reminded her of The Rock opened the door of the suite and ushered her inside. The other bodyguard sat on the couch. They were in the penthouse of the new Trump Towers in Manhattan. Ajaye came out of the back to welcome Asia. He kissed her hand.

"Asia, you are looking stunning this evening. I see you received my gift," Ajaye remarked, referring to the full-length all white fur she was wearing.

"It's beautiful, Ajaye, thank you," she sweetly replied.

He escorted her into the bedroom and closed the door behind them. The bedroom was large and ostentatiously decorated in typical Trump fashion. The view of Manhattan through the glass doors that led to the balcony was breathtaking.

Ajaye went to the bar.

"Chevis Regal, or Remy Martin?" he asked, letting her know he remembered.

"I'll take the Regal, you have a good memory," she replied.

He handed her the drink. Ajaye charmed, "Everything about you Asia, is a good memory."

She blushed at his comment. Ajaye held up his drink.

"To a job well done," he toasted.

"And the appreciation of an opportunity," she added.

They touched their glasses.

"No need to thank me, my dear. You deserved the opportunity and proved you were more than capable," he complimented.

Above The Law

They were celebrating the completion of the 600 million dollar wash job that Asia had just pulled off. The money, less the expenses of the many complex transfers and Asia's two percent fee, was in several offshore accounts she created.

"Are you cold, Asia? I hope you aren't just going to drink and run," Ajaye commented because she was wearing the mink.

"Oh," she giggled, "I'm sorry. Help me."

She turned her back to Ajaye and he helped her out of her coat.

Underneath she wore a burgundy thong and bra that matched her open-toed burgundy snakeskin heels. Ajaye's dick instantly began to rise.

"I wanted to thank you...Personally," she lustfully said.

Ajaye licked his lips and pulled her close; he ran his hand down her back and massaged her ass.

"You, Asia, are what dreams are made of," Ajaye crooned before he passionately kissed her.

She took in his kiss and then broke it.

"I need a refill," she whispered as she finished her drink and handed him the glass.

He took the glass to the bar and poured the drink. As his back was turned, Asia pulled the small hand-held straight razor from the underpinnings of her bra. He never saw it coming. It was as sharp as a scalpel. She filleted Ajaye's throat from ear to ear, his jugular spewed. He panicked and staggered while grabbing his throat, his eyes wide in terrifying shock. Blood squirted on Asia's bra and stomach. She knew it would, that is why she didn't wear a dress.

"Surprised, Ajaye? Tell the truth, you thought it was going to be the other way around, didn't you?" Asia taunted.

He wanted to call out for his guards, but he couldn't.

"How were you going to do it? Make it look like I committed suicide? Nah, you know nobody would believe that. Probably make it look like a robbery or late night break-in; probably throw in a rape for good measure. Yeah, that sounds about right," she surmised.

He was dying, but his rage was just coming to life. She betrayed him. He was beaten at his own game; everything she was saying was true. It wasn't personal, just business. She was a loose end in his eyes. Now, she had turned the tables and he couldn't accept defeat, even in death. He mustered all the strength he could and lunged at her with his arms out and gurgling on his own blood. Asia smiled; she let him get close and then slashed him across both eyes with the razor. The blood ran down his face and splashed her neck. He instantly dropped to his knees.

"You never knew what you were up against, did you? The best set-ups end when the mark thinks he's setting you up," she giggled.

He collapsed on his back, blinded and defeated. He was choking on his own blood.

Asia crouched beside him.

"Don't worry my African prince; I'll take care of those accounts for you."

The gurgling stopped and his body went limp. Asia stood; she brought the black silk spaghetti strapped dress out of one pocket and the nine with the silencer out of the other. She slipped the dress on and chambered a round. She calmly exited the bedroom.

The other guard saw her first. He went for his holster. His throat exploded from the first shot. The second went through his left eye. He convulsed and relieved his bowels.

The Rock got to his feet and got to his gun. He received a bullet in the forehead before he could let off a shot. He dropped to his knees and pitched forward on his face. Asia stood over him and put one more in the back of his head for good measure. She went back to the bedroom and retrieved the fur. She wiped off the visible blood on her before she left the suite.

Chapter Sixteen

Marlon was awakened from his stupor by being doused with ice-cold water. It took his breath away, but he was conscious. It took him several seconds to realize it was dark, he had some kind of black sack over his face, and his hands were bound behind his back. He saw the first blow being thrown before it landed on his face.

"What the fuck were you doing at the docks?"

"Fuck you," Marlon growled while tasting his own blood.

The second blow was to his jaw and rattled his skull. It made his consciousness blink like a TV on the fritz.

"Answer my fuckin' question!" the man demanded.

He said nothing.

"Oh, you're a tough guy?"

Marlon felt like throwing up after the man kicked him in the nuts. He would've doubled over, but his hands were tied around the back of the chair. He simply slumped, the pain exploded in his brain and body.

"Still wanna be tough?"

Above The Law

"It— It takes…a big man to b–beat a man tied to a…chair," Marlon struggled to say.

Two vicious blows to the ribs. A third and a fourth, he thought he felt his ribs crack.

"Why were you at the docks?"

"Fuck…"

Another jaw-shattering blow followed, Marlon felt himself being snatched forward. The next thing he felt was his head being submerged in a tub of ice-cold water. He helplessly splashed and heard the man say, "Who are you? You a cop?"

When he thought that he couldn't hold his breath any longer, the man snatched him out.

"Who do you work for? Who sent you?"

"Your mother," Marlon mumbled through swollen lips.

Splash!

"Who do you work for?"

Just when he thought he would drown again, the man snatched him out and put a gun to his head.

"Fuck it, he don't want to talk, kill 'em," he heard someone else say.

"You wanna die motherfucka? Huh? I'm asking you one more time, who do you work for?"

"I don't know what the fuck you talkin' about," Marlon barked.

Boom!

The gun went off close to Marlon's head and he felt the discharge. It didn't burst his eardrum.

"The next one's goin' in your head. Now talk!"

"Kill me. Kill me you bitch ass faggot! Do it!" Marlon raged. He was past the point of caring whether he lived or died. He was at the point where people either break down or say fuck it. Marlon was cut from the latter cloth.

Silence followed as Marlon's last words echoed in the room. He waited for another blow, a face full of water, or a bullet. There was nothing.

The bag was snatched from his head. His eyes adjusted and he saw the guy with the gun, a lumberjack of a white boy. He saw a shorter pit bull-like Latino. He saw Steve and Henry looking at him with suppressed smirks.

The adrenaline was pumping so hard, he threw up. Henry nodded and the lumberjack untied Marlon. He and the Latino left the room. Steve and Henry helped him to a broke down couch in the corner. He was in the small office that the men were huddled in for warmth.

"I'ma fuckin' kill you," Marlon hissed, he meant every word.

"You brought this on yourself, Porter," Henry calmly replied. "In life, we make our own hell. This is what happens when you don't follow instructions."

Marlon, grimacing in pain, looked at them.

"You knew... the whole time you knew," he accused.

"Of course we knew, but it wasn't for you to know! N.T.K., Porter, N.T. fuckin' K.! You could've blown it tonight! The whole goddamngoddamn operation, because you wanted to play hero," Henry spat. He was shaking his head. After a few paces, he added, "What if we would've been the Abdullah's people, huh? Did you stop to think of that? You'd be dead, we'd be blown, and the bomb would take a couple of hundred lives? Did you once think about that?"

Marlon knew he was right. If Fuquan had spotted him or if it would've been the Muslims at the dock, it would've all been over.

"I don't wanna see your fuckin' face for a few days. You go heal, think, do whatever you gotta do, but when you get back, you better have your shit together," Henry seethed.

He eyeballed Marlon for a few moments before leaving. Steve started to follow him, but turned back and said, "One good thing, Porter...you didn't break."

Steve walked out and Marlon rested his throbbing head on the back of the couch.

Above The Law

Asia beeped him. He didn't recognize the number, but he recognized the code triple 3's. He called the number back.

"Yeah."

"Baby, are you okay? Where are you?"

He was aggravated that his pain was so obvious, yet grateful that someone cared enough to be concerned.

"I'm in a hotel, a Howard Johnson, in Elizabeth I think, room 207."

"I'll find it. I'm on my way. I love you," Asia replied before she hung up.

"I love you too," he answered.

Within the hour, she was there. She had changed out of the fur and the black dress. Now, she wore a waist-length black leather shearling, skinny jeans, and three quarter Prada boots.

Marlon opened the door and she instantly went into motherly mode. She saw him cradling his head and moving gingerly.

"Baby, what happened to you? Who did this?" Asia asked as she helped him to the bed.

She held his face and the swelling made her heart sink.

"I'm good, Ma," he grunted, easing his head onto the pillow.

"You're not good. Where's the room key. I'll be right back."

She went to CVS and got some Ace bandages, alcohol, Tylenol, Band-Aids, and Midol.

He shook his head when he saw the Midol.

"What the hell you get this for?"

"I don't know Marlon, I'm not a nurse. I figured if it's good for cramps, it's good for ribs," she shrugged.

He laughed and winced in pain.

"Shit, it hurts when I laugh."

As she wrapped his ribs, she waited for him to tell her what was going on. When he didn't, she forced the issue.

"Marlon, what the hell is going on? And don't say trust you. First, you're dead and then you're alive, now you're half-dead. Talk to me, please."

He decided to shed some light on his situation. He didn't tell her anything about who he had become, but he told her everything about Zanzibar exports. He told her about the statues, the C-4, and the port.

"I don't know if he's a part of it, or just a front for some terrorist organization, but I want you to be careful, very careful. That money you're moving might be being watched," he warned her.

"Don't worry, baby, I'll be okay," she assured him. She didn't bother to tell him that Ajaye was no longer a factor. "So, how did you get away?"

It was a simple enough question, but sometimes simple questions led to a Pandora's Box full of answers, ones Marlon refused to provide.

"Ma, no more questions, okay? I'm here, that's all that matters."

"That's all that matters," she softly repeated. "Thinking you were dead drove me crazy. I don't want to lose you again."

"You won't," he promised and kissed her softly.

He kissed her lips and her neck. She whimpered in pleasure. Her lips parted and he traced the contours of her throat down to her cleavage with his tongue. She gently bit her bottom lip. Marlon was already in his boxers, it wasn't long before Asia was down to her skin. She gave his body a tongue massage, giving special attention to the bruises and abrasions. His dick was so hard that the veins stood out like the roots of a tree. She was so wet that she had already soaked the bed. Anticipation alone made her cum.

"I missed you soooo much," she passionately moaned while mounting him. She felt his girth fill her hole, causing it to expand.

Above The Law

She rode him, grinded him and gripped him. He sucked and gently bit her nipples as she held herself open for his massive strokes. No man made her cum again and again like Marlon did. No woman fit him like a glove, like Asia did.

"Marlon, I love you."

"Oh baby, I love you too."

They laid on their sides in the afterglow of mind-altering sex. Her body was comfortably cradled inside his. She slept as he kissed her neck. He looked closer and he saw what he thought to be a mole behind her ear. Upon further inspection, he realized that it was too big to be a mole and her birthmark was on her ankle. He examined it closer and frowned when he realized it was dried blood.

xxxxxx

February 21ˢᵗ

They awoke and showered. Asia brought back breakfast from IHOP. He threw her the keys to the Maserati and told her to go get it.

"Damn baby, a Maserati," she cooed. She was impressed. "There really is life after death, huh?"

He chuckled and had to hold his ribs.

"Just get the damn car, Anna Mae."

"Yes Ike."

Asia returned his rented Magnum. She took a cab to the movie theater in East Newark to get the Maserati. As she headed back, she pulled over. Her conscience wrestled with her loyalty. Her reasoning was conflicting with her emotions. She'd been thinking about it ever since she laid eyes on Marlon's battered body. Yes or no, do or don't. Her emotions eventually won. Her loyalty switched sides, from what Marlon wanted to what she knew in her heart Marlon needed.

She made the call...

"Ortega," he said as he answered the phone.

There was silence; she was stuck.

Ortega pried her loose.

"Ms. Walker?" he asked.

"Yes...I'm...He's ..."

"I understand, say no more. Where are you?"

She told him the location, even the room number.

"I'll be there as soon as I can; thank you. And Mrs. Walker?"

"Yes?"

"I hope you're not wearing your chinchilla."

At first, she was confused, but a smile of understanding blossomed across her face as she remembered D.C. and the Republican fundraiser. The man that was watching her, she saw him coming from the coat check as she and Ajaye were headed to it. That's how she knew the coat had been bugged.

Her thoughts turned to "American Gangster," the part where Denzel burned the coat in the fireplace.

Back in the room, they watched movies, played cards and made love.

"Why you so tense?" Marlon asked.

I hope I made the right decision, Asia prayed.

Fuquan beeped him and Marlon called and told him he was sick. Fuquan heard Asia in the background and laughed.

"And you got your own nurse," Fuquan playfully added.

Asia was nervous and fidgety. She kept checking her watch.

"Let me find out you got a hot date," Marlon joked.

There was a knock at the door.

"Yo, who the fuck..." Marlon scowled.

When he looked at Asia, he knew. He knew why Asia was nervous and checking her watch.

"Asia, are you expecting someone?" he quipped; his tone was dripping with a sense of betrayal.

Above The Law

She sobbed and shook her head.

"Baby, it's the only way. I swear it's the only way."

He stopped in the middle of the room; he was shirtless and shoeless with his gun cocked in his hand.

"What's the only way?" he hissed.

There was another knock.

"Porter, it's me, Ortega. Please, all I want to do is talk."

Marlon turned on Asia with fire in his eyes.

"You dimed me out!"

"It's the only way, PLEASE trust me, it's the only way," she cried. She repeated the words of the mantra that was her only defense.

"Trust you?" he laughed. The sarcasm in his voice cut her like butcher knife.

"Porter, I'm not here to arrest you," Ortega assured him. "Please, just open the door."

Marlon felt like he was stuck between a rock and a hard place, the rock being his past, which was represented by Ortega on the other side of the door. The hard place being his present and future, which depended on the decision he made in the next 30 seconds.

He decided to open the door and face him. Ortega stared at Marlon and noticed his gun. Marlon stared back at Ortega. He noticed Ortega's gun.

"I won't shoot you, if you won't shoot me," Ortega bargained. A slight smirk was hidden in the folds of his cheeks. "Can I come in?"

Marlon stepped back to allow him to enter. Ortega came in and closed the door behind him. He put the safety on and holstered his weapon. After a few moments, Marlon did the same.

Ortega rocked on his heels; his hands were clasped behind his back. He resembled a Latin Columbo.

"Well…I guess this is the part where I say I knew you weren't dead."

"Nah, this is the part where you tell me what the hell you doin' here," Marlon shot back. He knew he was wrong for treating Ortega with contempt, but his arrogance made him defiant. In that world, he outranked Ortega.

"I could ask you the same thing," Ortega retorted, "Especially since I watched them lower your casket into the ground. May I?" he asked, referring to the chair.

Marlon nodded his approval. Ortega sat while Marlon paced the room. Asia silently watched.

"Who were those two men who came to see you the night of your arrest?"

"My lawyers."

"Bullshit, they killed Fred Stevens. Did you know that?"

Marlon simply looked at him. He didn't know for sure, but he figured as much.

"Did you set it up?" Ortega asked.

There was no response.

"Aaron Snead got killed a few days later. By a rival gang member," he said with a tone that indicated he didn't believe that was the extent of it.

"You keepin' score? Because I sure am. That makes Fred dead, Aaron and of course you. All the major players in the investigation are dead or supposed to be. What a coincidence, only I don't believe in coincidences," Ortega explained. He was eyeing Marlon firmly.

"So what happened, huh? Who got to you to squash the investigation?"

Marlon laughed in his face.

"That's what you think? That this is about a few seats in the Senate or an election? You really don't know what's going on," Marlon smugly chuckled. He spoke as if Ortega was the naïve one.

Above The Law

"No son, I think it's you who really doesn't know what's going on. And there's nothing more dangerous than a man that thinks he knows something. He's worse than a fanatic and just as easily manipulated...like a pawn."

Ortega saw the glint of resentment in Marlon's eyes and he knew he had struck a nerve.

"You gonna arrest me?"

"No."

"Shoot me?"

"I hope not."

"Then I guess you got what you came for, C.Y.A.," Marlon chuckled.

Ortega stood up.

"Honestly, that was only part of the reason I came...to cover my ass. Do you blame me? I couldn't allow something like this to go down on my watch and not cross my T's and dot my I's. I also came because I know that you're in too deep. I've seen it before, in Nicaragua in the 80's. If you're not careful son, you're gonna find yourself with a bullet in your head that you never saw coming."

Asia, sensing that Marlon's pride wouldn't allow him to reach out for help, got off the bed and took Marlon's arm.

"Please baby, you have to tell him what's going on. You have to tell him about Zanzibar Exports," she implored.

Ortega looked at Marlon and asked, "Do you know who owns Zanzibar Exports?"

"Ajaye Aweys," Marlon replied.

"No, who *really* owns Zanzibar Exports?"

Marlon was silent. Ortega grabbed the doorknob and opened the door.

"I didn't think so; you have to get out while you still can. Maybe I can help, maybe I can't. But when the pieces all come together, you'll see that I'm your only hope."

Ortega let the words sink in before he walked out.

"Marlon, you..."

He coldly turned to her.

"You fucked up, Ma. I love you, but you fucked up. Go back to Chicago. Stay away from me, for your own sake."

Marlon got dressed and left, he slammed the door on his way out. Asia sunk into the bed, her heart was aching, and she cried for both of their sakes.

Chapter Seventeen

February 22nd – 1:15 PM

There was no bomb, at least not in America. Aziz told Marlon that and he believed him. A liar is good at recognizing the truth. Aziz asked him to come to 12th Street. It was the same house Fuquan had taken him to when he first met Fatimah. He hoped he did not run into her again there. Being that she was an Abdullah, he didn't want to get involved with her. He was already fucking her family by infiltrating them; he didn't want to add insult to injury.

The door opened and a big bearded Muslim brother escorted Marlon down to the basement. He didn't' even frisk him, it made him feel a little guilty. They fully trusted him.

Aziz and two other Muslims sat on prayer rugs. Marlon had to remove his shoes before stepping on the thick white carpet. He salaamed and shook hands all around. They spent little time in small talk and got right to the heart of the matter.

"You came through with that C-4 like a champ, Shukran," Aziz thanked him.

"Afwan," Marlon replied.

"But for what you're asking of us... to trust you, I need you to trust us as well."

Marlon nodded, he had expected some quid pro quo.

"It was definitely top choice. How did you get it?"

Marlon nonchalantly shrugged.

"My partner, he deals with the Russians over in Brighton Beach."

"Heck of a connect," Aziz said.

"Yeah, and definitely worth killing for," Marlon remarked, alluding to the Miguel murder.

He had to admit, it was a beautiful setup Steve had put together. Even down to the few days, that Steve spent in jail. It was a move that established trust, rep, and rapport all in one shot... literally.

"So why us? Why do you wanna be a part of the struggle? You may be Muslim, but you're not practicing. You don't even let your beard grow. What is it that you want? You think you can buy heaven with a bomb like some of these fanatics out here?"

Marlon knew Aziz wasn't being judgmental. He was just assessing the situation, and accurately at that. Marlon knew he couldn't convince Aziz he was some radical waiting to happen, so he did what good liars do, he lied by telling the truth.

"I'm not even gon' try to front like I'm that pure, Shaykh. It's not like I'm ready to strap on a bomb and run out into traffic, hell no. To keep it one hundred with you, I don't even know if there is a God. If there is, I believe his name is Allah. I do have principles, and even if it's egotistical to say so, I do know what's right. That's why I'm here."

"I appreciate your honesty and to keep it, as you say, one-hundred if you said you were ready to strap up and go out in traffic, I would've known you were lying," Aziz chuckled.

"Maybe you aren't a soldier for Allah, but you can be a mercenary for him. Our Arab brothers and their

Above The Law

organizations...many of them have become compromised. They are so infiltrated that it's next to impossible to obtain weapons from them without leading the CIA or the FBI right to our door. That's why you're such a blessing."

Marlon subtly flinched when he said, infiltrated, but Aziz didn't notice it.

"Even if your partner or his Russian friends have a little heat, the only thing the alphabet boys see is a bunch of wanna-be Scarfaces on the corner, monkey men," Aziz disgustedly spat. "He doesn't see the black man as a threat, but we are. The future of Islam is inextricably linked to the future of the African-American Muslim. The Arabs, in their foolish arrogance, think that Islam is their religion," Aziz laughed. "But Allah sees their arrogance and he is taking the mantle from their shoulders and giving it to us."

"To you?" Marlon quipped.

Aziz shook his head.

"I'm not that egotistical. I'm only a soldier."

"With his own army in several states," Marlon pointed out.

Aziz smirked at the mention of his power.

"They obey Allah. The truth is from Allah, only the mistakes are mine."

"So you want me to supply you."

"Yes and only us. That reduces the risk of the Feds getting on to us through any other customers that would be less careful. You'll be well taken care of."

Marlon pretended to think about it then shrugged.

"Okay, I can handle that. On one condition."

"Which is?" Aziz asked.

"That whatever I supply won't be used to kill civilians or innocent bystanders."

"You mean suicide bombers."

"Nah, they can blow themselves up all they want. As long as they don't kill babies and non-combatants," Marlon explained.

Aziz nodded.

Al-Nymayr doesn't do suicide bombing. It's… counterproductive, nor do we target non-combatants.

Marlon looked at him skeptically.

"I give you my word, ock," Aziz vowed.

"Even on what I already supplied?" Marlon asked.

Aziz looked at him for a few seconds and then said, "That's out of my hands."

Marlon's heart dropped. He thought he was too late.

"But you just said Al-Nymayr…"

"It wasn't for us," Aziz cut him off.

"I won't tell you who it was for, but I can tell you it wasn't for us. It won't even be used in America."

Aziz said the last words almost as an afterthought, not knowing that in those few words was the lie his life had become. In that instant, Marlon told himself Aziz was lying; he was just covering up his actual plans. It only took a hundred milliseconds to discard the thought. Aziz had no reason to lie, did he?

If he wasn't lying, then why was Marlon here in the first place? Had Steve and Henry been mistaken? Had the informant really been telling the Feds information? And then it hit him…

How did they know it was false if they didn't know the truth?

"And there's nothing more dangerous than a man that thinks he knows something…He's easily manipulated." Ortega's words resonated in his ears. Marlon's knees might have buckled if he hadn't been sitting down.

The entire time, Aziz was oblivious to Marlon's inner turmoil and he had continued talking. Marlon's mind refocused as Aziz said, "Suicide bombings are just like drive by shootings. They don't discriminate and too often miss the real target. Al-Nymayr means panther in Arabic and that's how we move...in silence. Patiently waiting and then we kill with accuracy. We want to protect the people, not terrorize them."

Marlon's mind was in another place as the meeting came to a close. They salaamed and the Muslim brother that showed him in, escorted him out. His mind didn't snap back to reality until he saw the green BMW X-6 pull up and double park beside his Maserati.

It was Fatima.

She lowered the window and he leaned on the roof of the car.

"As Salaam Alaikum, Jamil."

"Wa Alaikum As Salaam, Fatima. Yo, shit been so hectic, I was..."

She cut him off with her right hand and a giggle.

"It's cool, Jamil. It ain't that serious. You make it obvious that it ain't that serious, because if it was, you woulda called."

Marlon sighed.

"It ain't like that, believe me, a man gotta be blind not to take you serious," he remarked. He was eyeing her like a piece of candy he knew he would like to have.

Fatima was truly one of the most beautiful women he had ever seen. Her skin tone was so smooth it seemed to glow. It took everything in him to not to push up on her.

"Then what's the problem?"

"I'm sayin', you Fu sister."

She sucked her teeth.

"And?"

"And, Fu my man...I ain't wanna, you know, like..." he stuttered.

"Like what?"

"Ma, stop playin'. You know like what," he smirked.

She laughed in his face.

"Oh, *that's* what you thought? That I was like that? Oh no baby, don't even go there. I'm a flirt, not a fool. I seen your kind before Jamil, I know you ain't gonna do right."

He laughed because she was right.

"Oh, so you was just flirtin'?" he doubtfully asked.

"Jamil, I've been a virgin since I was fourteen."

"Huh?" he asked with a puzzled look on his face.

She laughed at his look.

"When I was fourteen, I fell victim to a pretty boy like you. After that, I promised Allah I would wait 'til I get married," she explained.

"Oh, I get it. You had me confused," he said.

"Don't get me wrong, I would've loved for you to be the one. You ain't husband material, not yet anyway. Especially while you fuckin' that nasty ass Hasana," she knowingly smirked.

Marlon looked at her with the question on his face. How did she know?

"Oh, don't think I ain't peep that slick shit you pulled at my party. I watch that bitch, 'cause I don't trust her. She got Malik's nose open while she hopping from bed to bed. She even fuckin' one of them Crip dudes."

Crip dude, he thought to himself. Hasana was definitely out of order. Not that Muslim woman couldn't be loose, but they usually kept it in their own circles, especially when you're the type of Muslim woman who wears full covering and frequents the Masjid. Fucking a gang banger doesn't fit into that equation.

Unless...

"Where Hasana from?" he asked.

"Damn sure ain't Newark," Fatima replied.

"She funny style, yo. I tried to tell Malik, Fuquan tried to tell Malik, but you know how stupid men get when y'all get a good shot!" She laughed at her own joke.

Above The Law

Later on, as Marlon gazed out the plane window watching the sun go down at eye level, he was in deep thought. The rays shot through the clouds giving them a golden hue. Earlier, he called Ortega. Like a Rubik's Cube, the colors were beginning to coordinate. He thought of chess and pawns in particular. Pawns that make it to the opponent's side can become anything they want.

"Somalian Defense Minister Disappears," was the headline on CNN's The Situation Room. The reports were coming in and being aired.

"Police and staff of the Trump Towers Hotel are baffled by the disappearance of Ajaye Aweys, the Somalian Defense Minister. Police say Mr. Aweys was scheduled to make a speech at the U.N. earlier today. When he didn't show up, several calls were made to his hotel suite. There was no answer and the investigation into his disappearance continues. Making his disappearance suspicious, a source close to the State Department says Mr. Aweys was under scrutiny by the Somalian Government for misappropriation of funds that total half a billion dollars..."

That was all Ortega had to hear because he knew the rest of the story. "Nicaragua all over again," he mumbled to himself. He quickly grabbed his Navy issued pea coat, along with his fedora and scarf, on his way out the door.

He headed to the United Center for the Chicago Blackhawks and Detroit Red Wings game. It was a rivalry game that was also a grudge match, good for at least one bloody brawl.

He was glad that Marlon called. He hadn't been expecting it, but he wasn't surprised either. Marlon was in over his head. What he just heard on the news confirmed it. Marlon said he had a hunch, but he needed Ortega to flesh it out.

"Meet me at the Blackhawks game, section 221."

"Hockey?" Marlon questioned.

"Last place in the world that anyone would look for a dead Black guy," Ortega chuckled.

The United Center was packed. The crowd was out in full-force to see the Stanley Cup defending champions take on their rival. Ortega settled into his seat. He ordered a beer and destroyed a hot dog while he waited. The first period went by with no score. Marlon walked in at the beginning of the second. He came in through the F Gate and spotted Ortega from the landing in their section. He moved in his direction.

"Hey, what the fuck's your problem?" Ortega overheard.

"Hey, watch it buddy!" another man responded.

Ortega turned toward the commotion. A scuffle in the row behind him broke out. There was some pushing and shoving back and forth. At the same time, Chicago scored a goal. Ortega was on his feet, and turned to cheer for the score as Marlon walked his way. A blow was thrown behind him. He turned to see the fight and reached for his badge. There were four white guys fighting each other. As they tussled, two of the men inadvertently fell into Ortega. By that time, security was notified and on the way. Ortega tried to move away and felt a sharp pinch in his chest. He flinched and grabbed his heart as one of the fighters moved away from him. Security arrived and Marlon was still six rows away. He saw Ortega fall into the arms of a security guard. The guy who was walking away glanced back and he and Marlon locked eyes. It was Steve.

Marlon looked at Ortega with regret. Security was on their walkie-talkies trying to secure medical attention. Ortega's body jerked and twitched. The Ricin that was

Above The Law

injected coursed through his veins and entered his heart. It would look like a heart attack at the autopsy. It would look natural, instead of the murder that it really was.

Marlon saw Ortega's body go limp. In his mind, he heard the drone of a flat line. Steve started walking briskly toward him. He backpedaled and Steve broke into a light jog. Marlon sped up his pace as well; he dipped and dodged his way through the crowd. Steve was in full pursuit. Marlon reached the main corridor and turned his jog into a full sprint. He sensed that Steve closing in and hit an emergency exit. The cold Chicago air smacked him in the face. He ran up West Madison Street and turned right on North Damen Ave. He headed for the L train. Steve was nowhere in his sight, but he wished he had a gun as he took the stairs two at a time to get to the train platform. He took the Brown Line southbound train. He sat down and sighed heavily. Ortega was dead, murdered by the men he was working for. Was he next? He didn't plan to stick around to find out. There was only one thing to do and one place to go. He had to run and go into hiding. He texted Asia.

Asia knew who it was without looking at her phone. The text read, 'The Temple of my Familiar.' It had a triple meaning. It was the name of her favorite book. It was also the name they called the spoken word café where they first met. That's where he was telling her to meet him. She sucked her teeth and dropped the phone in her lap. She stepped on the gas, headed for Canada. Everything had fallen apart. It was time to go. Why turn back? Why turn back? Why was she turning back?

'Cause I'm a damn fool, she thought to herself as she got off at the next exit and back onto Interstate 55 south heading back to Chicago. She was going back to him.

"Back to Chicago," she bitterly mumbled to herself. That's exactly where Marlon told her to go after she went out on a limb for him, to save him. He threw her efforts back in her face and didn't appreciate it. Maybe now, his mind had changed.

She did go back and packed up her things. She sold the Benz and purchased an Accord with cash. She transferred her portion of the 600 million dollars to several other accounts. They were all under several other names. Now she was on her way out, to make her great escape, until Marlon texted her and, like a fool, she went to him.

Asia arrived at Café Noire and anxiously walked in. Marlon sat in the corner, away from the lights and people. He made sure that the door was in his line of sight. She walked up to him ready to curse him, flip out, and slap the shit out of him.

He looked up with fire in his eyes.

"Ortega's dead."

Asia took his hand and they walked outside to the car.

They drove in silence for awhile. He didn't know what to say and she didn't want to say it. "Where we goin'?" he finally asked.

"With me," she answered, as if he had asked a totally different question.

He understood her answer.

"Ma, I can't run from this."

"It's the only chance we have."

An eerie silence filled the air.

"Asia, stop the car," he said.

"No."

"Asia."

"We can't, Marlon! If we —"

"Stop the fuckin' car!" Marlon barked.

Asia pulled over in a Denny's parking lot.

"Now what? Huh? What are we gonna do, Marlon?" Asia demanded.

"I'm not running from this...from them," Marlon seethed.

Above The Law

"They killed a Federal Agent, Marlon! A fuckin' Federal Agent! What do you think they would do to us?"

Marlon shook his head. He knew she was right, but it just didn't feel right.

Asia put the car back in drive and eyed him with the ultimatum.

"You want to go back? Go back."

He put the car in park and switched off the ignition.

"There's nowhere I *can* go, Asia! Nowhere! If they're gonna kill me, I'm already dead!" He laughed like a desperate man at the end of his rope. "I'm in too deep. Baby… ain't no comin' back."

"You had a way back, I gave it to you. I tried to save your black ass. I gave you me and you just threw it in my face!" Asia spazzed, she was releasing the torrent that had been building in her from the hotel room.

Her comments bewildered Marlon.

"Asia, what are you talking about? Gave me you? I love you, what do you mean, you gave me you?"

Asia broke down into tears; her rage was spent.

"You just don't know…"

Marlon felt like a man waking up from a dream. Everything was becoming clear at once.

"Marlon…for once, just listen to me. We have to go. I've got the money, twelve million; we can go away… just get away…"

"Asia, where's the Benz?"

"I sold it."

"Why?"

"Why do you think?"

Her eyes told the story, but his heart refused to believe it.

"Baby, I love you. I really do," she whispered as she reached over to caress his face. "Please just —"

Marlon abruptly grabbed her wrist. They looked into each other's eyes. He was hoping not to find what his mind told him was there. He turned her hand over and looked at it. Her fingertips were smooth and a reddish-pink. They were like his, no fingerprints.

She was just like him; she was one of them too.

"Damn, not you too baby," he mumbled. He dropped her hand in disgust and his heart sank.

He was sick and needed air. He quickly got out of the car. He felt the utmost sense of betrayal, as if he had been played from day one. He felt like his entire life was a lie.

"I guess I was just another Ajaye to you, huh?" Marlon laughed to keep from crying as Asia got out too. He shook his head in disgust.

"No," she firmly replied.

She killed Ajaye, but tried to save Marlon. She told him everything about the murder. He remembered the blood behind her ear as she spoke. She told him why she killed him. Ajaye was playing both sides of the fence. He was stealing America's money and selling weapons to the rebels. He was also smuggling drugs into America; he had it coming. She gave it to him at the Trump. She told him how the surveillance tape had been digitally spliced, how there was no record of her coming or going. There was no record of the cleaners who took care of the mess. The bodies were never found, nor would they ever be.

Marlon still didn't fully understand.

"When did they get to you, Asia? When did they turn you?"

Her heart wept for him. She wanted to lie, but knew he deserved the truth.

"Three…three years ago."

He grabbed his head with both hands and leaned against the car for support.

"The whole time, Asia? The whole time…"

Above The Law

She went to him, but he pushed her away. She told him how Steve had him profiled and she was briefed on everything about him. His favorite color, the type of music he liked, pet peeves, psychological quirks, his latent arrogance, his volatile temper and his need to be loved.

She used it all to get into his head, but the truth was they were alike in so many ways.

"I know it sounds crazy, but when I walked into that hotel room and saw what they did to you..." She shook her head with tears streaming down her cheeks. "That's when I knew it was real."

Now he understood what she meant when she said, "I gave you me." She did exactly that. Asia exposed herself for him. By bringing Ortega to Marlon, she violated The Department's protocol. Doing so meant only one thing, death.

She did it hoping Ortega could somehow bring Marlon out. She badly underestimated The Department. She didn't know they would go as far killing Ortega, a high-ranking FBI agent.

To them, everyone was expendable. They made their point abundantly clear. Even if the relationship they started was a lie, the sacrifice she made proved it wasn't anymore.

"I won't let nothin' happen to you," Marlon vowed.

She smiled through her tears.

"Baby, you can't save me. You can't even save yourself," she softly replied, without a hint of reproach.

He debated within himself. She exposed herself to save him, should he expose himself to save her? What if this too was a game? It could be an elaborate farce conceived by them. Was she worth it? His heart didn't hesitate, she was.

"Go to Cuba," he told her.

"Why?"

He smiled as if he had a winning Powerball ticket.

"That's where my father lives."

She knew his file said that his parents were deceased. He explained that his real father was a bank robber. He had joined the Black Panthers, they didn't call it bank robbery, they called it liberation. He liberated 3.2 million dollars from an armored truck. J. Edgar Hoover's Cointel Pro had a snitch in the Philadelphia chapter. His father jetted to Cuba before he could be arrested; his mother was pregnant at the time. She met another man a few months later and his name was on the birth certificate. Eventually, Marlon's mother told him the truth.

"But this is our little secret, baby," she stressed to him.

She then put them in touch and they stayed in touch over the years. Asia could go there and be safe with him.

"Go with me baby, PLEASE," she begged. She wrapped herself around him.

"I can't, not right now."

"Then what are you gonna do? Just let them kill you?"

He shrugged.

"Dead is dead. If I'ma die, I'd rather a muhfucka shoot me in the face for comin' than in the back of the head for runnin'."

She hated his analogy, but she understood. She kissed his cheek.

"You still love me?"

His kiss told her just how much he really did. It was like the kiss Alicia Keys sang about in "Like You'll Never See Me Again."

Chapter Nineteen

February 23rd – 11:00 A.M.

Marlon rode the Amtrak train into Detroit. It was the next train leaving Chicago at the time. He really had no destination, no purpose. He was a man without a past and possibly without a future either. He contacted his father and told him about Asia.

"You sure about this?" his father questioned.

"Yeah, I'm sure."

There was a brief pause.

"Okay, I'll take care of her. What about you, son?"

"It's whatever wit' me," Marlon cockily replied.

"Yeah," his father chuckled, "You got that from me, too."

He exited the train at the Detroit Station at 11:15 PM and walked along West Baltimore Avenue thinking about Al-Nymayr and the Department. He realized that they were really identical; they were both full of shit. He may've liked Aziz as a person, but it was bullshit to sell poison to the same people you said you wanted to save, especially in the name of a religion that stands against that sort of thing.

The Department was no better. In the name of protecting America, it partook in everything that was destroying America. They were no more than gangsters with a badge. Actually, they were gangsters that were above the badges. Ortega's murder proved that to be true.

Marlon had to admit that he fit right in with both sides. In his youth, he was a hood with heart. He then grew up to be an officer without scruples. Now, he was a dead man who they wanted to kill.

He laughed so hard at the thought that people walking past thought he was crazy.

"Maybe I am crazy," he mumbled.

Where would he go? What would he do? His plans went no further than one foot in front of the other. He was hungry and saw a convenience store. He went inside to find something to eat. He placed two cheesesteak burritos in the microwave and then grabbed a Pepsi and a family size bag of Lay's sour cream and onion potato chips.

While he was waiting on his food to finish, a short dark skinned female came in. She grabbed some diapers, baby formula, Newports, and a Pepsi. She walked past Marlon on her way to the counter. She passed the man behind the counter her credit card. He swiped it, shook his head, and handed it back.

"Declined," the clerk said.

"No, that can't be. Swipe it again," she demanded.

Marlon approached the counter as the clerk said, "No, not again." She dug into her purse frantically looking for money. She shook her head and sighed. Marlon stepped up to the counter.

"How much?" he asked the man.

"For that?" he pointed to what was in Marlon's hands.

"No, for her," Marlon said.

She looked at Marlon with tears of frustration welled up in her eyes.

Above The Law

"Twenty five," the man said.

Marlon paid for everything and they walked out together. She was still thanking him. She looked to be in her early thirties, but wasn't very attractive. She wasn't used to men doing things for her.

"Like I said Ma, you good. I was in a hurry," he lied.

"Can I give you a ride somewhere?" She wasn't trying to flirt; she was just being nice, not knowing how to repay him.

It was the kids in the car that got him. One was in a baby seat, almost a newborn, and the other, a toddler, in the back seat in a booster seat.

"Nah, I'm good. Where you work?"

"I wish," she shook her head. "I've been looking for weeks. It's so hard though. I had a part time job, but I couldn't get a baby sitter for those hours."

He took out his food and handed it to her. He kept the plastic shopping bag balled up in his hand.

"No, no, I can't take your food."

"I'm not givin' it to you," he smiled. "Just do me a favor, hold it 'til I come back."

"Come back?"

"Yes, please, just ten minutes."

She hesitated, bit her bottom lip, and thought how she owed him at least that much.

"Okay, I'll wait."

Marlon walked a block to the bank he just passed. He pulled out the gun he got from Asia and walked up to the security guard. He didn't point the gun at him, but it was clearly visible.

"Excuse me, I—"

"Holy shit!" the guard cursed and put up his hands. "Please, don't shoot!"

"I'm not," Marlon told him, taking his gun out of his holster. "Just do me a favor. Lay down for me."

The heavyset guard rapidly complied. Employees and patrons nervously looked on. A woman screamed and Marlon gestured for her to quiet down.

"Nobody's gonna get hurt. I promise."

Marlon turned to the first teller; she was an older red-faced white woman. He saw her arm move quickly back to her side. He smiled and handed her the bag.

"You just hit the alarm, didn't you?"

The woman trembled in silence.

"Don't lie," he urged her.

She nodded her head up and down.

"Good girl. Now, fill this up. And no dye packs. I just bought this coat and I ain't tryin' to fuck it up."

"O...o...okay," she stammered, as she filled the bag.

"Relax, it's cool. I'm a Federal Agent. I'm doing this for charity," he chuckled.

She nodded like a bobble head doll.

"Yes sir."

She handed him the stuffed bag. He casually walked out. He walked the block back to the woman who was still waiting. She was patiently sitting in her car. He handed her the bag and her eyes bulged like in the cartoons.

"Oh sweet Jesus," she reverently whispered, "What...what... why...how..." Questions jumbled in her mind all came out at once sounding like gibberish.

"Just go, Ma. Take care of them babies, okay?"

He didn't even wait for a reply. He headed directly back to the bank. By the time he got there, two police cruisers were pulling up. Marlon entered the bank behind them. He tossed both guns at the security guard's feet.

"What the hell? You?"

"It's him," the guard yelled.

"Where?" the officers asked.

"Him!"

"Freeze! Get down on the ground!"

Above The Law

Marlon snickered at the officers.

"Okay, I'll play along."

They roughly cuffed him and snatched him off the floor.

"You have the right to remain silent…"

As they drove to the station, the driver glanced through the rearview and laughed. "Man, are you high or somethin'? You've got to be the dumbest son of a bitch this side of a woman's cunt! What the hell were you thinkin'?"

Marlon shrugged and smirked as if he knew something they didn't.

"What did you do with the money?"

"I gave it away," he replied.

The passenger cop shook his head.

"Certifiable crazy," the cop said.

Marlon may've been a man with no past or future, but that also made him free. He had nothing to lose. He thought about going to prison. He thought about maybe calling a reporter, or even writing a book. He knew no one would ever believe his story. He was headed to jail, but he knew he wouldn't be there long. Upon entering the front door of the Wayne County jail, he confirmed what he already knew. Henry and Steve were already there. They wore blue suits and flashed their Federal blue badges.

"Thank you officer, we'll take it from here," Henry said.

"Take it from here? We haven't even booked the guy?"

"He's not your problem. He's wanted in several states for robbery and murder," Steve explained.

The officers exchanged puzzled glances.

"Look guys," Henry smoothly said, "I'm not trying to muscle in on your collar. You guys caught one of America's most wanted, you're fuckin' heroes. But we have jurisdiction. Talk to your Sergeant."

The driver went to talk to his commanding officer. The other cop looked at Henry while Steve gave Marlon an icy glare. The driver cop came back and sighed hard.

"We gotta cut 'em loose, Ed."

They uncuffed him and Steve recuffed him tightly.

"Don't forget, you spell my name, Officer D…e…"

Marlon was in the back seat as Henry drove. Steve was riding shotgun.

"When you do it Steve, put it between my eyes, none of that coward shit like you pulled with Ortega," Marlon furiously spat.

"Don't tempt me, Porter."

"Tempt you? Man, motherfuck you!" He turned his head toward Henry. "And fuck you, too! Fuck the Department! Y'all ain't Homeland Security. You're fuckin rogues! Fuckin' out of control cowboys!"

Henry chuckled and glanced in the rearview mirror and replied, "If we're rogues, who'd they call to make the Sarge cut you loose?"

Marlon was at a loss for words.

They drove back to Chicago and went directly to a safe house. Marlon sat strapped to a lie detector once again. Steve sat in front of him and Henry paced the floor with a cocked .40 caliber.

"Here's the deal, Porter. You lie one time and I blow your fuckin' brains out. We clear?" Henry said. He stood behind him and leaned over his shoulder.

"Yeah."

"One time, Porter," Henry reiterated.

Steve took his vital signs, everything was normal.

"You ready?" Steve asked.

"Yeah," Marlon dryly replied.

Henry put the barrel to the base of Marlon's skull.

Above The Law

"Is your name Marlon Porter?"

"Yes."

Normal.

"Are you a male?"

"Yes."

Normal.

"Have you ever informed anyone of your affiliation with The Department?"

"No."

Normal.

Steve took out a folder and opened it. He handed a picture to Marlon. His heart was caught in his throat; it was a picture of Asia and Steve. They were fucking, doggie style. Marlon ice-grilled him, Steve taunted him with a smile.

"You a fuckin' asshole," Marlon gritted.

Steve ignored him.

"Did you know that Asia and I had sexual relations?"

Marlon was silently seething. Henry put pressure on his skull.

"Answer the question," Henry told him.

"No."

Normal.

Steve held out another picture and Marlon reluctantly took it. That one was of Asia sucking Steve's dick. Marlon knew what Steve was trying to do, and he steadied his nerves.

"Do you know where Asia is at the present time?"

"No."

It was normal. Marlon had beaten the machine. Steve looked at Henry, who was skeptical about the results.

"Ask him again," Henry said.

"Did Asia tell you where she was going?"

"No."

Normal, he had ice in his veins because murder was in his heart.

"Would you tell us if you knew where Asia was going or if she contacted you to inform you where she was?"

"Yes."

The results were normal once again. Henry nodded and removed the gun. Steve turned off the machine and Henry stepped around to face Marlon.

"Glad to see we're still on the same team," Henry remarked.

"And what team was Ortega on?" Marlon retorted, with bitter sarcasm.

"Ortega's blood is on your hands, Porter. We told you not to go back, but you disobeyed orders. The only reason you're not dead is because it's crunch time and we need the informant," Henry explained.

"You've wasted a lot of time on this bullshit. If the bomb goes boom, that blood's on your hands, too," Steve added.

Did they know that there was no Al-Nymayr bomb to be detonated on American soil? Was he one hundred percent sure Aziz was telling the truth? He couldn't take the chance that he was. He had to follow his hunch and find out the truth.

"Don't worry, it won't. But what happens to me after I stop it?"

"The Department takes care of its own, Porter. Don't worry, we'll set you up in something really nice as a cover until you go active again," Henry assured him.

At that moment, Marlon knew they would kill him. *The Department takes care of its own, in more ways than one,* he thought. Marlon smiled to himself. It was all about who got who first.

"Okay, I think I know who the snitch is."

xxxxxx

Above The Law

The day was overcast, the sky a gunmetal gray. It was about as good as February could be in New Jersey, but the breeze off the Hudson didn't go unnoticed. Fuquan stood in Liberty Park; he was leaning on the rail and gazing across the Hudson at Manhattan Island.

Marlon walked up to him. They salaamed; gangsta hugged and then leaned on the rail.

"Yo, what up ock, what happened to your face?" Fuquan asked.

"That's what I wanted to talk to you about. Me and my partner got into it," Marlon explained.

"Who, the white boy? The white boy did that? Let me find out you let a cracka whoop your ass," Fuquan chuckled.

"Fuck outta here, yo, never that. But yo, it's deeper than that. Ever since that Miguel shit, muhfucka been actin' real shady."

"Shady, how?"

"Like…he think… I don't know, but he don't think Miguel dead," Marlon played Fuquan.

"Word? That's crazy! That shit was done to hold him down!"

"Exactly. Only he don't see it that way. But if the muhfucka don't trust me, how I'ma trust him?" Marlon rhetorically asked.

"You think he might dime you out?" Fuquan probed, he was thinking about the possible fall back on his family.

"Nah, the dude solid. I'll give him that, but I'm thinkin' he might try to move on me," Marlon surmised. He was serving up the bait that he knew Fuquan would nibble on. He did exactly that.

"So we move on him first!"

"Then we lose the connect," Marlon reminded him.

"Damn," Fuquan shook his head.

"But," Marlon smirked, "If he were to…disappear, I could go to them Russian dudes like yo, Mike's gone, what up. I'm spending a hundred grand a whop. Boom, we got the connect for ourselves," Marlon explained just how he planned to do it.

Fuquan nodded, he liked what he was hearing.

"What you mean, disappear?"

"I'm saying, I just can't kill him in his apartment or no shit, 'cause then they find the body. The Russians ain't gonna fuck with me after that. If he never surfaces…" Marlon dropped a nickel in the Hudson to demonstrate, "Then they won't think twice about fuckin' with me."

The plan was beautiful and Marlon knew it. It had just enough truth to cover the lies.

"So how we make it happen?" Fuquan wanted to know.

"I'ma get him to think Miguel ain't dead, like me and Miguel plannin' on flippin' on him. He gon' follow me, and when he see me pick up Miguel —"

"But he sleep," Fuquan interrupted.

"Mike don't know that. Don't worry; I got this. We just need two muhfuckas that you don't care about for decoys," Marlon replied. Fuquan understood a little better. He smiled and gave Marlon dap.

"Yeah, that shit slick. Okay, say no more. Let's make it happen."

Marlon was ten steps ahead of him.

xxxxxx

An hour later, Marlon was in another safe house with Steve and Henry in South Orange.

"You sure Malik is the informant?" Henry quizzed.

"No. That's why I'm going at him like this," Marlon explained.

Above The Law

Henry pensively pinched his lip. A quick glance passed between Henry and Steve.

"Explain it again," Henry told him.

Marlon smiled to himself. That is where he had the expertise. Steve and Henry may have been well versed in international espionage, but in the ghetto, they were blind as bats. It is why they needed Marlon in the first place. Why they had come and gotten him originally. Now, he was simply using it to his advantage.

"Malik's got a side thing going on with the Crips. He's working it through his girl Hasana. She came to me with it, trying to get me on the team."

"What's that got to do with being the informant?" Steve impatiently probed.

"I'm getting to that. Crips bang under the six-point star, Bloods under the five-point star. Who else is famous for the six point star?"

"Jews, the Star of David," Henry answered.

"Exactly, but the Islamic banner carries the five-point star. No Muslim would back the six over the five. That's what gave him away," Marlon explained as if it was obvious.

In actuality, it was bullshit, but believable bullshit to someone that didn't know any better. It was esoteric enough to seem like something of great significance and simple enough that it was seemingly right in front of your face.

"But isn't he already selling guns to the Crips?" Steve asked.

Marlon waved him off like that point was irrelevant.

"That's all hood politics. You can't not sell 'em guns. But on a power move, never would Muslims move with the Jewish star."

Henry nodded in agreement; the last analogy sealed it for him. It made it palatable to his political taste.

"But you're not sure?" Henry asked.

"Nah. That's why I'm gon' set up a meeting. It has to be somewhere secluded. I'm gon' talk to him and accept his deal. I'll need you guys to secure the area of electronic monitoring; make sure he's not wired or anything. Once I signal you that he's the snitch, you signal me that there's no surveillance. If all is well...BANG...end of the story." Marlon smirked as he pictured a very different ending.

They thought about the plan and then nodded.

"And if he's not the informant?" Steve probed.

Marlon shrugged.

"Then it's back to square one. But I'm telling you, this is it," he smiled.

His plan was full of double meanings.

Chapter Twenty

Getting the decoys was simple. The only stipulation was that they had to be the same size as Malik and Marlon. Fuquan picked two dudes from Sly Street, Wan, and Tim. They were wanna-be thugs, ripe for the picking. He used their greed against them.

"We get half?" Wan said.

Fuquan nodded.

"Yeah, we gotta meet 'em tonight, only I gotta handle something. You go meet 'em, pick up three pounds of Loud and keep a pound and a half. I don't give a fuck, I don't smoke."

"Say no more, we wit' it," Tim happily agreed.

Fuquan knew they would be. He checked out what they wore. Tim had on fatigue pants, a green Polo shirt, and a brown leather jacket. Wan wore black Nike sweatpants, a silver Raiders hoodie with a matching jacket. Marlon and Malik would be wearing the exact same thing when they made the switch.

The decoys were in place at Malik's house, while Fuquan schooled Malik on the plan. Steve and Henry followed

Marlon to Malik's house. Marlon got out in front of the house. He was wearing fatigue pants, a green Polo shirt, and a brown leather jacket. He entered the house with a smile.

"The white boy fall for it?" Fuquan snickered.

"Dead on his ass," Marlon laughed. He gave Fuquan dap.

He gave his keys to the decoys.

"Take my Maserati, the connect know my car," Marlon told them.

Their eyes opened wide, a Maserati, it was getting better by the minute.

Wan and Tim walked out of Malik's house. Steve and Henry saw the clothes and thought they were seeing Marlon picking up Malik. The Maserati pulled off and Henry followed. Marlon heartily laughed as his plan was coming together. He left through the back door and headed for the rented Dodge Charger that was parked two blocks away. He reached the car and headed in the opposite direction.

The decoys reached Weequahic Park and checked their watch. It was 9:03 PM. Fuquan told them to wait, watch, and make sure there was no police. If none were seen, flash the lights at exactly 9:15.

"I'm tellin' you, my dude, as soon as I get my paper right, I'ma cop me one of these shits," Tim boasted.

"Nah yo, you want hot shit, get the Aston Martin. That's what a gangsta like me gonna be pushin'," Wan shot back.

"You crazy as hell. An Aston Martin can't fuck wit' a Maserati."

"Fuck a Mas-a-fuckin'-ratti!"

They argued back and forth like they really had enough money for a used Hyundai between the two of them.

"Damn, it's 9:17!" the driver cursed. He flicked the headlights in rapid succession.

Above The Law

"Here we go," Steve smiled, feeling the early surge of the adrenaline rush he always got before a job.

He gripped the P7M8 in his gloved hand. He and Henry were more than ready. They thoroughly checked all angles, except the one they took for granted.

They checked the park before the meet and followed the Maserati at a safe enough distance to make sure it wasn't being tailed by the Feds. They checked the park again and secured the perimeter with the Ironclak, a handheld device that resembled a cell phone and allowed them to check the area for digital, electronic and microwave surveillance.

Satisfied that the area was clean, they awaited Marlon's signal.

Steve checked his watch it was 9:15. He and Marlon were synchronized, but there was still no signal.

"I guess he ain't the guy," Steve remarked.

"Guess not," Henry reluctantly agreed.

At 9:16, Henry leaned forward to start the car.

"Back to the drawing board," he shrugged.

Another few seconds passed and it was 9:17. The headlights of the Maserati flickered several times.

"Turn off the fuckin' car! It's him!" Steve excitedly growled.

"Why is the signal late?" Henry asked.

"Who knows? Maybe he was giving the guy a hand job. The bottom line is the mark is here, Porter is here, we get two birds with one stone," Steve sneered.

Henry blinked his lights, giving who he thought was Marlon the go ahead that all was clear. They waited for the gunshot. Fifteen seconds went and nothing happened.

"What the fuck is he waiting for?" Steve impatiently growled.

Forty-five seconds…

"I don't like this," Henry remarked.

One minute, 8 seconds…

Steve grabbed the door handle.

"What the hell are you doing?" Henry asked.

"This guy's blowing our window of opportunity! We gotta move! For all we know, he's had a change of heart. Maybe he can't stomach killing Muslims. I don't know and I don't care! He gave us the signal; he's our guy. Everything else is collateral damage," Steve broke it down for Henry.

Henry couldn't deny his partner's logic. Marlon did confirm that Malik was the snitch. The mark was less than 100 yards away. Now that he had been exposed, they couldn't let him leave. Maybe Steve was right, maybe Marlon had gotten too close to the mark and couldn't do it. Maybe the signal without the gunshot was Marlon's way of saying, 'This is the guy, but I can't do it. Come do it for me.'

Only, Marlon didn't know he was also scheduled to die. His usefulness had expired. He was a temporary measure and upon completion of his mission, he was to be terminated with extreme prejudice.

Then Henry understood his own moment of hesitation. He felt a twinge of guilt. He liked Marlon, although he had no qualms in killing him, he just wished there was another way.

"Okay," Henry agreed. The entire mental wrestling match took less than five seconds.

"Where the fuck is these muhfuckas? I blinked the fuckin' lights," Tim huffed.

"Blink 'em again," Wan suggested.

Tim blinked the lights once more.

The second flickering only confirmed in Steve's mind his own assumptions.

"He can't do it," Steve whispered to Henry, as they crabbed their way through the trees, approaching the Maserati from the rear.

"But we will," Henry replied.

Above The Law

"Yo, I gotta drive this muhfucka up Chancellor one time my dude," Tim remarked with fervor. "They gonna be on our dick!"

"A'ight! I'm wit' it!" Wan eagerly agreed.

Little did they know, they would never see Chancellor again.

Steve and Henry moved like silent assassins. They were ninja-like in their approach. When they reached the car, a barrage of bullets entered through the glass and doors tearing through skin, flesh, and bone. It was painless and instantaneous. Two head shots for each decoy sent them to the afterlife. They were dead before their brains soaked Marlon's headrests. Their eyes wide with the death stare and their mouths wide open. For them, it was life's last surprise. The tilt of their heads and the glare of the overhead streetlights gave Henry a look at the silhouette of two unfamiliar faces.

"Oh fuck ..." Henry exclaimed. The realization hit him before he saw the infrared dot on Steve's forehead. Behind Steve, he could see the movement of shadows.

Steve saw the same thing on Henry's forehead and the same shadowy movement behind him. They tried to lift their guns, but it was too late. Bullets whizzed and ripped through them as Fuquan's team opened fire.

xxxxxx

"As Salaam Alaikum, Hasana."

"Wa Alaikum As Salam, Boo. Wow, I was beginning to think you wasn't feelin' me like I am you," she flirted into her Bluetooth as she left Aisha's hair salon on Clinton Avenue.

Marlon already knew exactly where she was. He was parked on 18th Avenue and looking at her as she walked to her car.

"Nah Ma, in fact you been on my mind heavy…you and that thing you talked about," Marlon replied. He watched her every move.

She stopped short with her car door open.

"Yeah?"

"No doubt."

"So what's good then?"

"I was hopin' we could meet somewhere and talk."

"Sounds good. When?"

"Now."

She happily giggled.

"Where are you?" she asked Marlon.

"Doesn't matter, but I'll be at Cooper's Deli."

"The one on Grove and South Orange Avenue?"

"That's the spot," he answered.

"Gimme twenty minutes, Boo."

"As soon as she hung up, he watched her make another call before she pulled off. He leisurely tracked her movements and observed her behavior. He didn't expect her to tip her hand so easily.

She parked on Grove Street. He drove by and circled the block. When he came back around, he parked behind her and down the street a half a block. He watched and waited for ten minutes before he called again.

"I'm here, Boo," is how she answered the phone.

"Ma …you, my bad, but some shit just came up that I can't put off," Marlon lied.

"Oh, okay," she answered; he could hear the disappointment in her voice.

It's all about who get who first, he thought.

"I'ma definitely get at you tomorrow though."

"You betta," she giggled.

"Peace."

They ended the conversation.

Above The Law

He waited for her to pull out. When she did, he did the same. She took South Orange Avenue into East Orange and double-parked. She was trying to see if she had grown a tail. Marlon fell back off her. She made a right and another right. It was a standard maneuver; he anticipated her next move. He didn't follow her when she made the third right. He made a left and then another left back onto South Orange Avenue. Traffic was light, but the darkness of night camouflaged him.

There was no doubt in his mind now. Too much had given her away. The more she tried to blend in, the more she stood out.

She pulled into the driveway of a small brick house on a quiet street in West Orange. He parked on the street two houses down. He crept, stealth-like, to her backyard. She was still in the car and he tried to see what she was doing. There was a lot of movement, but it was too dark to make out what was going on.

Hasana stepped out of the car; she was no longer covered head to toe in Muslim garb. She had on tight fitting capris and a House of Dereon shirt. She looked totally relaxed. It was her safe haven away from Newark, away from scrutiny, away from Hasana.

She was too relaxed. She should've known that a lie must be lived at all times. When the lie drops its' guard, the truth is revealed. She dropped her guard and Marlon slipped easily past her defenses.

"Scream and you're dead," he menacingly whispered. His silenced nine was at the back of her neck.

Her body tensed in fear.

"What—"

"Shhh… Open the door, nice and slow."

She complied with her assailant's demand. Her body remained stiff and she was visibly looking for a way out of her situation, like a cobra looking for a chance to strike. Marlon wouldn't give her the chance. He saw the Brink's home security keypad and turned her to him.

"Jamil? Why are —,"

He interrupted her.

"Disarm the alarm. Send the distress signal and you'll be cold before the police get here," he bitterly told her.

She looked at him and he could see the wheels turning in her mind.

She was thinking about her cover. *Does he know? It this just a test to see where I live or to check me out?*

"You wanna deal...We deal on my terms," he expressed. He was reading her mind and trying to assuage her fears about her cover.

Her tensions eased at his statement and her guard was back up. The lie was back in place.

"Is that gun really necessary, Jamil?" she asked as she entered the alarm code and it stopped beeping.

He lowered the gun, but it remained locked and loaded. She approached with seduction in her eyes. He subtly raised the gun to his waist level and she stopped advancing.

"Is there anyone else here?"

"No," she answered.

He made her give him a tour of the house, from top to bottom. They ended in the basement.

"Who are you?" he asked. He focused on the slightest twitch in her demeanor.

"What?"

It was a question of clarification to buy time. He wanted her to realize she'd have to earn each additional breath.

Pzzzpt!

The bullet grazed her thigh just as he had intended. She screeched in agony and fell to the floor; blood stained her blue capris.

"Oh fuck! Jamil!"

Above The Law

Her eyes were like those of a cornered cat that had been declawed; she was helpless. Her gun was in her Islamic cover, in an inside pocket. Marlon put the tip of the silencer to her right knee.

"I'ma ask you again. Who are you?"

"I – I, I have money!" she blurted out.

"Thirty thousand...upstairs...in my safe," she was breathing hard as blood was coming from her wound.

"I got money. What I don't have is an answer. But fuck it, that's how you wanna play your hand..." he shrugged and put pressure on her knee like he was about to shoot.

"I'm a Federal Agent! If you kill me, you're fucked!" she barked, masking her fear with the protection of authority.

He humorlessly laughed in her face.

"What a coincidence! I'ma Fed, too!"

She didn't believe a word he said, but she quickly replied, "Then get me to a hospital. You have a fellow officer down!"

Marlon said nothing. He merely stared at her while she grimaced and squirmed in pain.

"Jamil, please!"

"Marlon, my name is Marlon."

"Please Marlon," she sobbed.

"What's your name? Your real name?" he calmly asked.

"Regina."

"Regina ...what?"

"Re...Regina Wingate."

Without warning, he shot her through the palm of her hand. She arched her back and howled in pain. She was cradling her spurting hand.

"Why are you doing this?" she screamed.

"Regina, Regina, listen. Stop crying and calm down. Now tell me...Do you want to live?"

"Yes!" she said through clenched teeth.

"Then you're gonna brief me on your investigation. If I think you're lying or holdin' back the truth, I shoot you. Are we clear?"

She vigorously nodded her head, took a deep breath, and began.

It started in Connecticut. She was a Field Agent undercover in Hartford. The target of the investigation was a set of Crips. They were selling exotic weed and guns. So she got connected with their connect, Malice. She got in his head and in his bed. She found out about Malik and worked her magic. She had them both and neither knew of the other. Malik's guns led to the Abdullah's heroin-jackpot. The investigation was two years in the making. She was in almost as deep as he was. Her handler called her Donna Brasco; a Fed joke referring to the infamous Donnie Brasco. Malik was a gold mine for her. He was in love and wanted to impress her with his own importance.

"Our shit comes straight off the boat, Ma ..." ".... This Somalian diplomat ...." "Zanzibar Exports..." They had thousands of hours of surveillance tapes based on his information; they called it his greatest hits collection.

"Mar – Marlon, I'm losing a lot of blood," she begged.

"Then talk faster."

He didn't say it in a cruel way, but more like a disinterested suggestion.

"He...told me about you...about Washington Heights," she said. She looked him in the eyes, her look saying she already knew he was a killer.

Marlon nodded he assessed the situation. She was going to try her magic on him, like she did with Malice and Malik. Federal agents that become sexually involved with their targets, destroy the case. Her handlers had to have known she crossed the line, but what was more important, the integrity of the investigation or the dismantling of an international drug ring?

Above The Law

Everybody pretends to be crazy sometimes, he thought to himself.

"What about Zanzibar Exports? What do you know about that?"

She licked her parched lips. The usually golden hue of her skin was now an ashy brown. The pain was evident.

She told him it was big. They gathered concrete evidence that someone high-ranking in the government was protecting the Somalian Defense Minister and turning a blind eye to his conduit for Afghani heroin.

"He...he used his diplomatic status to...to get it in. Past all the red tape, past customs..." she grabbed his hand and gripped it with surprising strength.

"Can't you see? Re – Remember Congresswoman Maxine Waters found out about the C.I.A. helping the narcos smuggle cocaine into L.A.? It's hap – happening again ... in Afghanistan."

She knew, or thought she knew, but Marlon knew better. He would allow her to die believing what she thought she knew, although the truth was far more sinister than she could ever imagine.

"Who else knows? Who do you report to?"

She grimaced and turned her head in disgust.

"They didn't believe m – me, not about Aweys. I knew dates, I knew ti – times when he was expected to land at Kennedy with a plane full of the dope. But they wouldn't let me pursue it...They drug their feet. It was sickening."

The truth, if she had known it, would've been sicker.

Zanzibar Exports, exporting Afghanistan heroin through Uncle Sam, the operation's godfather. To help the Somalian government defeat the Islamic horde in the horn. *What is more important,* Marlon thought, *dismantling an international drug ring or combating global terrorism?* There were shades of gray everywhere.

He decided that the truth would die with her. Her death was the solution; it was inevitable. The look in her eyes told Marlon she knew it was over. He dropped his head. She squeezed his hand, which she had not let go since she grabbed it.

"Jamil...Marlon...Who are you?"

She knew he wasn't just a street dude, a gangster. But she still didn't believe he was law enforcement.

He looked her in the eyes. That question would haunt him for a long time. He shook his head and answered with confused sincerity.

"I don't know."

He got up and shot her at point blank range through the head, followed quickly by a shot to the heart. Her back arched and her body quivered. The force of impact tilted her head up and then it rolled lifelessly to the left. Her eyes remained open, a trickle of blood oozed from the hole in her forehead. A pool of blood formed under her head where the black projectile destructively exited. She was a pawn who didn't deserve her fate. It was ironic that she died enforcing the law of a country whose security demanded her blood. It was the ultimate variation of a theme.

Marlon had completed his task, but he didn't like it. Who was he? The question haunted him, accused him, and exposed him at the same time. He was above all laws, foreign and domestic, except one, the law of justice. The security demanded her blood, but justice demanded his.

Marlon stood and put the gun to his head...

"Don't do it, Porter. You'd be doing your country a great disservice."

He didn't flinch because he wasn't surprised. He knew they would come. He sensed someone close by the entire time, but he was beyond caring.

"It's over," Marlon replied, without turning around.

Above The Law

He heard the footsteps against the cold concrete of the basement as they approached. The man gently brought Marlon's gun hand down as he stepped around and faced him.

He was shorter than Marlon. He had a salt and pepper buzz cut. His cold blue eyes were like that of an Israeli Prime Minister. He was dressed in Brioni and tasseled Italian loafers. Marlon knew he was in the presence of power.

"For some," the man replied, "For others, there are choices."

"And you are the man with the choices?" Marlon quipped.

The man smirked.

"Every man makes his own choice. I'm the General, the Director of The Department."

Marlon heard movement behind him. Three men entered carrying bags.

"Let's go upstairs and let them clean up," the General suggested.

Marlon and the General went up to the living room.

"I'm sure you already know that Steve and Henry were ambushed in Weequahic Park earlier," the General told him.

Fuquan had texted Marlon as he followed Hasana/Regina. It was one word …Khalas, meaning enough, the end, el fin … it's a wrap.

Fully automatic Mac 10's, the same guns Steve sold them. He who lives by the sword…

"Shit happens," Marlon shrugged.

"They were going to kill you on my orders," the General admitted in a matter of fact tone.

"Then why am I'm still alive?" Marlon shot back.

"Because you've proven to be an asset, more valuable to me alive," the General replied. He sat down on the couch and crossed his legs.

"An asset? You mean a killer willing to help you keep your dirty little secret?" Marlon quipped.

The general smirked.

"Yes, among other things.   Freedom comes with a price."

"Yeah, we definitely wouldn't want the fact that the American government is working with Al-Qaeda known," Marlon remarked.   He revealed what he knew to be the real cause of Hasana/Regina's death.

The General nodded in agreement.

"Not necessarily the American government. It has been said that truth, in times of war, is so precious that it needs a bodyguard of lies.   Allow me to explain.   During Regan's Presidency, he signed Executive Order 12333, or 'twelve threes.' It banned any person employed by or acting on behalf of the United States government from using assassination. Politically it was understandable, but it effectively tied the hands of covert ops, period.   However, in 1986, Oliver North and William Casey wanted to put together a stand-alone, self-financing entity that would operate independently of Congress and its oversight Committees and Appropriations process. That entity is the Department and we answer only to the Potus."

"Potus?" Marlon asked.

"It's the military acronym for the President of the United States.   P-O-T-U-S," the General explained.   "We're like the Mossad in Israel.   Officially, we don't exist. Realistically, the world knows we do and that gives our enemies pause.   Now, the American government's foreign policy concerning Somalia has been to extend aid to the Somalian government.   It is the politically correct thing to do because they are fighting the Islamic rebels who are backed by Al-Qaeda," the General explained.

He uncrossed his legs, leaned forward, and rested his elbows on his knees.

He continued, "But the Somalian government fucked up. They invited the Ethiopians to send troops. It was under

Above The Law

our behest, of course, Somalia should've known better. Somalians and Ethiopians hate each other. It was equivalent to the Bloods bringing in Crips to control their set, asinine. This turned the Somalian people against the government. They may not have wanted an Islamic presence, but it was a <u>Somalian</u> Islamic presence and was more acceptable to their taste than the Ethiopian-assisted government."

Marlon understood.

"So, overtly, the government backs Somalia, but covertly, we support the rebels. So if the Horn does fall to Al-Qaeda, we've already infiltrated it and have a foothold on destroying them," the General chuckled.

"I couldn't have said it better myself," Marlon added with a smirk.

The General went on to explain how Aweys was the Somalian branch of Al-Qaeda's biggest pipeline. How, with him dead, they would need another connect and The Department would be there to supply it.

"We will make them totally dependent on our resources and then we will totally annihilate them from within," the General predicted.

"So where do we go from here?" Marlon questioned.

The General stood.

"There's a small island in the Caribbean about to gain its independence from Britain. I want you to go down there and convert it into a smugglers' paradise."

"What about Asia?" Marlon probed, hoping for the best, but knowing hope was an indulgence he could no longer afford.

"She violated the code, she broke the rules. She exposed you to Ortega. That can't be tolerated."

"I understand, but —"

The General stiffly eyed him.

"Make no mistake, Porter. She will be found and dealt with. And if you have contact with her and you don't deal with her yourself, *you* will be dealt with."

The line had been drawn and Marlon had every intention of crossing it.

"If I decide to handle that Caribbean thing, I don't expect to be in the dark about anything."

"Granted."

"No leashes," Marlon added.

"Consider yourself unleashed," the General replied with a smile.

"Now tell me how you knew I was here?"

The General laughed.

"I like your style, Porter, so I'll humor you. Your watch, it's been fitted with a tracking device."

Marlon took off the watch and handed it to the General.

"No leashes," he reminded the General.

Marlon walked away and the General said, "Henry and Steve were two of my best guys. How do I take that?"

Marlon paused at the door.

"Everybody's expendable, sir...No exceptions," he replied before he left.

The General's face remained emotionless, but in reality, he had already chalked up the loss. If Steve and Henry weren't sharp enough to recognize the setup, then their expendability was already an established fact.

"Shit happens," the General said to himself.

Outside, Marlon climbed into his car. His beeper went off. He checked the screen. It read 77777777.

He smiled, started the car, and said, "I'll see you soon."

About The Author

Hailing from Newark, New Jersey, Kwame Teague is the award winning, critically acclaimed, and Essence #1 bestselling author of the street classic Dutch trilogy. His other novels include *The Adventures of Ghetto Sam, The Glory of My Demise, Thug Politics, the Dynasty series and ? – Pronounce Que. He writes under the pen name Dutch.*

In Stock Now!

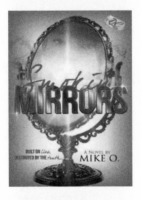

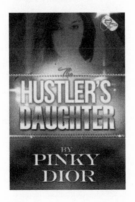

Order Form

DC Bookdiva Publications

#245 4401-A Connecticut Avenue, NW

Washington, DC 20008

dcbookdiva.com

Name: _____

Inmate ID _____

Address: _____

City/State: _____ **Zip:** _____

QUANTITY	TITLES	PRICE	TOTAL
	Que, Dutch	15.00	
	Smokin Mirrors, Mike O	15.00	
	Dynasty By Dutch	15.00	
	Dynasty 2 By Dutch	15.00	
	The Commission, Team DCB	15.00	
	Trina, Darrell Debrew	15.00	
	Secrets Never Die, Eyone Williams	15.00	
	Dynasty 3, Dutch	15.00	
	A Killer'z Ambition, Nathan Welch	15.00	
	A Killer'z Ambition 2, Nathan Welch	15.00	
	Lorton Legends, Eyone Williams	15.00	
	Convict's Clique, Nathan Welch	15.00	
	A Beautiful Satan, RJ Champ	15.00	
	Above the Law, Dutch	15.00	
	A Beautiful Satan 2, RJ Champ	15.00	

QUANTITY	TITLES	PRICE	TOTAL
	Tina, Darrell Debrew	15.00	
	A Hustler's Daughter, Pinky Dior	15.00	

Sub-Total $_____

Shipping/Handling (Via US Media Mail) $3.95 1-2 Books, $7.95 1-3 Books, 4 or more titles-Free Shipping

Shipping $ _____

Total Enclosed $ _____

Certified or government issued checks and money orders, all mail in orders take 5-7 Business days to be delivered. Books can also be purchased on our website at dcbookdiva.com. Incarcerated readers receive 25% discount. Please pay $11.25 per book and apply the same shipping terms as stated above.